RHL

... so light of touch, so full of insight into human strategies for coping ... unusual, composed and engaging ...

The Bulletin

... the novel has the charm of early work such as Gustave Flaubert's *Novembre* and Jack Kerouac's *The Subterraneans.*

The Weekend Australian

... a quirky, touching story ... thoroughly entrancing.

The Big Issue

... both sad and hilarious ... a daring and moving work.

The West Australian

Written with wry humour and great depth of perception, this moving and often hilarious novel is a must-read.

Melbourne Weekly

First published 2004 by
FREMANTLE PRESS

Fremantle Press Inc. trading as Fremantle Press
PO Box 158, North Fremantle, Western Australia, 6159
www.fremantlepress.com.au

First edition reprinted 2004, 2005 (twice), 2006.
Second edition first published 2008. Reprinted 2010, 2011, 2012, 2016.
This edition first published 2021. Reprinted 2022.

Cover photograph © Matsu Photography.
Printed and bound in Australia by Griffin Press.

 A catalogue record for this
book is available from the
National Library of Australia

ISBN 9781760991401 (paperback)
ISBN 9781760991418 (ebook)

 Department of
**Local Government, Sport
and Cultural Industries**

Fremantle Press is supported by the State Government through the Department of
Local Government, Sport and Cultural Industries.

RHUBARB

CRAIG SILVEY

 FREMANTLE PRESS

this book is dedicated to Parvin Khan

It seems that almost everyone has a patch of rhubarb tucked in a corner of their garden.

Rhubarb: More Than Just Pies
Sandi Vit, Michael Hickman

RAPIDEYEMOVEMENT

A vigil slips. But only because it has to. Only because sleep can't always be staved.

Moongleam bleeds silver through cheap lace curtains. The window is shut, the trapped air hot. Dry and stifled.

This is a child's room. Still. With a child's adornments, but without a child.

On the wall is Mickey Mouse, redshorted and ringed by numbers. His arms frozen wide open. Splayed, like he's ready to be dissected. The thin red secondhand doesn't move or tick or tock. It just offers a determined, stunted flicker (stuck, stuck, stuck).

But Mickey grins a plastic grin and points gleefully at the numbers Three and Nine.

It's three forty-five. It's lightyears from midnight.

There is no music.

The bed has sloughed its covers. There are only two sheets (plastic under polyester) and there she lies. Supine. Thin and sweatglossed. You can see her rack of ribs embossing cotton.

She lies and she doesn't toss, doesn't welter. She's pinned rigid, like she's strapped down, held, like she's ready to be —

If you look close though, you can see how her eyelids fibrillate. Rapideyemovement. They flicker like a projection reel. Behind them there's mutiny. And noise. Things are surfacing from a shallow burial. Things are spilling from sacks, undone and unbidden. And she's pinned rigid. She might twitch.

Warren is here. Driven by duty and worry. He keeps watch, because her sleep is his vigil. A guard dog by night; because Warren can't go where she is, he can't weave her away from Things. Dreams don't need guide dogs.

So he sits: staunch and patient and a little thirsty. Eyes large and lazy in the dim light. He makes occasional nuzzled enquiries, but mostly he just sits. Head cocked, ears pinned, still.

It's later, when her breathing breaks into heaving, when lungs press brittle ribs; that's when Warren begins to shuffle with restless unease. That's when Warren feels queasy. And that's when Warren farts (poofffft) and whines softly. He forbears a flurry of barking, like a fist in his chest.

And he'll trundle off to gather a ratty leather harness. He'll trundle back and deposit it carefully on the bed near her open hand. And he'll sit. Stay. And wait.

BIG RED ARROW

It still feels dark when Eleanor eases the front door shut.

It's three forty-five. Her skin is moist from the shower. There are red scratchmarks on her arms and her belly. Warren is harnessed and Ready.

The pavement is cool beneath her bare feet. And Eleanor is ushered downhill by a thick easterly breeze bearing pollen, bugs, dust and monoxide. She moves quickly through streets she knows. This is a straight and wellworn path. She glides silently with somnambulist detachment. Roundshouldered and tilted forward, like she's towing something. Her chest is tight.

Warren does not glide. He has the detachment of the barely awake. His loose bodyfat jostles and his wet eyes are blinky. His head sways low to the ground.

There are four things Warren hates (in order of irritation):

1. Early mornings.
2. Seagulls.
3. Children.
4. Martha Gardener.

Warren yawns. His tongue curls, then unfurls; as though the yawn is a royal presentation.

There is no traffic, so Eleanor doesn't pause for kerbs or crossings. She doesn't Stop or Give Way. The breeze chills her back, makes her skin taut. She is ghosted by pale streetlights. Warren quells the urge to sniff roadkill. A cardoor slams distantly. Reticulation ups periscope and hisses. She charges beneath an overhanging jacaranda whose discarded lilac nipples adhere to her callused feet. Sticky. But she doesn't stop, because moving helps. And so does water. She's almost there and she knows.

Warren steers her past two hirsute men unpacking crates of vegetables. They watch her slip by round a corner.

Closer now. Past a sleeping cafe. Past the shadow of the hospital. Past the pungent fishwaft from the markets. She turns and her pace quickens. She smells baking Turkish bread. Warren lingers.

On the dewy lawn of the Esplanade Reserve they weave beneath Norfolk Island pines. She grips the harness tight because she can smell the salt now. Warren stumps along at her left. His hackles fan as seagulls wheel above and squawk discord. He harrumphs with feeling.

They whip through the railway labyrinth. Dip between parked cars. They jaywalk Mews Road, giving berth to a taxi pulling out of a nightclub. It whispers past, its back door streaked with vomit. A weak, incipient sunhaze spreads off the hills behind them. Warren stops for a flight of steps.

I know, she says. Come on.

And she's on to the thick boards of the harbour platform. Impatient and breathing hard. The nails of her dog clickclack as he canters alongside. The last crossing is four steps long. She pulls left, away from the listing shore of Bathers Beach, and follows the path beside the low limestone mole that looms close to her right. Blunt rubble peppering the sand ruins the rhythm of her steps. She sniffs. A tiny nosestud gleams. The breeze gets sharper.

She slows, then stops. Makes her estimation and bends. Clicks her fingers. Points.

Okay, is it here Warren? Look, where is it? Here?

She taps granite. And Warren's tail whips as he snuffles the clefts along the seawall. Metres away, he scratches at an open cavity.

Eleanor reaches in to her elbow and removes a handline and a small plastic tacklebox. She drops the harness. And Warren watches her calves flex as she climbs the rock wall in the half-light. The tackle rattles. He sets off slowly after her.

Eleanor quickly locates her rock; a jutting slab of granite with snug ergonomics. A wide throne in the lee of the mole. She sits and its smooth skin is cool. She cradles the cheap plastic container in her lap, wipes away the sand. Her fingers move with careful method. Pinching the line, she threads the sinker and hook easily, though her ties are messy. She clasps shut the tacklebox. Stands. Her back arches as she rolls her shoulders.

Eleanor's toes curl like a diver's over the edge of her rock. Biting her lower lip, she windmills the line and flings it deep. It uncoils from a beggar's hand. She hears the rig slap and fizzle, and feels the swallowed weight slide. She sits, settles, and, leaning back, keeps the baitless line taut in her fingers.

Warren is at the crest of the seawall, negotiating his next Leap of Peril. The cumbrous harness hampers his mobility. He squints into the wind and assesses his options. He is heckled by vermin. He glares upwards malevolently. Their wingflaps are a pisstaking applause. He growls.

Eleanor offers gentle encouragement nearby. Warren farts in distress. He leans, paws at the edge, overbalances, slips, recovers and scrabbles over to where Eleanor reclines. She shifts across. He lays his head in her lap and sighs with drama.

Nicely done, she says, and rubs his snout.

Below her, she can hear lapping files of wavelets; in rhythm with the weighty undertow she absorbs through this thread, like a pulse. Eleanor never winds the line, just holds it. She doesn't expect to catch anything and doesn't want to. Shutting useless eyes, she inhales. Wedged between a rock and a big, wet place. And she can't smother the thought that this, even this, is getting harder.

***

It is well into the morning when Frank clambers the groyne with creaking knees and a straight back. His arse is tingling unpleasantly. He is accompanied by a fetid white bucket and a thermos he keeps separate. He peers over to where she should be. Sees a short scruff of honeyblonde hair. The long tips of her ears are peeling pink. The polished tan of her shoulders is stark against her tight white singlet. So small and childlike she is, seated beside that great dribbling lump of dog. Sometimes he finds her here curled and sleeping, still fisting the line.

I know you're there, Frankfurt.

Frank smiles. Morning Elly, love. Christ, you don't miss much.

You're not exackly stealthy over those rocks, Spiderman. Anyway, I've got eyes like a hawk.

Yes, and I've got a dick you could limbo under. I see you have a line out. How goes the world of perpetual disappointment?

Same old shit. Yourself?

Well, he announces, and rests his bucket. Speaking of shit, I've had a wonderful morning having my prostate digitally examined.

Eleanor laughs and turns her head towards him. Sorry. How was it?

Oh, you know, strange at first, but then he worked into a rhythm, you know?

I see.

We've set up another appointment next week. Booked a motel. I haven't told my wife as yet, but she'll understand.

Well make sure you wear something nice.

I'll try, but my arse swallowed my last G-string.

Good chance he'll find it for you.

True, Frank laughs. He has a high, infectious giggle. I'll tell you what though Elly, it actually felt very very pleasant coming *out*. And one good thing must be said about Dr Buggery — he loosened things up lovely. I've never crapped so smooth. It was like ... velvet or something.

I am truly enlightened to hear it, Franklin. So, how is Helen?

Frank shrugs. Yeah, she's well. Says hello. Flat out with the Christmas, you know. It's at ours this year.

So why aren't you helping?

I am, love. Trust me, I am. How's your mum then?

Estelle's good. Out and about, you know, same as Helen.

Frank bends stiffly, retrieves his bucket. Listen, you want some bait, or are you still praying on a suicide?

I'll be fine.

Well, I'm orf to get jiggy with some squid. There's a bit of a run owing to some recent vessel activity, apparently. I'm oready late.

God speed. Jig well.

You take care, Elly love.

You too. Bye.

Frank keeps his smile as he climbs down gingerly, propping his hands on his thighs. His stumpy stockiness is going to fat. A landslide of the chest. A slit of belly pokes out in a wide grin from under his greasy shirt. His thongs flick sand and crumb the back of his legs.

Frank walks like he's pushing an invisible wheelbarrow. He frowns and rubs his saltandpepper stubble.

She worries him, Eleanor. Always has, though he could never say why. She's not brittle. Volatile, maybe. And it seems her fuse is shortening. Maybe it's the heat, he doesn't know. But he's always had a concerned paternal urge to beat his sliding chest, tuck her under his arms and run with her. Alternatively, he knows, he could headbutt a landmine, which would detonate just as thoroughly. He's seen her tumble badly from the top of those rocks, and the first thing she did was lash out furiously at the people trying to help her up. Frank has always sensed that abrupt boundary with her, and he's always been mindful of it.

Frank climbs the south end of the groyne, offers affable greetings to a row of anglers and leaves her be.

She reels the line on to the plastic spool. He worries her, Frank. She thinks of him, thinks of his wife, and worries because she knows.

Eleanor collects her tackle and spool, pushes herself upright and stretches. She can hear Warren snoring solidly at her feet. She smiles, sly, and turns slowly. Her foot finds a furrow and she sneaks over the seawall. Shelves the tackle. Then she whistles.

On the other side, Warren wakes, sniffs at her absence and scrabbles up confused. He circles. Panicking, he scans the mole before barking at the water.

He pauses; glares over his shoulder hearing his name called. And he belts up and over the seawall without reservation or vertigo.

She's laughing. He lunges in to nip her toes. Still giggling, she fends him off, takes his legs and tips him. Rolls him on to his back and scrubs his softwhite underbelly. Warren's pink slab of tongue lolls flaccid from his open mouth. Eyes glazed. Inert with ecstasy. He comes up schnitzelled. Shakes the sand from his coat and sneezes. He trots away and sits metres apart from her. His tail sweeps and he grins.

Okay. Very funny, Mr Guide Dog. Come on, let's go.

Warren canters back, point made.

The heat is thick. A waning breeze brushes her face. And Eleanor curls fingers round the aluminium harness to leave with her shadow behind her. The ribbed cloud overhead is like scattered sheepfleece.

They move back the way they came. Strolling. Less urgent. Restaurants yawn open for early lunch. Eleanor smells suncream and fatty batter. Rich men in high shorts boast their boats in the harbour. Tourists amble and reprimand their children. Warren quells the urge to maul a grounded flock of gulls.

The pavement is toasted. Warren stops her for a tight fluorescent cluster of middle-aged crises on bicycles (with shaven legs to lessen wind resistance) who clot the road. Behind them, motorists bawl invective and search for parking.

Away from town, Eleanor stops at a bakery to buy a loaf of sourdough and some water for Warren. He is sneaked some leftover pastry, like always. He chews with moist eyes.

The suburban streets are sleepy and quiet. She keeps to the dappled shade and weaves her way, choosing roads at random. She doesn't feel like going home just yet. She hears a distant whippersnipper and the piccolo trill of darting wrens. Freckled kids pull faces at her and giggle from their frontyards. Warren cuts his eyes at them.

Sweat coats her lean body satin. No hips, no thighs, no breasts. She has retained the taut, waifish figure of a distance runner, which she used to be; but that was before rhubarb, before sacks, before teflon, before Everything. She lost Running, and kept Distance. And Appearance. She is the same size she was at twelve.

Eleanor wasn't always blind. She's seen enough, too much. She lost her sight the same year his cirrhotic liver haemorrhaged.

He drowned in his own blood. It happened at an airport, where he worked. She wasn't there, she didn't see it. But she'd lost it all before that anyway.

When Estelle told her he was dead, Eleanor said: No. He isn't.

But she was a child then. With long hair. Jenny wasn't, technically, but she was gone by then. Jenny had always been the swimmer. It was like she was built for it. She surfed too, an excuse for early mornings.

Jenny sends a letter once a year; each as useless as the first one she left, the night she stole Running from her younger sister. But all she really wanted was the Distance.

And once a year, Eleanor doesn't reply. So Jenny doesn't know about Warren, about livers, about wombs, about rhubarb. About staying.

They wend stealthily through the streets she grew up in. Streets she explored as a child on a pink bicycle with an embarrassing florid basket (though she never shaved her legs to reduce wind resistance).

Though they are now gentrified and renovated, she *knows* these streets. At will, she can conjure a cerebral map of Fremantle, a network of space and place and roads. And always inside it somewhere, there's a Big Red Arrow pointing at a tiny figure, and three Big Red Words that say: **You Are Here.**

A map with a perimeter, a boundary; and like Frank, she stays within it. She knows her way west to the seawall. East to White Gum Valley. North to the river. And south to South Beach. This is her vicinity; the square she lives in.

She knows these streets because she inhabits them. She's in them every day. She depends on it. And it's not the warm lure of community, though people know her (first) name and call out to her sometimes. They speak briefly, harmlessly, with a fence between them and her. She is often vague with constant fatigue, so people think she's either stoned or stupid. She is ruthlessly evaded by the tight of arse, who assume she is a collector for the Blind. And on a good day, she is only curt with those who offer charity. She doesn't *need* community, or even want it. It's just a simple need to be outside. Moving.

Because Eleanor can remember that unbearable period of no movement that kept her inside, back then, after she lost her sight.

She had refused a cane. Refused all assistance from groups and associations. Confined, she went nowhere. After a vapid year indoors she broke. Choked by claustrophobia, Eleanor had burst outside and attempted to navigate her own way. Her chest was pounding. Incredibly, she rounded two blocks before she was hit by a parked bus. She was taken to hospital with mild concussion.

When she woke, only darkness and the reek of urine were familiar. She had no idea where she was. She screamed.

A week later, a patient, ruddycheeked Englishman called Clive arrived at her door and introduced her to a younger, wilder Warren. Despairing, she agreed to be helped.

That first day, Clive evaluated Eleanor's mobility. They set out cautiously in the morning. She clutched his arm, but kept him apart. She had a straight, dead, unwavering stare. She scowled and spoke only in sparse acerbic mumbles, protecting a proud, childish dignity. But it didn't last. She couldn't contain her relief. They walked fast. Clive was astounded by her orientation. She was confident in her space. Stubbornly assured. He felt her soften and thaw as they strolled the main street bordered by peoplepeopleplepeople. She was overawed and it stirred Clive to see it. They walked all day. She asked quiet questions.

Warren was about to be fired from school. He had just failed his exams gloriously. He just didn't cut the mustard.

He struggled with fitness because he didn't have any. He was always hungry. And he could never grasp the ability to piss on cue. He was scolded for skirmishes and chewed orange markers. He had tapeworms and attitude: the class badboy. But Warren's greatest weakness was Distraction. He weaved the straight line like a drunkard. He just had to sniff things, lick things, chase things, roll in things. He couldn't help it. He inhaled arses like they contained secret hidden treasure. And, despite being neutered to ward the temptations of the flesh, Warren maintained a discerning eye for winsome bitches.

This was his Last Chance.

Clive began training them at a park nearby. They adopted each other immediately. Their trust was instant. Separately, they were awkward to instruct, but together, the task was facile. He taught her to listen, because Sound, he said, was her semaphore. Clive was firm, funny and generous. They worked hard. And at the end of each day, he began teaching her braille beneath an old eucalypt. She absorbed it hungrily. Reading was like being outside again. Another world at her fingertips. And the darkness was like a backdrop. Like a projection screen. It gave more room for illusion.

In Eleanor, Warren had suddenly discovered his duty. He slipped into his harness like it was armour. It was never again chewed or buried. He became fiercely protective and took his job seriously. He learned to quell urges. He led from the front. He took the bullets.

He remained overweight. He still pissed when he needed to piss. But he was never again Distracted whilst in the harness. Warren cut the mustard and graduated at the end of that summer.

Eleanor was moving again. And moving helped.

Now, nine years on, Warren is cocking his leg in a tuft of tallgrass, pissing for neighbourhood primacy at one of his many urinal checkpoints. He marks a broad territory. Sir Warren, (fearless) Knight of the Yellow Empire. Vigilant Protector of the Visually Impaired.

He uncocks, and trots on ahead.

Warren's lifelong gripe is the name Warren. He feels mocked by it. He'd like a name like Major or Boris or Conrad; something darker and harder. Something wolfish. Something that wasn't a habitat for rabbits. A name that invoked the respect he truly deserved as a faithful public servant. Because Warren has issues with Respect, too. The way he sees it, he doesn't get enough. He senses a distinct lack of civic reverence for his position. And it's the very reason he hates:

3. Children.

Children. He is assailed by them. In the street, under tables, everywhere, trilling masses of sticky poky fingers. They cuddle prod stroke hug, while he quells sinister urges and Eleanor is too happy to oblige. Like he's a showpony or something. They ask for his name and she tells them Warren-The-Pooh. Then assures them he *won't* bite. Tells them he *likes* children.

Couldn't they all see he was a professional? On duty? A working dog with responsibility? He should have fangs, a menacing scar, studs on his harness. He should be ploughing furrows among scissoring shins. People should be moving for *him*.

After all, he had someone to guide. And guard. And save.

***

It's noon. There are seven days to Christmas, thirteen left in the year, the century, the millennium, when Eleanor Rigby stops and hears it for the first time, carried on a hot offshore breeze.

(Yes. Eleanor, too, is mocked by her name. Though she's not too big for it. She's so small she's been jinxed by a Beatle. And in fact, it slaps her twice, front and backhand, because her first name, derived from the Greek, means *Light*.)

Faint it is, from here.

It competes with the click of insects, a million offbeat metronomes. It gusts in fluid snatches. She frowns, concentrates. Shutting useless eyes, she inhales. Breathes cloying heat. Smells carob and salt and frangipani. Her armhairs hackle. Her bloated lowerbelly crawls. She is strangely held by it. Sound, like voice. Semaphore. Reverbs in her head, makes her suddenly restless. It's not a sound she recognises, but she's heard it, she's felt it before. Even knows it, maybe.

Bent and tentative, she moves closer.

NAPHTHALENE

Ewan Dempsey is making moonshine.

But it's not illicit, or whisky. He's brewing an organic cleaner.

On a sibilant stovetop, water simmers in a huge stainless steel pot. Over which, Ewan tears open two plastic bags and empties them of fresh rhubarb leaves. He compresses the frothing mound with a potato masher before setting the lid.

Ewan turns up the heat and gets out of the kitchen. The evening is cool. A web of fairy lights draped loosely over next door's peppermint tree gives his backyard a twilight glow. He hears voices over the fence.

Crossing anklehigh lawn, Ewan ducks his head for the Hills hoist and keeps it bowed to enter his small tin workshop. He kicks three more bags of leaves inside, tugs the lightcord and closes the door. The air is musty with stale heat. He breathes timberdust and turpentine. In the dimness, it appears as though there is even less room to move. Within reach are rows of stacked planks reclining on the opposing wall. They all bear a tight straight grain, like a corduroy uniform. His bench is a clutter of assorted debris. The dust is a thick pelt. Tools, dovetails, rags and scrapwood are scattered throughout. There are shelves with pine moulds, power tools, rusted tins of adhesives, fasteners, chemicals. Rods of dowel. Gleaming zincalume templates. And bodyparts: ribs, necks, heels. The beginnings of backs and bellies.

Ewan makes cellos. Or, closer to the truth, Ewan makes one cello over and over and over again. To his right, on a thick wire turnbuckled taut, is a row of wet replicas. Three bare, limbless torsos; mirthless and inert, recently varnished and hanging like a public execution.

Clones that each bear the same shape, the same size, the same hue and tonal shifts as Lilian; the Working Model. Even the grain is of eerie, uncanny sameness.

And Ewan can sell them upon completion, because they will never ever sound the same as her.

Lilian's voice is made unique with History. Two hundred years of it. Two lifetimes for Ewan. He can reproduce her sound only by playing, and that way he keeps her.

It was Jim who named Lilian, because she used to be his. Her full name was Violiliancello. Jim said cellos deserved names, because they were the closest instruments to the human form and voice and temperament.

Ewan's cello was called Kamahl. He was a midget.

A moth stirs to clap its dusty wings at the globe. Shuffling across, Ewan stoops over an inchoate scroll that is set firmly in a cushioned vice. A spread of sketches, diagrams, guides and identical models surrounds it. At his feet, there are stacks of workbooks and a spread of ageing pages filled with notes and dimensions. Scaled posters of her form hang like the curvy centrefolds of other sheds. He is watched sternly by the hanging panel of headless torsos.

He takes a scalpel and shaves slivers in careful, cautious increments.

Ewan can sell them only if the bodies are exact. And exactitude is a tedious process. His discards far outweigh his accomplishments. There is two years of work in that stern hanging gallery. His work is not Profitable, nor an Enterprise. His product has no name, he takes no orders. The precious few he has completed have been shipped to Europe and, as far as he knows, snaffled iniquitously by affluent private collectors. His instruments, like his playing, could be world-renowned if anyone knew.

Matching the grain is the most exhaustive, impossible task. And made expensive due to his demands, though cost has never been a problem. Lilian's belly and back are racks of thin herringbone welts which all converge in symmetry down the centre join. Her neck is a wider asymptotic grain, with three linear chestnut knots. Jim called them The Three Sisters. Difficult to replicate.

The majority of his timber he has delivered from a poplar plantation down south; and most of that is destined for firewood. He also has a retired millworker, whom he has never met, scouring woodpiles for the elusive grain. He has dusty, listless collections of maple, ash, willow, apple, walnut, alder, pine. Even a sheet of oak. Timber that has come close, but without cigars. So the rare wood that fits is precious.

Ewan works a solid half-hour and the viced scroll looks barely scratched. He stretches, then, clutching an armful of empty winebottles, he slips outside. The voices are louder next door. He smells citronella and mosquito coils.

Inside, at the stovetop, he unveils a bitter plume of steam and coughs himself lightheaded. Cuts the gas. The house is hot and still with ambient silence. Using the pot lid, Ewan waves away the rising steam like a onehanded cymbalist. Peers in. The leaves are a limp khaki. He tongs them out, drops them into the bin.

Ewan sprinkles in some soapflakes as a wetting agent. Stirs.

A Dissolution.

It's an annual brew, RhubarbLeaf Moonshine. Ewan boils the leaves for their constituent oxalic acid. And he uses the mix to remove the dark, seated waterstains from his delivered timber. It clears the marks without affecting the quality of the wood. (It also drills aphids.)

Ewan drops in a tray of iceblocks, waits for them to melt. With a ladle and a small funnel he transfers the thick limpid liquid into the winebottles. Presses a cork into each and gathers them up.

Outside he is faceslapped by cool air and bad music. He hears a party next door. Leaving the bottles by the workshop entrance, Ewan creeps towards the fence, picking carefully through a cluster of cannabis. He stays in the shadow of foliage.

Beer, barbecue, mingling, fondling. The backyard is floodlit and festooned with Christmas lights. The small crowd looks young; most of them pissed already. Some nod their heads to the Hits of the Eighties. A loud group throw darts at the pinned picture of a crucified Marilyn Manson. Shots of something clear are taken for any dart to the genitals. Sausages are turned religiously. Kylie wishes she was so lucky, lucky, lucky.

Ewan watches them for a time.

There is a sudden collective groan as a bent figure in a Santa suit spews through a flywire door. Ewan winces. The flywire acts as a sieve, apportioning the liquids from a mosaic of solids. Santa passes out, grinning through a sickly beard. He is dragged to the lawn, kicked twice, narrowly missed by a flung dart, and left alone.

The door is wiped and left open. The party resurges. Marilyn's impaled erogenous zone expands steadily. The Proclaimers proclaim. And someone near the barbecue squints in Ewan's direction, waves a slopping beverage and slurs:

Heyheytallguy! Cummin havva drink!

Ewan ducks his head and walks inside.

His elderly Kelvinator buzzes and burrs, complaining through cracked seals. Ewan bends, opens a cupboard and breathes the grey cardigan fume of naphthalene that he somehow inherited. The entire house exudes it. Ewan moved into the quiet limestone cottage when he was fifteen, and for eight years he has been steeped in the inexorable odour of mothballs, dust and mouseturds. And more recently the coiled excrement of possums.

But Ewan is used to having things bequeathed. He has inherited all there is to inherit. Almost everything he owns is a leftover. Even Lilian is his through default, though he never asked for her. Jim had her sent. Ewan never asked for any of it. For the money he was given as restitution for his (and his father's) stake in the family firm; or this house, offered to him on the proviso of his continued absence from both church and business. There's a blue Volvo in his garage that was bequeathed by virtue of his father's leaving on a plane via taxi. He sits in it sometimes, revving, doors shut, a signed softleather bible in the backseat, and thinks of his own ways of leaving.

Ewan is twenty-three and tall. And sometimes he is Angela: plump, middle-aged, shy. Or Lewis: black, buffed, bashful. Or some other generic, harmless name (John, Lucy, Matthew, Linda) whenever he sits in on internet chatlines to watch other people converse. He logs on, sees his name quickly swallowed and forgotten by the rolling sprawl of text and he reads, safely detached. Truly invisible. Contact with a screen between. He watches mutely until he is unceremoniously booted. And when he is done, he physically disconnects his modem, drops it in a drawer.

In the cupboard, the choices are bleak. He rubs high cheekbones. Snatches a can of chickpeas. Checks the use-by, then opens and drains them at the sink. With a damp cloth (and habit) he wipes the dust from a deep granite mortar and slides in the chickpeas. Adds three cloves of garlic, some cayenne pepper. Bashes the ingredients with a cracked pestle. The floorboards creak. He adds lemon, olive oil and a dash of balsamic vinegar. A sprinkle of paprika. He thuds a 4/4 beat.

And he's not really hungry. It's just the process of preparing a meal.

Like his cellos, Ewan's days tend to take the same shape. The same circular trajectory. He leaves each day as he found it. Finds each day as he left it.

Could be why he feels a sudden unease. Because compared to its predecessors, today seemed to be relative disorder. All it took was the heat, two possums and the early absence of rhubarb.

He had planned to make Moonshine early, so he could slip back easily into the day's rhythm. He woke just on dawn. And like every morning, Ewan pinched and packed a solid, spicy conepiece just outside the kitchen. He slowly pulled the creamy bucket and embraced the day, waiting for his hulking chrome espresso machine to warm up.

His coffee was dark and dense. He welcomed it, having slept badly, kept awake by two possums in the roof cavity above him making sweet loud love all night long.

The delivery was late.

Ewan waited, waited, waited, but the leaves didn't come. He cut a grid into a mango cheek and ate it at the kitchen sink. Waited. The heat seared. He prowled awhile. Watered plants. Worked briefly in the shed. Just before noon, he came inside to play. He felt unctuous with sweat. And itchy. It beaded in the dark rims under his eyes. It was stifling inside, and difficult to breathe. He opened no windows. Stripped his shirt and wiped his face.

He headed down the hallway. First room on the left. He sat and took up Lilian, began tuning. And just as he tightened his bow, he heard the strafing ratta-tat-tat of possums overhead. The heat permeated. He felt agitated. He tried to concentrate; couldn't. But he had to, he had to play, it was noon already. The possums scrabbled louder. Angry, he rose and lifted his chair. Escorted Lilian down the hallway. And for the first time, Ewan went outside, to his front verandah, to play.

He stops bashing. The mix is now a smooth babyshit paste. Ewan tears crusty bread and scoops into his quickfire hommus. He chews absently and feels suddenly nervous. He wonders how long she was there. Listening.

Listening while he was way back when, with Johann Sebastian, his very favourite. Eyes shut, intent. Intense. Trying not to notice the different, distant, broader acoustics of the open air. Trying to forget where he was. His foot tapped Time into a spill of grevillea. He played two concertos (bach to bach) and launched stiffly into a third, but it exhausted him. His arms fell slack. Sweat covered Lilian's shoulder and ebony fingerboard. A thin bead of it dropped from his chin like a tear. He heaved.

Then he saw her and panicked. Her: small, shorthaired, barefoot, bra-less, white singlet, long frayed cargoshorts. And a dog: doleful and pink tongued. She gripped his fence like she was holding it up. Very quiet and very still. Her strange, urgent expression. And how she stared, blue-eyed, at him, through him. She heaved with a sense of withholding. He stared back, blood belting, in silence. He felt dizzy. Naked. Felt weight in his belly. Felt ashamed.

They broke away at the same moment. He stirred, lurched to the door and the bow slipped and skidded on the verandah boards. He fumbled pushed forced the door open and closed. He did not see her leave just as sharply.

He leant on the door and breathed. Lilian shook in his hand.

Then he heard a knock behind him. He pushed away and wheeled rigid. He waited. Was it her? The rapping came again, louder and more insistent. He slid down the hall. Another knock:

Scuse me, Chief? Hello, I have your, er, rhubarb *leaves*? That you ordered? Hello?

Ewan gathered himself. Breathed. Moved. He rested Lilian on her side. Took some cash from inside a dictionary.

Leave them there, he mumbled shakily and slid something exorbitant under the door. Okay bye.

He watched the wad disappear.

A pause, then a whisper, What the *fuck*? Are you sure, sir? This is, er …

But Ewan had moved away.

He rinses the mortar. Drinks tepid tapwater from a recycled jar.

Thinks of her. *Listening*. So close, so explicitly. And that bilious melancholy settles again. He feels restless, afraid even, just thinking of it. He dries his hands. Can't shirk it. His stomach feels pestled. He walks outside, for no reason, then straight back in. Searches for something, but he isn't sure what. He washes the mortar again. The fridge rattles out a grand finale. Silence. Still.

And it's always with unease that you hear her the loudest, like a surge. Shivering upwards. And you're moving, moving with somewhere to go. The hallway is four steps long. The door swings open and the verandah is silver with moongleam. You bend and reach and take your bow still taut. And poised there you take a moment to look out. See the orange wharfglow over the harbour, like an artificial sunset. And beyond it, darker, a looming front; rain laden and sliding closer. Your face is washed by a strong seabreeze. Then you're scanning the foreground, again not sure of what you're looking for. But the street is empty, quiet, still. Like it should be.

The door is shut and locked. And you turn to breathe the same trapped static atmosphere. Four steps. Conviction. And you are sitting and she is weightless and you are setting her endpeg on a phonebook (A–K) because you're too tall otherwise. You are clamping her hips with your knees and her shoulders fall back into your chest where she fits. Encased. Your frame surrounds her, ursine. Your arms and legs like the limbs she doesn't have. Freckles of rosindust are scattered on her belly beneath the bridge, like a galaxy of dim stars. You smear them away quickly with a sweaty palm. You scrounge inside an old suitcase, pull out a yellowed sheet of Kodaly you inherited, and set it on the stand. But you close your eyes against it (the darkness, like a screen) and project Memory. Bow kisses string. And Zoltan, long left fallow (six months), he hits you *hard*. And you remember, Jim used to say The old stuff finds the vein quick. Your hair stands on end. Nimble fingers curl and dive and shimmy down her neck. Fluid and firm. Notes lift and fade in this dim room like smoke. And she whispers things in your ear that only you can hear. Only you.

SKYBLANKET

Sliding in stealthily off the coast is a fat slab of cumulus, its belly warmed by the sun's passing. Deep, dense and dark it is; the result of a northern cyclone. Ribs of waves usher it forward with frothy lips. It creeps low and bulges with volition. Gorging on stars and moonlight. It belches cool air.

People snuggle into thick sheets and eiderdown, wary of the looming doona above, thankful for the heat ease. They wait.

Eleanor Rigby is baking muffins in the dark. Banana and cinnamon muffins. She sifts flour and whittles away night hours. Her breath is bitter with thirst and stale coffee.

Through open windows, Eleanor feels the cool humid change and its promise of rain and is not thankful. She hopes it passes quickly. She has never liked winter. Rain has always just further hemmed her confines, kept her inside.

Eleanor slips outside to strip her washed sheets from the line. A sudden chill shudders her shoulders. She is spat on intermittently from above as she gathers the bundle in her arms. And buried hidden in the scent of rain and fresh linen is a winter memory: of her mother, fondly folding linty sheets with memories of her own.

On wet weekends she often waxed sentimental about Inverness, the shire in Scotland where she had grown up. While it made her two daughters churlish and restless, winter always made her wistful. She spoke with a renascent sweetness in her smothered accent. Rain always reminded her of Home, she said, which was a Guest House her family ran in Drumnadrochit. She told Eleanor that people from all over the world stayed there, and told her tales of their own Homes. They had all come to see the Loch Ness Monster. She told Eleanor that Loch Ness was the most beautiful place she had ever seen. And Eleanor believed her, because her mother had seen the world. She showed her sepia photographs of the family lined by the loch, and surprised her daughter by their resemblance at the same age. She told her that the only Monsters at Loch Ness were her brothers who chased her up and down the headland with handfuls of mud.

Once, when it rained on her birthday, she gave Eleanor a ribbon of their original clan tartan, which she tied carefully into her hair. She promised her that they would go to Inverness together one day, when it was cold here and warm there, to see Loch Ness.

Eleanor said that it sounded like Happy Ness was just round the bend.

She imagined it. A Place. Where merry redbearded Scots in merry tartan kilts jigged and skipped in bright highlands, singing merry songs while munching buttery shortbread. In Happy Ness, they tossed pillarlike cabers and watched them cartwheel merrily downhill into a sparkly lake. Kersploosh. And according to Eleanor, if Happy Ness was a Place, then there must be other Places too. Like Cold Ness. And Wet Ness. Quiet Ness. And nearby Wilder Ness. And it sounded like you didn't have to go far to find Kind Ness. But you had to travel a long way to get from Near Ness to Far Ness. Big Ness loomed over Small Ness. There was a road that led straight to Mad Ness (where pale nude people with darting heads spoke only to themselves). And the boisterous people of Guin Ness (who liked Bitter Ness), sometimes passed Drunken Ness on their way there.

You had to climb the grassy slopes of Steep Ness to get to High Ness (where Godly Ness, of course, was next to Cleanly Ness) and shielding your eyes from the sun you could see Vast Ness. In the shadow of that mountain lurked Sad Ness, Empty Ness and Lonely Ness.

As the sun went down, the lush Green Ness turned into a dusky Dim Ness.

And it didn't matter where you were, reasoned Eleanor, because at night-time, everyone was in Dark Ness.

And you could walk through all these places in Dark Ness, when the sky was ink and the air was shadow. If you were lucky, you might bump into somebody nice. But you could walk for miles and miles and miles and still be in the same place, never to be seen.

And some people can't get out.

Bed made, Eleanor moves back into the kitchen to beat her mix without reflection. The television is off, so Estelle is sleeping. Warren warms his rump by the preheating oven.

She grits her teeth against a prickling pain in the base of her belly. With her foot she prods her dog out of the way. He licks spilt sugar from linoleum while she slides in the tray and slaps the door shut.

There is no breeze. She slowly packs things away. Warren circles, circles, circles and slumps back in front of the oven. The house is suddenly silent.

But in Dark Ness there is music playing. Only she can hear. A murmur, sad and saccharine. The sound of lullabies and comfort singing softly insistent in her head.

And then it spills, like a weeping confession. Straightdown, in heavy crackling sheets. It batters nodding leaves and drumrolls every roof. Slick streams of it follow contours, collecting Summer's dust and shit and residual heat. It washes cars and evicts earthworms. Hippies in colourful Punjabi suits laugh and dance in it with their thin arms raised and waving. They are stung by occasional bullets of hail. Thunder rumbles. Birds bathe with ruffled wings and dip their beaks into shallow pools. Surfers prep their boards. And Santa is woken on a back lawn. He giggles nervously, shivering, squinting, and wonders if he is drowning, wonders why he can't move.

People peel back their curtains just to watch the hissing swathe. One of them is Ewan, shirtless, sleep eluding him again. His room is still sultry with preserved heat. He observes a stolid, dignified frog squatting on his verandah, regarding the summer rain with suspicion. He is interrupted though, *again*, by the irritating source of his sleeplessness. Above him, more plangent than the roof-pounding rain, is the scrabbling and orgiastic squealing of those two relentlessly fucking possums. He glares at the ceiling. They have woken him at intervals throughout the night, and their current depraved foray moves him to a murderous, irrational anger.

From the kitchen he drags three stacked chairs and positions them beneath the manhole in his room. They groan and creak as he climbs them unsteadily. He lifts the manhole cover like a waiter carrying a tray. The ceiling is high, but he is just tall enough to peer into the roof cavity. The storm is deafening. Ewan slews a torch like a beacon and flinches as he spotlights two possums in reachable proximity; caught in their sordid act, frozen mid thrust. Joined unmistakably at the nether regions. One crouched, one upright. Ewan stares at the possums. The possums stare lazily at the light. With moist pink snouts and rigid bushy tails. They continue to stare as Ewan confronts his quandary. He is now unsure of what to do with them. He finds something unnerving about their haughty indifference.

Shut the *fuck* up! he yells at them finally, but he can barely hear his own voice.

And just as the two possums turn their heads to resume, a languid wolfspider wanders inquiringly on to the face of the torch, casting a sudden shadow large enough for Ewan to drop it in shock, lose his balance and topple forward, falling safely on to his bed. The manhole cover claps back into place. He is followed by a shower of dust. The spider totters out and down the hall (incidentally, to be eaten by the dignified amphibian).

Ewan lies with a pillow over his head.

It's three forty-five when the rain eases and thins to drizzle. And in a child's room, it's three forty-five when a vigil slips again. Twice in as many days. But this time, it's not exhaustion; she's disarmed, suddenly, by the ceaseless sound between her ears. A voice captured on an offshore breeze. Even louder now. Her subconscious finds a beat in the flicker of a stuck clock. Her eyelids, though, are mercifully still. And in the cool air, she sighs and gropes, pulling a sheet over herself. A cover, if only thin. It clings to her skin.

And under the same clearing cloudlayer, for the first time, Eleanor and Ewan both sleep on past dawn. Both their sheets stay dry. And both are woken late by resurgent heat.

MISSING

And so it is accompanied by a dog and stunned confusion that Eleanor worms into a pair of cheap sandals and closes her front door. She rubs the strange crust of sleep from her eyes. She is not used to being undone. Not used to waking dry. Or calm.

The lingering damp colludes with the heat. Hopeful green shoots present themselves in strips of washed-up soil. The air is syrupy.

Hovering is the immutable stink of sheepshit, spread by a squadron of trucks with a frightened freight of bleating live trade, and settling in the wharf. Woolly carcasses with dim heartbeats. There is no breeze to move the damp fetid air. It remains trapped beneath the bruise of an overcast sky.

Eleanor moves languidly, without conviction, though she knows where she's going. And she knows the way, despite having no sound to chase this time. Her head is silent now, save the burr of urban airconditioning. She sweats from a furrowed brow. She has Questions.

Warren sniffs at a rehydrated turd. It is not his.

She walks through a tight match of frontyard cricket and smells suncream. Past a boat enthusiast (with high pants) about to reverse his vessel into a limestone letterbox. And on towards Brunos Famly Cornerstore, which slumps in a perpetual state of implosion in the middle of the street.

Bruno, the ex-Romanian pseudo-Italian Australian Citizen, is negotiating dust beneath his store verandah. He was once described to Eleanor by a member of his slim custom as the lovechild of an inflatable whale and a soft-serve icecream.

He sees her nearing, leans on his millet broom and calls out:

Ha! Is my fayvorite Blind Midgit! Buongiorno Bella Hallynor! I am well, but the world it smells like shit today.

Eleanor waves sickly and keeps walking.

Ah! Hallynor, you know aye haff a new joke for you. Are you ready?

Eleanor keeps walking.

Okay, here it comes, here it comes, okay: Why doan Blind People skydive?

Bruno leans forward and pauses. Eleanor keeps walking.

Because it scares the shit out of their dogs! Aha! Is a good one yes? Ha ha!

But she is past him now, and she is not stopping. Bruno laughs on undeterred. He smiles and indulgently admires her arse. He suspects she didn't hear him (because Bruno assumes the blind are deaf too), which means he can tell his joke again. He vows to speak even louder next time.

He moves inside to berate his wife.

In a nearby neighbourhood, in another cornerstore (actually on a corner), Ewan is softly asking the man behind the counter the best way to take care of the two possums in his roof. The man laughs loudly. Ewan takes two steps backwards. He clasps his discomfort together in his hands to stop it making them shake.

The man reels off options, even offers to remove them himself. Then he leans forward, looks up and speaks conspiratorially. Ewan nods and leaves.

He considers the Last Option. Admits he is ready to drill them, good and proper.

He walks briskly down the short street to his house. It is thankfully quiet. Con's Cornerstore is his longest excursion outside. He usually goes at dawn, when nobody else is there.

Ewan stops as soon as he sees her. His belly sinks.

Again she is clasping his fence. And waiting, in the same place, like she hasn't moved since yesterday. She moves only to fan away flies, her face set in a hard blank stare. The dog sits attentively.

Ewan shrinks back into a nest of bottlebrush. Watches from a distance. The air is thick and sticky. Sweat rolls down his back. Bees skirt his head. He does not move.

They both wait.

Finally, he sees her dog lose patience and nuzzle at her thigh. Then pulling at her. She lingers, then takes up the leash. Says something short that he doesn't hear.

And she is walking towards him. His blood belts just under his skin. He leans further back into the bottlebrush. A butterfly flutters by. Closer she walks. He holds his breath.

Ewan looks down and watches as she walks past. She is as high as his ribcage. And she is right there. He could touch her. The dog eyes him warily. She rounds the corner before he moves. A bee stings his earlobe, and zips away to die. Ewan rushes inside to stop the shaking.

***

The streets are busy tonight with Yuletide preparation and the cooler, rarefied air. A steady seabreeze dissolves the septic sheepstink. The road is filled with the glares of headlights and impatient drivers. People diffuse from stores and restaurants littered with Christmas motifs to stroll listlessly along South Terrace. Eleanor is among them, munching on the samosa she has just bought from the markets. Embroiled in the fold and sway and brush of the crowds, more cautious than usual. The pavement is still warm underfoot. Tufts of her hair spring from beneath a short beige headscarf. She smells bad perfume, new books and eucalyptus from a shameless souvenir shop. Smells the garlic from a passing doner kebab. She walks beneath painfully carolling muzak.

Warren negotiates a sea of knees and shins and shoes. Narrowly avoids an imminent collision with a fast approaching pram. The saved toddler displays its gratitude by tugging hard at his ear. Warren quells a snappish growl, and resumes the dodging of self-absorbed meteors. (Of course, if he received the Respect he truly deserved, he wouldn't have to; he'd be cutting swathes through these people.) Instead he stops and starts and stops and waits, made all the harder by guiding a sponge with legs.

He weaves her around a tight group of women catching up with shrieks and hugs. They pause outside the stale beersmell of a corner pub. Eleanor turns and listens hard by the kerb.

Dyou need a hand, love? someone asks nearby.

No, she spins and says shortly. Then: No. No, thankyou. She offers a quick weak smile.

She prepares to motion Warren forward, but hesitates, stopping sudden and stolid. She shuffles back as a stream of Dickheads in hotted up sedans announce themselves with fat bass and pace. Cruising the streets looking for Blind People to kill.

She waits, then slips quickly to the median strip. She palms a traffic bollard. They play the game again.

This time, a spluttering kombi stops to let her pass. A dreadlocked head pokes from the window. Righto! he yells. You're good to go.

Eleanor flushes with hot embarrassment, in a headlight spotlight. She can feel the heads turning. She skips across with her head down. Offers no thanks.

Warren's relief is palpable as they move along the kerb to wait just outside the milling entrance of Gino's. He sits and sniffs lustily at the smorgasbord of aromas, watching the passing of fragrant plates with moisteyed envy. Eleanor rubs his snout. The waft of coffee is rich and heady. She feels pierced by interested stares. A novelty.

Finally she smiles. Steve arrives with a burst of familiar cologne.

Hey good lookin.

Ello Steve. There a table for me?

Steve smiles a set of deep dimples. He is hairy of chest and arm but balding prematurely. He carries a cream crate of cups and plates and cutlery and his rolled-up sleeves are wet. Steve is always happy to see her, as she is him, though she gives no intimation of getting closer. He takes pride in looking after her as covertly as possible.

Of course there is a table for you Elly, my dahling. You know we got to look after our lowest paying patron. Sitting outside yeah? Of course, of course. Steve stands on his toes. Okay, I believe I spy an opening. Come right this way ma'am.

And with his hand gently pressing her spine, Steve guides Eleanor to a table. Warren stumps along behind, sniffing his calves. Steve is careful and patient and aware of the stares. People offer knowing smiles, shunt their chairs in for them. Shuffling, he embeds her into the crowd. A centre table facing the street. Eleanor sits. Steve clears the table and wipes it. He crouches and rubs Warren's chest.

So how are you anyway?

Oh, you know. Blind. Hot. Tired. How's yourself?

Steve rolls his eyes. Oh, Elly Elly Elly, it's getting bloody desperate. It's all this heat. I need a woman.

Still nothing?

Elly, I tell you, at present, if it was raining virgins I'd be stuck in a gutter with a poof.

You poor man.

Oh! Don't get me started. Steve glances around, softens his voice. It's been so long I've forgotten what sex *is* Elly. I don't understand, I mean, take my word for it okay, I'm *very* good looking. For fucksake, I'm Italian! How hard can it be? It can't be me, surely.

Perish the thought.

Then what is it with you wimmin? Tell me, come on, what is it you want?

Coffee.

But that doesn't help *me*.

Sorry. I'll keep an eye out for you.

Steve laughs. Well, that'd be a load off.

Bad pun Steve.

I know, I know. Okay, so, coffee yeah? Coming right up. There's another bad pun. I'll be right back.

Thanks.

Steve backs up, evading talking heads with his crate. He'll be back with coffee and a dish of water for Warren. Maybe some chocolate, or something from the kitchen if it's not too busy. He'll pretend to take the money from her purse, and she'll pretend she doesn't know he's pretending. He'll make her laugh. And leave her be.

She is quickly forgotten. Swallowed by the surroundsound swelling of noise and bodies. She is framed by full tables. She hears a chunky blues guitar to her left. Beside it, two phlegmatic old Italian men roll a stockpile of unfiltered cigarettes with iodine stained fingers. They mutter incoherently about soccer and the stock market, breathing the fruity odour from their tobacco pouches. Their rheumy eyes twinkle.

Directly behind her, a jaded homeless man is reading Tolstoy with a ragged Pekinese on his lap. She can smell him on the breeze. He drinks sourness from a carafe of dark red wine. His lips pucker. He reads frenetically. When he finishes a page, he tears it down the spine and calls out the page number, like he's announcing a raffle. He looks around, expecting someone to leap from a nearby table waving the corresponding page number. When nobody claims it, he screws up the page and tosses it over his shoulder.

Occupying her right is a caustic boyfriend-girlfriend tiff; a game of backgammon between two thin men wearing dun cardigans and thickrimmed glasses, who laugh histrionically whilst surveying the tables around them; a maternal reprimand from a family of five; a table of girls who share passionfruit lipgloss; a table of boys who don't; a table of boys and girls warily watching the freak in the corner; and a church group. They all mesh into a discordant blather.

At the centre of it all sits Eleanor Rigby. She is strangely insular. She's not listening tonight. Doesn't even hackle at the insidious trill of a mobile ringtone.

Steve brings strong coffee. She smiles.

The soy is curdled, she accuses. And you call yourself Italian.

How do you know?

I can smell it. Strong. Like the scent of your Desperation.

Nasty, Elly. Nasty.

Steve smiles and pretends to take money from her purse. He tells her he can't chat because the kitchen is busy tonight. She doesn't appear to hear. Steve observes her straight, vacant stare. He opens his mouth, but pauses and slips away.

Blind Girl in a crowded cafe. Brings her spoon to the lip of the sugar dispenser. Measures by weight. One. And a half. Stirs. Doesn't seem to blink. Sips. Ringed by life and noise.

Eleanor surfaces upon recognising a bottom-end riff from the table to her left. A cover song. It is accompanied badly by a woman on amphetamines spanking a tabla. And followed up with a gritty, accented voice that is tonelessly Godblessing Mrs Robinson (because Heaven holds a place for those who pray, heyheyhey, heyheyhey).

The church group perks up.

And Eleanor grimaces on behalf of Paul Simon.

But this too (like linen and rain) unveils another buried hidden vestige. And tonight the tune strikes her as a cheap, eerie coincidence.

Revived is the memory of an eight-year-old vinyl junkie. She loved the feel of the stuff. Its hiss and crackle. The way she could play it without speakers, without cords or electricity. Eleanor had a pile of records taller than she was. Armed with saved pocket money, she looted dusty stores and op shops and the trestle tables of garage sales. She wheedled discounts and snaffled bargains. Loaded her LPs into an embarrassing florid basket and rode them home to play on her mother's old wind-up gramophone (a grand old mahogany heirloom, tinkered with and abandoned by Eleanor's inventive Uncle Victor, who slowed its rotation and adapted its pin so it could play 45s and LPs). She felt music strongly. She was eclectic and discerning. She had Billie Holiday, Ella Fitzgerald, Elvis, Otis Redding, James Brown, Chuck Berry,

Cat Stevens, The Smiths, The Cure, Abba, the Beach Boys, Split Enz. She loved jazz. When she played her Dizzy Gillespie records, she would hopskipjump up and down the hallway blowing a wild Air Trumpet.

She hated Bing Crosby and Sinatra. Loved The Rolling Stones, Neil Young, Bob Dylan, Queen, and kept her Joni Mitchell records near the top.

She loved the Beatles. Ringo was her favourite because he was the narrator of Thomas the Tank Engine on Channel Two. She bought Revolver because it had her name on it. When she saw it, she went very quiet and very still. She tingled all over. She touched her name to make sure. Looked around to see if anyone was watching. Like it was a secret. And she raced back on a pink bicycle, wound the brass winch and set the pin only to find that it was the saddest song in the world. She was crestfallen. She listened only once. On the album sleeve she scribbled out her name with a black pen. She kept it at the bottom of the pile, under Burt Bacharach.

But her very very favourite by far was Paul Simon. She knew all the songs off by heart, especially the ones he sang with his friend Gary Funkle, the tall man with the afro. (She explained to Jenny that he was there mostly to keep Paul company.)

Her very very favourite album was Graceland. She bought it for twenty cents. It gave her dreams of Africa. Some songs she heard, her chest would tighten until it hurt. It was difficult to breathe or swallow. She stood in front of the gramophone absorbing with her eyes closed and she felt like bursting. Fortified and restless. Some songs she poked her head inside the huge open horn and sang as loud as she could. And if she was asked where Happy Ness was, she'd say it was that moment just there: yodelling into the snout of a gramophone.

But then the gramophone was secretly wheeled into Jenny's room. No one missed it. Winding it up became Preparation. And vinyl changed. It became the stuff you put in front of noise of a night, like Dark was stuff in front of Light. Just loud enough. It lulled and hushed you both to sleep. Fortification and rest. Door closed. And with Jenny there, held and holding, you could stay there safe.

This much she understands:

That music could be somnolent now. That it might lay her down. Like last night.

But what she can't seem to grasp is how a stringed voice on an offshore breeze might undo her and keep her under, safe. How to explain the blankness? The closed sack. Mutiny effaced. A screen with no projection. How to explain that? The sound that stuck to teflon. The sound that arrested her, and she couldn't *be* arrested. She was too far away. She was bolstered by Distance; which had shortened as she drew nearer to listen. She didn't think. She just went. Pushed and pulled. Hard to believe that something could spill through the outside air like that. That fleshy, woven flow, in the key of D. Pervasive. It flensed her as she stood, head in a gramophone. It hit hard in an empty place. And the sound of it was too many things at once. It was coarse but earthen but watery but dense but lilting but tenebrous. It was a quelled riot: contained and falling apart. It was tense and gentle, it was soft strident brittle.

It was how she felt. And that was it. It did what the Beatles couldn't. And it came in volts. Tore at her, and she tore away. Strange time to have your period start. She left quickly. So did he. (She suspected he was a he. She just felt these things.) After an awkward, shaky silence. With a fence between.

And she's been back there four times today. To that same silence.

Steve brings another coffee at the end of his shift. She flinches.

Easy, Tiger, he says and she smiles. You okay, Elly?

Dandy Steve.

Want somming to eat?

No no, I'm fine. Thanks Steve. She tips the sugar.

Well, don't jump off any cliffs orright?

No, I tried that, but my stupid dog wouldn't let me. She stirs and sips.

Shit, you're not going to sleep tonight are you.

Any sort of luck.

***

Stores have shut their hinged mouths. Slowly the crowds have filtered out. Behind her, the homeless Pekinese owner hawks and spits thickly into the empty carafe, a generous tip. He looks at the tiny young woman in front of him, and with raised eyebrows he considers propositioning her for a quick fuck, but thinks better of it. He departs stiffly, leaving scattered paper balls of *War and Peace*.

Eleanor hears chairs being stacked around her. Warren is asleep.

Across the road, outside the pub, a hoary gentleman in a black greatcoat patiently paces the bus stop. And with an uncanny resemblance to Tom Waits, he gargles the lyric:

Ah ken git no, sat is fack shun
Ah ken git no, sat is fack shun

over and over and over again. A marching beat. It seems to Eleanor as good a mantra as any.

She hears the dingding of last drinks. Drains her second coffee.

And if she permitted it, if she let it run its course, this feeling now could Give Way to another unwanted segue. And backbackback she would go. Greeted by another winter memory. At night. And she would be sitting right here. With misty drizzle and a cold wind. The smell of wet dog and peppermint tea. She would be huddling into a colossal woollen jumper (Steve would say that it looked like you shoved your head up the arse of a plump sheep and pulled down hard).

It would be a busy wet weekend.

And a Hero would be approaching.

Slowly.

Pinkly.

Nudely.

On a skateboard. He would round Market Street, on to the Terrace. And it would erupt around you. Cheers and shrieks.

The Hero would wear nothing but a trailing red cape and an old leather aviation helmet. Arms stretched like wings, cruciform, like Jesus. Waitresses would stop. The rumour would spread up the strip. It would clear tables. A crowd three deep would form down both sides into a loose guard of honour. Lining the kerb, waiting for him to come back. Everyone would be up. And louder as he returned, with a broad grin under a handlebar moustache. Women would scream and point. His genitals would resemble a peanut atop a walnut. A camera would flash. A Mexican wave would follow him, as people laughed uproariously and watched him disappear. They would take their smiles back to their tables. They, they, they. You.

You would be sitting. You would have no idea. Warren, head darting, confused. And you would laugh like the self-conscious dance. Like you didn't fit. Restrained. A timorous, brittle thing, like the Hero's gonads.

And it would hit you, hotly, suddenly, the shame of it. Your polarity. Your farawayness. Of being so fucking *close* to something, but totally missing it. Like you weren't really even there. Half in two worlds. Detached. Apart. And not A Part of either.

And a nude man on a skateboard would rub it in your face: that you were alone in your disjunction, separate in any world, in any place. Apart.

And against your will it would make you think of just how much of your day comprised simply missing things. Just how much eluded you. Just how many kicks you were behind the play. Unravelled, you would entertain these thoughts.

You would be sitting with a guide dog and a slipped guard. And ambivalence.

Eleanor Rigby, the girl who kept Distance above all, would feel excluded.

Would. Would if she permitted it. If she let it run its course.

Now, jacked on caffeine and fairly busting, Eleanor rises. Warren wakes.

She'll miss the impatient scowl of the Czech waitress taking her cup and saucer.

She'll cringe as she slips cautiously into the thick stink of the adjoining public toilet. She'll take Warren with her. And hovering awkwardly above the bowl, she'll miss reading the scrawl of scatology on the back of the door; the phone numbers of local whores, carved initials, a passage from the Book of Revelation, and a selection of quotes badly spelled.

In Fresh Air, she'll wander aimlessly for a while.

And miss a lusty stare. The moon in a puddle. A news-stand headline. She'll miss her dog being pinked by a neon glow. On the Esplanade Reserve, she'll miss seeing the string of lights draped straight down the length of the Norfolk Island pines, so they look like a line of giant upright cucumbers.

Earlier that night, she missed the chance to peer into a Lebanese restaurant, where judicious husbands pretended not to be seduced by the frenetic titwobbling of a bellydancer. She missed glancing at an indifferent woman in the far corner, flicking raven hair that could have belonged to her mother, once upon a time.

She missed seeing her reflection in that window, and missed the shock that would have floored her. She would have touched her face, wondered where the roundness went, when the sharp angles took over.

She missed what the hell people were *wearing* now, though it sounded as though women still wore heels.

She'll miss a swung fist and a scuffle down a dim side street.

The hoary gentleman misses his bus. He keeps pacing.

In King's Square, she'll walk briskly by without seeing a sprawled group of Aborigines under a thick Moreton Bay canopy. They sit and slump on a lifesize chessboard, made from Black and White pavement squares. Used commercially for lifesize people to play lifesize games of chess. They don't care for any square. They seem unaware of the board; the game and its rules. The White Queen is absent. The Black King lies curled. Beneath those squares is Dirt, or Nyungar land, and they sit with that board between it: lolling, yelling, sleeping. Waiting to be moved, again. Clutching paper bags in the shape of bottles. Sniped at by Moreton Bay figbombs. Wedged between a Church and a Town Hall.

She'll miss surveying that bitter triptych. Bells will chime. She will be surprised by the time.

There are smaller chessboards for smaller games on tables nearby. Elderly men sometimes sit there waiting for contestants. She sat there one day, without knowing the other side was occupied by a petulant old turd with grubby bifocals and a set board. She started when he spoke. He told her she couldn't play because she couldn't see the pieces.

Bollocks, she said.

He beat her in four moves. She reset the board. Chess was hard at first, but it just took practice. And fierce concentration. Keeping the grid set in your mind. Knowing it. Keeping it there. (Now, *Scrabble*. Scrabble was a headfuck.)

They met on Tuesdays. Spoke only to move the pieces. She infuriated him by walling up her King, and moving her Queen out early. They were both stubbornly competitive. When he started cheating after she forced her first check, Eleanor left him alone. She would have claimed a Moral Victory, but she nabbed one of his onyx handcrafted knights. She settled for a Stalemate.

She'll miss a patrolling police wagon eyeing her with suspicion.

She'll miss a couple nestling a bong on their verandah swingchair.

And there are some things she can't bear missing, like the gone and left. Like Theo. Like Jenny. Absences too big to fill.

She's tired of missing. And missing the Missing. And maybe that's why, right now, she spends too long gripping this fence, waiting for a sound that she has to hear again.

But if it was there, she missed it. There is now only a faint scrabbling and the whisper of a chill breeze.

She pulls away. Misses a pale face staring from behind a peeled back curtain.

THE AMAZING AND WONDERFUL, COOL
AND FANTASTICAL ALEXANDER POPOFF

Back here:

Ewan loves to watch Jim's fingers. Sliding, punching, rolling, tickling notes so they sing like nothing else ever has. He loves the way Lilian rises and falls and settles into Jim's shallow frame. Clicking into place, like she fits. And the limpwristed fabric sway of the bow. A loose, liquid extension of his arm.

And Ewan sits opposite on the same Turkish rug, their Magic Carpet. Socks down, school tie removed. Watching and smiling with Kamahl, his midget. His toes curl and he is lost in it. A feisty rush fizzles up his back, imbues him with an unbearable energy. He wants to runaround and dance badly. Do something with it. And it's so easy to see that she is more than woodandstrings, the way she sighs stretches sings breathes life. And Jim is just warming up.

These are the Adventures of Zoltan and Wolfgang (pronounced: *voolfgung*). They happen every Tuesday afternoon. After the school siren, there are three linking buses in suburban Sydney with the urgent freight of a child and a cello. They can't go fast enough.

At the last stop, a boy, to whom everything is yet to be bequeathed, leaps through the hiss of hydraulic doors. Kamahl bumping in his celloshell. Brisk walk. Quick steps. Two raincoats when it rained. And there's Excitement bubbling deepdown somewhere in his chest. A knack on the latch of a chickenwired gate. The velvety pelt of a damp mossy path. Letting himself in through the front door. Yelling *Ahoy!* down the dim hall. The savoury smell of past meals and tea-leaves and the tincture of weed.

And there's Jim: thin, dishevelled, scruffy. He walks stiffly, with a pronounced limp. Like a pre-greased Tinman, but with a heart. He grins. He is nineteen. He has the complexion and stippled arms of a junkie. He feels the cold, and so always wears a V-neck jumper.

They shake hands sagely, such is the Traditional Greeting.

And how for art thou, thy noble Zoltan?

Truly spiffing, sir. And thou?

I feelst like shite as ever. Would thou please haveth a seat thither?

And Ewan sits. He watches him play, Haydn today, as he shells his halfsize cello and prepares. Smiling. Lilian is lovely to him, in timber and timbre. A shudder gusts from his spine. A cloak of tingles to start the lesson.

He winds his bownut and watches as Jim's stiffness and coldness disappear before his very eyes. Like magic.

But trace backbackback from the tips; away from that manic vibrato and the flurry of Jim's fingers, through the arthritic jolt of wrist and joint and tendon, up the knotted atrophy of that forearm, and there's a different rush in this room. A slower, seeping, pulsing rush. It stems from a tiny tear in a tiny cluster of vessels. There, in the hinge of the arm. A calm collection of blood. A silent, stealthy contusion. And nothing is going to stop it.

Doctors call it haemophilia. Jim doesn't. And he knows enough about Doctors to disagree with bitter conviction. Haemophilia. From the Greek: *haemo* — blood, and *philia* — affection. And Jim has no Affection for his Blood. Dumb Blood, he calls it. Terminally Stupid. A few factors short of a bloodclot.

And Jim won't know about this bleed for a few hours. While plasma spills and spreads with every dopey bloat and lapse from that ticking Tinman heart. With no plug. No clot. Nothing. It's a slow, excruciating, pointless stampede of cells. And it will continue to flow, building pressure under the skin. Distending the muscleflesh until it is taut and tight with the surfeit. Unable to break the skin, it will push back inwards. It has nowhere else to go. It will suck into the joints and strangle nerves.

Jim's pain is constant. Bleeding has fused his joints and caused debilitating arthritis which slowly drains his dexterity. It has gnarled his fingers and produced an awkward gait. He appears impossibly old.

It's when Jim recognises the Additional Pain that he does the plumbing. It is easier now than it ever was. When he was a child, it meant a tedious cryoprecipitate transfusion in a hospital. Now, the missing factor has been isolated into a concentrated powder, which he mixes with distilled water and administers intravenously with a butterfly needle. A Dissolution. A styptic swallowed in transit, flushed and filtered into the bruise. A precious plug.

But back here on a Tuesday afternoon, Ewan is not wrong when he sees the stiffness disappear. Jim goes to another place. Like magic. And Jim gets his pigment back, as he plays for analgesia on a cello called Lilian.

Jim told Ewan that Lilian was the oldest and most infamous cello in the world. Her History According To Jim was as inaccurate as it was entertaining, and randomly amended.

Jim said that Lilian had been carved and fitted by Elvish craftsmen longlongago, using a secret enchanted wood called *Brabuhr*, which was found at the guarded helm of a perilous promontory. They said it had special healing powers. She was savoured by the elves for the sweetness of her voice. However (alas), she had been stolen by a giant who lived on a cloud and used her as a viola. Later, she was bartered to a village of dwarfs for seven gold ingots and a small pony. They lived in a town called Lillianput and used her as a double bass.

Jim said she had passed through many hands and generations since. She had been fondled by Eros. Plucked by monkeys. Hidden in a secret cave on the isle of Monte Cristo. Pilfered by pirates. She had been a gift from Caesar to Cleopatra. A talisman for a tribe of Pygmies. She had been plundered by Vikings (*Ahoy!*), pillaged by Normans and rescued by the

Gnomes of Zurich. She inspired Bach and made Stradivari weep with frustration. She had been part of a quartet that played on the *Titanic*, and sank with it. She froze into an iceberg, and for forty days and forty nights, she was flotsam against the tide. She washed up in London, on the river Thames.

And perhaps most famously (Jim liked this story), she had been part of a wedding present from Kaiser Wilhelm to the Russian Empire, when they handed over a dud wife to the last tsar.

After initially being stowed away by Nicholas (nephew of Alexander II), she was later played by a lascivious monk called Rasputin to ease the discomfort of their Dumb Blooded son Alexis. But Rasputin, it was said, was really playing in order to shag the tsar's wife, Alexandra. Rumour was he had her under a spell. When Nicholas found out, he was suitably unimpressed. Summoning his Royal Bouncers, he organised to have Rasputin killed.

They tried poisoning him during a midnight tea party. When that failed, they tried biffing him around, then tried shooting him. They tried everything, but he just wouldn't die. Despairing, one of the guards picked up Lilian and stabbed him through the heart with her endpeg.

Subsequently, Jim explained, Lilian was hailed as a catalyst for the Russian Revolution. She became a Bolshevik Mascot and was openly adored by the proletariat. St Petersburg was renamed as Liliangrad (but Lenin later stole the show).

She was later exiled to Britain. Allegedly, she lay low in an antique store for a while.

Jim said his great-grandfather won her in a poker game with a leprechaun. His father gave her to him on the day of his birth. His mother gave him haemophilia.

Jim was equally imaginative with his own origins. He said that his father was a man called Sisyphus, who courted and made sweet love to a dung beetle. And they called their child Jim, who was forever destined to walk backwards, pushing a great ball of shit uphill.

Ewan laughed because it was silly. Jim laughed because he was bitter.

Jim's life was a series of tradeoffs. He was, he said, relentlessly fucked by irony.

Jim was desperate to relieve his arthritis. But each remedy held a catch, a reaction. He swam routinely. Slow, stiff laps which eased the joints but exhausted him to a state of anaemia. He smoked a spliff after every meal, but relief from the spicy anodyne was fleeting, and becoming harder to achieve. Painkillers were Effects with Side Relief. He was trading ailments.

For years he had been religiously applying rhubarb root to his wrist, knee and elbow joints. He swore it reduced the inflammation. However, it also eliminated stagnant blood and invigorated its flow. It made bleeds harder to staunch. It took as much as it gave.

And it was his most effective prophylaxis for pain that caused Jim the most damage. She was two hundred years old, made of wood and strings and varnish.

The sound of her, the playing of her annealed him. Numbed him blissfully for the duration. He needed that sound to fill his lungs and convince them to push back outwards. But she taxed him heftily. She pressed against his chest, she wore red sores into his knees and grated his joints. Right under his nose as he juiced the sound from her. She tore tendons and vessels and ligaments. Bleed by bleed. Leached the use of his body while he sought reprieve in hers.

But it was his lifeblood that provided Jim's most thorough fuckover. It almost made him laugh, that the blood that saved his life would end it.

At the beginning of the glorious eighties, Jim had just embraced the new powdered concentrate. It was processed from a much broader blood pool, which meant more donors. There was HIV found in the blood supply. After concerned enquiries, Jim and his family were assured by doctors and health authorities that the concentrate bore no risk of contamination. Jim continued with the new treatment. Jim contracted HIV. So did another two hundred and sixty Australian haemophiliacs.

Dumber Blood.

And it sat. Heavy. Dormant. An unarmed bomb. It waited.

Jim was twenty-three when he died.

Back here, on a Tuesday afternoon, Ewan has his cello ready and waiting. Jim lays Haydn and his bow to rest. The first thing they do is engage in the Ancient Oriental Art of Tu Ning. It doesn't take long.

Jim urges Creation in his lessons. He tells Ewan that he is not concerned with levels and stages. He is training him for his Artistic Licence. They have never played a scale in a lesson. They play pieces, of course, but the emphasis is on interpretation. Jim is still strict on technique and tone, on posture and the alignment of energy. But he tells Ewan that the basis of it all, the *point*, is to Create. To do something with it. To make something that has never existed before, in all the History of the world. Something that wasn't here yesterday, wasn't here the day before or five minutes ago. Out of thin air. Something real and alive, like music. That was yours alone and couldn't ever be taken away. That was magic.

Ewan knows that his instrument is alive. Even Kamahl, who is a midget. Jim has shown him how. By lightly running his fingers down a string and drawing the bow, he can make harmonics hit him like sparks. Like electric charges on the tips of his fingers. It makes an ethereal tinklytingly sound. Sugarsweet. The sound of a segue into a dream scene.

They play. They giggle whenever someone mentions the G-string. Or the Nutcracker Suite. They joke and talk loudly. They fart. They drink tea with biscuits. They work hard. Jim tells stories about the great composers, of players and movements and orchestras. Tales of incest and intrigue and reckless debauchery. And Ewan just soaks it all in.

Jim said he was once beaten in the pool by a brick with flippers.

He was slow. Chopping through that university pool was like hacking through honey. Thick honey. Against a *tide* of thick honey.

Shivering, he would shake his head in a changeroom full of wet athletes, their huge healthy bodies against his pale emaciated frame. Their wide shoulders that did not scrape and ache with movement. Though Jim felt no resentment. He loved swimming, and loved to watch competition by virtue of his own disappointment. He recognised the rhythm in it.

Jim took Ewan to an international meet in Sydney one weekend. They sat far back and way up in the congested, humid stadium. They ate steaming overpriced chips with vinegar and cheered lapafterlapafterlap. Jim felt light in the vaporous air, and a little stoned. He tried to conceal the agony of his wasted knees wedged behind the seat by concentrating on the action. The podiums, anthems, tight races, tight times, women in tight swimsuits.

The two of them giggled whenever they heard the word Breaststroke. And they lost it completely when the announcer announced the name of a young Russian upandcomer (from south of Liliangrad): Alexander Popoff.

Fanta sprayed from Ewan's nose over the neck of the man in front. Jim almost choked on his chip. They checked their program and there it was: Popov. Ewan was frankly astounded that Popoff could actually be someone's name. They laughed until irritated people asked them to stop.

And as they cheered and watched him win all his races easily, the Russian suddenly became an enduring legacy they took home with them.

He has evolved into The Amazing And Wonderful, Cool And Fantastical Alexander Popoff: an epic performance at the end of every lesson. A concerted jam. A tribute. And it is different every time. According to their mood, they sometimes precede it (hand on heart, in a dubious Russian accent) by singing the following lyric:

Ohhh! I am the
Amazing
And Wonderful,
Cool and Fantastical
Alexaaaaaaander Popoff!
And I'll never ever ease (bup dadada dum)
Through those cold Russian seas (bup padada da)
For I go up to my knees (buppada dadada)
And I almost freeeeeeeze! (dum dum dum dum)
And I fear, that my baaaaaaaalls
Should dropoff!

Ewan watches Jim with a grin. They bow and begin.

And at the end of a Tuesday afternoon, from here it is anything. Anywhere.

Baroque. Rock. Ragtime. Something Arabic. Something Celtic. Vaudeville. Jim might have Ewan jigging like a dirty Dubliner. Or have him waltzing Kamahl across a dusty rug. They might do the Funky Chicken. Or some country slide. They may jazz it up. Ewan might hold down a bass line and Jim might scat all over it. They don't know.

Sometimes they traded riffs. Threw them back and forth. Echoed ditties. Softloud. Loudsoft.

They played Name That Tune. They rhapsodised. Played

lullabies. They were Blues Kings and Pop Queens. They were synchronised and syncopated, harmonised and dissonant. They abandoned the theory. Paced it up. Slowed it down. Switched keys at will. They remixed Bach and Brahms and Schubert. Jim once played a Hendrix medley. And Rachmaninov backwards.

Sometimes, just to see Jim play fast, Ewan would say: *Honestly*, Wolfgang, thou playst like my grandmother. I challenge thee to a Duel!

Ba! he would say, Ewan whose army?

Ha! That's Ewan Dempsey to you good sir!

And Jim would always win.

Ewan liked to play with his eyes closed. And Jim would smile and shake his head at the ease of his talent, his ability to invent. To experiment with tone and dynamics and rhythm. Sometimes tight, sometimes messy.

At the end of a Tuesday afternoon, they will take something they know to somewhere they don't. They never confer. And so learn to trust their understanding of each other, to let it evolve.

It is a semblance of their mood. They might move slowly in plaintive minor scales. Sometimes they have to stop for laughing.

Look at them! They are the greatest virtuoso duet in all of History! Zoltan and Wolfgang! Watch them weave their myooozical edifice of splendiferous improvisation. Out of thin air. Gasp and bask as they discover it, uncover it, merkinball it. The Amazing and Wonderful, Cool and Fantastical Alexander Popoff. A serious thing with a stupid name. Whatever it is, it's theirs (and Alexander's) and more important than they know. Ewan is in love with it. It is the best thing in the world to him.

It lifts and evanesces, like smoke. But its transience doesn't matter. There is always more to come.

It is always dark when they finish. The dregs of their tea always cold.

Jim will always say, Shit, Zoltan. Where *did* the Time go?

To Brazil. I think we scared it off.

And exhausted but full, Ewan will pack away his cello.

Jim ruthlessly overcharges Ewan's parents. So at the end of every lesson, before he takes him home in a red Renault, he always pares off a cut and gives it to him.

Then there was a cavernous coldblue leather suitcase. Open, for Ewan to pack all the Shit He Didn't Need. Then closed, so he could drag it and pack it into the cavernous boot of a coldblue Volvo.

In the front seats on a cold July morning, there sat Ewan and his father. Loss sat in the backseat, next to Kamahl. Heavy. Amorphous. Invisible.

They only took hand luggage to the other side of the country, because everything was going to be New.

As the Volvo severed away, there was no waving, no turning, no goodbyeing. It was a Tuesday. Ewan was very still, and very quiet.

Jim said he didn't understand the term Life Expectancy. He preferred Death Expectancy, because that's what he had.

Jim advocated an entertaining funeral. He intended to literally go out with a bang. He told Ewan he wanted a jolly procession in the evening, at the head of a cliff overlooking the ocean. He said he wanted his casket stuffed with fireworks and attached to a hang-glider. His pallbearers would throw him off and light a long trailing fuse. And everyone would sip sweet port and Ooh and Ahh at the bursts of colour.

They laughed. Then Jim started to play Yesterday, by Paul McCartney. He sang with a sweet voice:

> *Leprosy …*
> *I'm not half the man I used to be*
> *There are limbs falling off of me*
> *Oh, Leprosy, came suddenly*

And they laughed until they ached.

***

It's midnight. Can't sleep. There are now four days to Christmas, eleven left in the year, the century, the millennium, as he plays for a counterfeit memory on a cello called Lilian.

He smells mothballs and dust. Can't smother the thought that this, suddenly this, is getting harder.

SWALLOWED

Mutiny again.

In the wake of heavy breathing, a sack is spilling. Opened by shut eyelids. With a projection reel flicker, exposing the quartermoon whites of her eyes.

(Stuck, stuck, stuck).

In Dark Ness, dreams are forged from stored images. They unsettle stubborn sediments and trap them.

She is summoned and shifted to a cloudless, starless night. She sees a girl standing, faceless, on a thickplanked jetty with no rails. A fat gust hooks at her gooseflesh and sucks at her long hair. Sweeping coldness skimmed from the water's surface. Sand blusters up from the decking, stings her skinny legs.

No ears. No nose. No mouth. No eyes. Barefoot. The rawboned body of a child, hugging out the cold.

A ribbed tide is pressing towards her, burnishing the jettylegs. It smears the shore, stains it a darker hue. Lapping and slapping. The sound of dim fists.

Silverdusted dunes look on like a grandstand. Bleak in the moongleam. A Golden Retriever playing the part of Warren tumbles down the declivity, tripping, rolling, sliding. The girl laughs with no mouth as she looks on with no eyes and waves to no response.

The water is suddenly messy with assorted flotsam. Murk. Seaweed. Feathers. Celestial reflection. She is overlooking Bathers Beach; this jetty where the seawall would be. There is no warm wharfglow. And only a broad stretch of water behind her.

Also bobbing are a television, a satellite, tampons, trash. Bottles without messages in them. A grinning inflatable whale with a coiled cap of softserve icecream. A refracted surge of herring. A gramophone with a snuffling lily snout. And a dog playing the part of Warren paddling in circles; a furry eddy.

Alone on the jetty, the faceless girl sees a Big Violin coursing silently towards her. Almost submerged. Its strings are broken and spread like whiskers, too light to tear the waterskin, though these floppy oars seem to row in stunted strokes. It parts a shimmering, furrowed V in its wake. It comes closer. She is not afraid.

She glances up and sees the defunct Roundhouse atop a granite knoll. And the circular convict prison spins like a merry-go-round, with bright flashing lights. Pulsing above it is a Big Red Arrow. And three Big Red Words: **You Are Here.**

The tide rises. Lapping and slapping and louder still.

She feels heat between her legs. She clamps them shut. It scalds. It's blood, she knows, but she can't see it. Smells its ferric scent. Feels it sticky and itching. She turns to run but her feet they are stuck, stuck, stuck to this jetty. Her head pounds. Feels heat and she tremors. So hot, so cold. Long hair lashes sweeps wraps. The dog playing Warren barks like Warren. Reams of beerfrothed waves claim more shore, like an Englishman with a flag. Louder they are. The sound of fists.

Tries to wrench free, her legs betray her. Naked, she falls. Crusted with sand and dried bait. Flat chest hurts. Hands between her legs, stopping, stopping.

And there's Theo at the end of the jetty. Tall. He casts no shadow. His bald head with a hair curtain, unruffled by the wind. He smiles and points to his eyes. His pupils dilate constrict dilate constrict. Big then small then big.

With his left hand he uncaps the bald part of his scalp. Lifts it off. It makes the sound of a cracked egg. He dips his other hand in. He cups gold yolk. Dripping viscous. It flares suddenly with light. He laughs, proffers it to her.

Rhubarb, he says.

The jetty groans with the lapping and slapping and she screams it with a mouth she doesn't have. Her faceless face strains and flushes red. The Roundhouse spins madly.

And it rains rhubarb. In thick strips from a clear sky.

Splish. Splash. Splosh.

It fells a seagull. Theo laughs, though he's not there any more. The dog playing Warren chews on a floating fat stick of it, and squints at its raw tartness.

Hot and hairless, she sees the Big Violin approaching and she quietens. It passes beneath the jetty. The gaunt girl scrambles, feet freed. Fire on her fingertips. She reaches as it re-emerges. A touch. Her finger licks the scroll, but it eludes her. The girl spends her balance on that hope. Gravity shoves her again.

Splosh.

Her fingers fizzle. She's under. Darkness. Swallowed, she's sinking. Gulping and thrashing. She is scratched by barnacles, but they're chewed back fingernails above the crust of this dream. Heat heat heat heat heat.

Mutiny shut by open eyes. Heaving, it subsides.

Just in time to be shamed by boiling jets of urine. Marinating her thighs.

Sweating and shivering, Eleanor frowns and sits up. Arms knotted across her chest like a fleshy straitjacket. Different dream, same result.

Unnerved, she quickly wipes herself with the sheet. Pulls on random clothes. Warren is there, harness in his mouth. She slips it on, buckles it. She takes no shower. Gets moving. Instinct takes her outside.

Breathes deep. Warren yawns (tongue curling, then unfurling) and keeps up. The pavement is cool. No sunrise to warm her spine. This is not a wellworn path. She is seething and ashamed and resolute. She knows the way.

Estelle wakes to the sound of a slammed door. She wonders if someone has broken in, or if it's just Eleanor leaving. Either way, she can't help but feel nothing.

Because it's late, he mutes her voice with clothespegs across her bridge. Just to muffle the volume. A gentle gag. He puts his faith in Schubert.

She's come here. Instead of her rock, instead of the Big Ness of the ocean and its weighty waterlap. And from a beggar's hand, she casts a different line.

She has found the gate and walked through. There is no fence between. She follows Warren, creeping up a centre path. She is still damp, with a faint acrid reek.

One. Two. Three steps. A verandah. She can smell mint and the blush of a bougainvillea. Moves to the right. Settles under a window.

A small sound might expire from her mouth as she hears it; recognises it.

Eleanor Rigby rocks herself gently to a minor key. Knees to chest. Hugging them. Her rough, matted hair damp and dark at the roots. A straight, blank stare.

She doesn't know why she's here. But it's working, it's working. It's soft. A wash; lambent on her skin. It fills her till she stills. She lets it.

Warren's nose twitches and tweaks as he patrols the verandah, overcome by new smells. He licks a nugget of rosin. It looks like toffee but tastes of turpentine. He only licks once. He chews on a bush of basil instead. Sniffs at a coir mat, and the gap beneath the door. Trotting to the far end, he sniffs the bashful face of a dusty garden gnome.

Warren lifts his head and confronts a possum.

Standing. Startled. They eye each other off. Ears lifted in inquiry.

Warren, tickled by gnomedust, sneezes hard. It scares the possum, which scampers through his legs, up a verandah support and on to the roof. Warren shifts quickly with much scrabbling. His fanning tail swipes a broomhandle to the floor. The scuffle is Loud.

The music stops.

Ewan, angry, charges down the hallway intent on the death of two possums.

Swinging the front door open violently, he reels seeing that blind girl, bending, recovering her dog. Right there. He could touch her. Ewan steps back, sick to the belly, holding the door. The dog looks chastised and worried.

She turns, looks down. I'm sorry, she says softly as he closes the door on her.

OTHER PEOPLE'S SMILES

Estelle was Eleanor's mother.

She is fifty-seven and she has seen the world.

Everything has gone pear shaped for Estelle. Age has crudely compressed the healthy, plump curvature she once wore. It has also leaked her of oestrogen and thieved her dense dark hair, replacing it with thick cobweb strands that she ties without brushing and puts behind her.

Her skin remains pasty pale. It is carpeted by a fine, downy white hair. She has lost the ability to blush. Her eyes are the grey of her teeth. She coughs occasional oysters the colour of mustard.

Estelle was Eleanor's mother. And Jenny's. Though she's neither anymore. She can't be a mother to anyone or anything. Gestated or gestating. That too was thieved, but not by Age.

It's true: she's seen the world, Estelle.

She just hasn't been anywhere.

For twenty-seven of those fifty-seven years, Estelle smeared herself a cosmetic facade, drizzled on a bland odour, pinned on a misspelled nametag (Esteelle), and battled traffic in a green

Datsun to develop photographs for a small franchise.

For twenty-seven years; a passive purveyor of Glossy Windows. And it's through them she's seen Everything.

She's seen the sights and sites of every continent. Seen all nations in all weathers. Seen the towers, the bridges, the statues, the mountains, the rivers, the churches, temples, mosques and casinos of the world. Landmarks, each with a beaming tourist in front and in focus.

Estelle has observed every surviving period of architecture. She's printed the Pyramids on so many occasions she has ceased feeling daunted by their construction. Surveyed Paris from every angle. Seen catacombs, coliseums, gazelles, volcanoes, New York hotdogs, the embalmed cadaver of Stalin. She's printed the planetary podium: the First, Second and Third worlds. Seen slums, beggars, Bengali rug vendors, Roma tomato festivals, nude raves in Amsterdam, amateur paparazzi. She's seen it all, Estelle.

She has printed more sunsets than she will live through. More hooked fish than she could ever eat. More weddings than a minister. Seen good art and bad art. Suffered the brooding portraits and barren landscapes of the serious weekend photographer. Filled a box with the shots she has been moved to reprint, to keep just for herself. Shots she had to simply sit down and stare at.

She has exposed the truly bizarre. From cult ceremonies to cowtipping to excretion to morbid shots of car accidents. And porn, of course. More than you could poke your stick at. She's squinted at more positions than the Kamasutra, back when she could blush.

She fended off rolls of it from propositioning voyeurs. Learned to explain exactly why she would not develop three reels of close-up vegetable fetishism, let alone have it enlarged.

And smiles. Always smiles.

Other people's smiles. Happyfamilies. Happychildren. Happyblissfulmarriages. Setup smiles. Forced smiles. Gummy, gaptoothed, wide, thin, lipstick, cheesy smiles. Rows and rows and rows of teeth. And she smiled back.

For twenty-seven years, Estelle was privy to the recorded moments of other people's lives. She was inside their homes, sharing something intimate, even if they were saying Cheese. She was there at reunions, holidays, birthdays, graduations. She was there at the beginnings of lives, smiling with doting parents and pink chubby bubs. And it bore a strange feeling of inclusion, developing their photos, playing her small part. They handed her a small container, a ribbon of pickled Moments; and she made them endure, gave them back frozen, coloured and alive.

It was only the happysnaps of highland holidays (Inverness, Loch Ness, Happy Ness) that ever invited a chill flush of envy and longing.

She spent a lot of time looking. Spent a lot of time borrowing vicariously. Towards the end she relied on it.

And that's what it was for Estelle (or Esteelle). That was how she remained for twenty-seven long years in a monotonous occupation. Printing photographs suited her shy, tacit understanding with the world. Her Look But Don't Touch arrangement. It offered her the certain safety of their not looking back. And

Distance. She could glean from each exposure with impunity. See the world. Go nowhere.

It filled long days. She drove home slowly.

In the first hour of her first day, Estelle spilled coffee over the print machine and very nearly fucked it completely.

She kept her job because:

> 1. She quickly soaked up the mess (with a teatowel embroidered with the native flora and fauna of Queensland).
>
> 2. Nobody knew about it.

It was two weeks later that it died. It crackled and sparked and singed the carpet, smoking blue plumes from its gills. It was wheeled out with solemn silence. Cause of Death was unsubstantiated. The manager eyed her with suspicion. Estelle said nothing and never drank coffee again.

She was a timorous but amenable assistant. She displayed a flair for processing rather than sales and service. She enjoyed the varied expressions of customers sifting through photos she had printed.

She remained. Steady and unimpressive and without ambition. It was longevity, not perseverance that had her relocated and promoted. She reached her plateau as Store Manager.

In the first hour of her first day as Store Manager, she was stung suddenly by the ebullient grin of an auburnhaired man. He smiled at her. And she smiled back, because he was in a photograph and she was alone. In a sea of teeth it somehow stuck for Estelle. His face and arms were pale and thin and stippled with an archipelago of freckles, like cigarette stubmarks on a toilet cistern. He was laughing.

There were four more shots of him in the roll. The man had beady eyes that wouldn't look straight at you. But they looked safe enough.

In the second shot, he was sitting among a stand of old growth-forest. He cupped a steaming mug of tea. A fern fondled his shoulder. There was seeping blanket of fog that covered his feet. It looked like dirty snow. The rest were angular snaps of cars and machinery.

Estelle had felt nervous when he arrived to retrieve his prints. She blushed. Found she was slightly taller and heavier than the man on the other side of the counter. She commended the photos, something she had never done. Offered him tips about shutter speeds in different light conditions. He thanked her and explained that he had been a timber worker before an accident damaged his spine. His claim for compensation had recently been dismissed. He said he'd just found work in an airport, but he didn't intend to stay. They chattered on, subdued and awkward. It was almost with relief that he left with her name and number scribbled on the negatives sleeve.

Estelle was thirty-three then. She lived alone in a small redbrick flat. Life was leaving her behind.

The following week, for six minutes, Estelle abandoned Safety. In the wake of her first orgasm, she decided the warm heaving afterglow she felt was love. She could feel the tips of every nerve crackle and spark. She smiled, convinced that this sentience, this awareness of her body was a gift. She was seized by impulse.

Thoroughly up the duff, she was married and mortgaged within three months. They honeymooned in Bali. There were a lot of photos.

Estelle had caught up to Life.

Soon after, a curled up foetus was discharged from her womb. It happened in their new bathroom. The smell of silicone and iron. It didn't have lungs yet, but she knew it had breathed in there. Felt it, in that nascent, corded connection. Developing. And in her role as nurturer she had failed. She took up smoking and was silently devastated.

Jenny was conceived with a determined lunge over a dining table spread with newspaper, tax forms, placemats and Guilt.

She slipped slickly into the world. She wailed and flailed. And when Estelle held that brittle body tender in her arms, something bold and warm shifted inside her. Too late, she realised Love was not an orgasm.

Eleanor arrived early in a shock of blood, with barely any coercion on Estelle's part. The tiny body was cradled in stained gloves. Eyes open from the beginning. Wide and bewildered. Her pink glow almost neon. Estelle wept and laughed.

Childbirth was her most powerful accomplishment. Estelle felt defined by it, creating those two lives. Lactating gave her the shivers, gave her melons sudden purpose. Her two daughters were precious possessions, and irrevocably *hers*.

She was a proud and solicitous mother. Dogged in her shelter. She was often awed that someone so overtly shy could produce two such raucous beings. She loved them with all she had left. They were the only momentum shunting that little Datsun homeward.

As they grew, she watched them pivot towards each other, like clockhands nearing midnight. Long and Short, hugging, holding, clinging time.

She envied them their Close Ness; a place with little room for her. They never looked back in each other's company. And so again she was observing from a Distance. Estelle felt piqued at their fierce independence.

However, she understood their need to be outside. During her annual paid leave (which invariably coincided with the bulb season), she herself spent a fortnight in the garden, procuring tulips with sheepshit and soil conditioner. She also grew varieties of herbs and vegetables and nurtured native shrubs. She experimented with colourful perennials in the frontyard. And beneath the lemon tree in the back corner, she fought tirelessly with a resilient patch of garden rhubarb. She wanted to clear the ground for leeks and aubergines, but the roots were seated deep. She routinely pruned back the thick stalks with a pair of pink secateurs she was bought for Mother's Day, but it always reemerged flourishing. It did not occur to her dig out the roots. She just kept cutting it back, cutting it back, cutting it back.

It's still there.

After hours one evening, Estelle abandoned Safety for another six minutes, up against the print machine with a zealous Sales Rep called Rob. She was a timorous and amenable assistant, desperate to have a gap filled in her life, desperate to re-enact her first innervating encounter.

But Rob gave her neither Love nor Orgasm.

And he left just as he'd ejaculated: awkwardly. And quickly. With a bumbling trail of apologies and a gluggy wad of semen on her shirt, on her nametag and on the control panel of the print machine. Her nametag was obscured to read EEL. It could have been his.

Estelle got to keep her job because:

> 1. She quickly soaked up the mess (with a teatowel brocaded in a goose motif).
>
> 2. Nobody knew about it.

The print machine did not die (though Rob, in his own way, very nearly fucked it). It did not smoke or spark or singe the carpet. And Estelle was the manager, so nobody eyed her with suspicion.

Estelle does not know where her eldest daughter went missing. She knows why.

For Estelle it came as no surprise, she had been disappearing for months. Estelle had scoured her vomit from the shower plug. Watched her fading; so silently and gradually and fiercely intent. Saw the dearth of her girth, from a Distance, without intervention.

Neither does she know how her youngest daughter went blind. It was on the same night Estelle skipped menopause, the same night Jenny went missing, the same night he left them.

That night, her uterus couldn't be revived by a swab of frozen peas or a half dozen painkillers. Useless deadwomb, switched off like a light. Floating like a bellyup jellyfish. Her prized possessions were a daughter she couldn't see and a daughter that couldn't see her. So she couldn't be a mother, to anyone or anything any more, gestated or gestating. She died inside.

But it didn't matter, she was numb by then anyway. See, she'd disarmed herself of feeling long before, with a grim resignation. With a cold conviction. With nothing left to lose. Silently, gradually, fiercely intent. It was no accident. She did not claim for compensation. She'd resigned her spine and scraped out her nerves. Pruned her neurons for a hollow anaesthesia. Cutting back, cutting back, cutting back.

She felt nothing at his funeral either. She was there alone. And even when it got real, when she noticed the weight of that bodyinabox. And when he was lowered. Carefully (too carefully) into a hole. To be sealed. Buried. With dirt. And gravel. She should have felt a lot of things.

But she didn't. And that was Estelle's tradeoff.

She retired from her long, modest career with hugs, kisses and bestwishes. She received flowers and wine and an engraved company bracelet. It said Esteelle.

She drove home over the speed limit. The Datsun shuddered.

The housekey shook in her hands. And Estelle vomited over the rubber welcome mat. It was obscured to read W OME. Through blurred eyes she read W OMB, and even then there was the luxury of feeling nothing.

***

Television.

It seemed such a logical transition. Bigger, glossier, louder, pixellated windows that *moved*.

And since retiring, Estelle has been aligned directly in front of her new widescreen oracle. In a static slump, thumbing channels from her choice of remote (each sealed in Glad Wrap to prevent dust), accompanied by a terracotta ashtray and tissues to catch her coughed wads. She is swallowed by a wide lounge bowed by her constant weight. It is stained with spilled food and odorous with stale farts.

Estelle sold the Datsun for a satellite. She skims her pension for monthly instalments.

She watches it all, Estelle. And goes nowhere. In the safety of her Living room, the world comes to her. It's all look and no touch.

And just by sitting here, she learns to cook felafels, advises Steve Waugh on his back foot drives (he needs to move his feet), travels to Mauritius, hums snappy jingles, watches petty court squabbles and addresses the Real Issues on talk shows. She watches avidly as Jerry, Ricky and Oprah berate their baleful, moaning guests whilst bolstered by a pointing mob that screams for retribution. She likes hip teen dramas with their savvy, voluble dialogue. And those American law series with their fastpaced narratives and infallible resolutions. She is inspired by handy hints from Lifestyle programs (hence the Glad Wrapped remote controls) and concerned by news and current affairs, but with a blessed television brevity (her attention is quickly diverted by advertising).

And it's the Soaps that are her true poison. All the sex and lust and deceit and bad hair. The fickle and fallacious, the sickly and salacious, she's immersed in them all. Estelle didn't find it difficult to follow the slow, circular plots. She slotted right in and stayed. The Young and the Restless for the Old and Inanimate. She has forged sisterly alliances with Ashley, Kristen and Marlena. She scowls at Stefano and Ridge (and that mordant bitch, Neena). She sighs for Kurt and Thorn and Blake. And for poor, misunderstood Erin.

She is easily bought by the cheap (cue the) music at emotional checkpoints, and the complicit quickzoom close-ups. She loves the lusty flashbacks, the perfect plastic bodies with their catalogue of expressions, the dramatic pans and fadeouts.

Estelle also likes to watch the classic black and white midday movies. And in crowded scenes set in bars and restaurants, she sometimes likes to watch the extras acting in the background. She sees their lips moving and smiles to herself, knowing they are just simulating a conversation. It's an old stage trick. They aren't really communicating. They clink glasses and laugh theatrically, all the while saying: rhubarbrhubarbrhubarbrhubarb.

Over and over and over again.

Estelle has embraced television. And it hugs her back. It gives her more Distance, more safety, and an even deeper sense of solidarity. Like she's part of a broad community that is just for her. She is warmed by stations that assure her that they *care*.

In her favourite sitcoms she laughs along with everybody else.

They share an umbilical bond. Transmitting nourishment. She is loyal to it, and it keeps her inured.

Estelle and television, Estelleandtelevision, in perfect symbiosis, they coalesce into one: Estellevision.

She sits, ashing her fags sedately. Her glued gaze does not waver. The TV Guide is her daily inventory, which she highlights in fluorescent yellow strips, pondering the time clashes. At night she drifts to a shallow sleep to Late Shows or golf highlights.

Her world is flat. Scripted. Remote Controlled and Glad Wrapped. She wants no further part in the spherical one.

Two weeks ago, a plumber arrived to fix the P-trap under the kitchen sink. Eleanor arranged it. Estelle retreated to her bedroom, and sat waiting for him to leave.

She and Eleanor seldom speak now. When they do, it's a short question followed by a short response. Sometimes during the news, they will share a silence without intimacy in the blare of the television. But mostly they are unaware of each other. She comes and goes, comes and goes.

Estelle hacks oysters into tissues and her hands tremor when she needs a cigarette.

She will be leaving in three days.

BRUNOS FAMLY CORNERSTORE

Bruno is a big man.

Sweaty fat bulges from wherever sweaty fat can bulge. He wears thin red braces that slope over his ample belly and bite into his tight grey trousers. His clothes spread the damp from his dirty pores. Bruno's dewlap is pelicanesque, like a giant spare scrotum. It swings like a sign. His face makes way for a big, congested Roman(ian) nose. He breathes exclusively through his mouth.

Bruno has the mother of all combovers. To conceal his polished pate, he has procured a long strip of greasy hair on the side of his head, like a misplaced mullet. In the mornings, he curls and coils this around and around and around his scalp, not unlike a softserve icecream. He glues it down with cheap hairspray that reeks of chemicals. And throughout the day it slowly rises, puffing out to resemble a messy turban.

He basks daily behind the raised counter of his Famly Cornerstore, effusing Brut and self-importance. The regal and reverent store owner. Bordered by strings of garlanded salami (left side) and Italian sausage (right side). They dangle like preserved turds, bunting mute in the breeze.

Beside him is his faithful imperial cash register. It still chachings! in pounds and shillings. However most cash is on a direct route to his back pocket, the till just holds his float. He has fourteen different signs that threaten shoplifters with prosecution. And another eight with security camera warnings, though he has no security cameras.

As far as Bruno is concerned, he is a supremely successful local businessman. So much so, he has recently been compelled to write his own empirical thesis, *The Retale Gospel According to Bruno: A Gide*. It occurred to him that, throughout the years, he has divulged reams upon reams of invaluable economic wisdom from his counter pedestal, for next to nothing. His priceless pearls, shucked and tossed freely to the masses. And, as he will tell you, bargains are bad business.

So in fits of inspiration, he now spends random evenings with a bottle of cheap red, huddled over his keyboard, ruminating. His stiff index fingers point accusingly at the scrambled letters as he tap, tap, taps out lines of badly spelt didactic tautology. Often he will pause to pour and recline, entertaining visions of his seminal text setting an unprecedented benchmark among the small-business community (followed naturally by his swift rise to fame, and a subsequent move into the political ring). He's pawed at the glut of glossy books from these so-called Professor of Economics charlatans, and it's clear to Bruno that it's all theory and no *experience*. They haven't been exposed to the public. They don't know what The People want.

And Bruno does.

In chapter one, *Understanding Consumor Relations*, he outlines his *Three (3) Points Vital To Retale Success:*

> *1. Profit Obtained Is Profit Justefied.*
> *2. Anyone Under Twenty-One (21) Will Steal From You.*
> *3. The People Will Respond Only To What They Want To Hear.*

And what they can *identify* with. Like Famly. And Corners. And flags. And *Community*. You had to give them what they want, or at least advertise it. And it didn't really *matter* if you were a struggling first-generation cornershop slumped in the middle of the street, what mattered was the *values you prenseted you're potential custom.*

And so Bruno sees himself as the axis of a thriving community. A point of local orbit. He's cast himself in a diplomatic, Man Of The People role. Although he doesn't *serve* so much as *take People's money.* Vouchsafing effrontery and happy banter from his higherup counter (chaching!), spreading a set of cigar-stained dentures and sending The People on their way.

And that's good business.

Bruno glances to his left as someone strolls through the transparent plastic strips of the entrance.

Ha! Is my fayvorite Blind Midgit! Buongiorno Hallynor!

Bruno likes Eleanor. She has an arse that could crack walnuts. He is always excited to see her. She is a good little size. And if you asked Bruno, he'd tell you that the best thing about Blind People was that they couldn't see price tags. He has no qualms about ripping off Blind Midgits. After all:

1. Profit Obtained Is Profit Justified.

Morning Bruno. Still alive then.

Like an ox, Bella Hallynor. Like an ox.

Under the manic whir of the fanblades, Eleanor breathes the strong amalgam of scents; the fusty dust, the fresh food, the spices, the chickengrease incense from the rotisserie, the perspiring storeowner. She brings in three blowflies and a doleful dog.

Diversification (chapter five) is Bruno's booming mantra. To Eleanor's left is a forest of fruit and vegetables. Cauliflower, sweet potato, corn, fresh coriander, field mushrooms, a canopy of broccoli. A ramp of Roma tomatoes. A cluster of garlic cloves. Carrots, gnarled and hairy like the legs of a pensioner. He has seven varieties of lettuce and twenty-three different kinds of cheese (because that's what The People want: *Variety*). Fruit flies hover and dart among loose packed nectarines and rockmelon and mangoes and Carnarvon bananas. Hanging are small hessian pouches whose mouths brim with cashews, macadamias, almonds and coffee beans. There are clear containers of ground spices with high prices. Pillows of Turkish bread. And beneath a display of artichokes and mutant knobs of ginger, thicksticks of rhubarb recline in a black bucket of water.

If it has a shelf life and might sell, chances are Bruno has it in stock. That was why he assembled the hardware aisle back in '83, which was the same year he stopped fitting between them. The shelves themselves are turgid with tins and bottles and obsolete kitchen accessories. And barrels of olive oil. Jars of marinated capers, sundried tomatoes, oily aubergines. Everything that could ever be pickled. Salted fish. Condiments. Talcum powder. There's a fridge full of cold drinks. A magazine rack spread almost entirely with porn (it's the boom industry). For all the Famly to enjoy.

Nothing is on special. Nothing ever was and nothing ever will be on special. Bargains are bad business.

He has everything. Homemade almond biscotti. Sesame seeded Frenchsticks. Ratty Christmas decorations. Icecream. In the back corner, hidden, nestled between the overpriced Catholic ornaments and the dusty Taiwanese fireworks, is a cavity stacked with rusted rabbit traps. They grin with blunt teeth.

Right out the back sits a self-built hutch housing three docile chickens for whom he spares no expense. When Bruno takes from their nests, he lifts each hen gingerly and distracts her with soft words and a palm of crushed (grade-A) lupins before pocketing the warm egg. He thanks them in turn by name and taps their beaks. But even with a surplus, Bruno never sells the eggs.

Next to the hutch is a large weatherproof chest with a brass lock. Bruno will never open it, nor touch it. His wife will never enquire after it. And fortnightly, a tubby bogan called Darryl will arrive in the evening to remove its contents. In a worn vertical slot, he will then post an envelope into the back of the adjacent hutch. Later, excited, Bruno will shuffle outside and look left and right before tucking that envelope between shirt and sweaty manboob. For twelve years his premises have been a go-between for soft illicit drugs. A torpid whale with a hair turban and clean hands. Though he does it less for the money, more for the thrill of the old days.

Bruno was born in Constanta, a city in Romania bordering the Black Sea. But if you asked, he'd tell you he was born and raised in a village just outside Rome. He grew up in a decadent shithole that is stained in his memory, with an indifferent father, two elder brothers and three auburn chickens that he loved dearly. He was a small child. When he was upset or angry, he used to piss on things. He was regularly caught and beaten.

When he was old enough to leave home, he smuggled himself on to a merchant vessel and into the seaport of Naples, Italy. He was never Romanian again.

Bruno looks back fondly on ol' Napoli. And the older and softer he gets, the harder and younger he was back there. Taller. Leaner. Quicker. The closer the shaves, the greater the threats. He wears that image like a coat, like a cloak.

Bruno was a burgeoning shitkicker among the resident mobocracy. They were Famly. He did jobs and took a commission. He thieved and dodged and survived. Stole from stores just like the one he owns now. Bruno boasted to be a distant nephew of (Uncle) Al Capone. He swaggered with his shoulders squared, he walked big in the loom of Vesuvius. Tried hard to be a gangster, tried harder to be an Italian.

One night outside a tavern, Bruno was glassed across the forearm by a pissed patron who swore he would kill him. Bruno, naturally, believed he was a wanted man. He vowed to lie low. Two days later, all too suddenly, Bruno found he was soon to be embracing fatherhood. To three separate women. One of whom was the daughter of an Employer. Now, Bruno really was a wanted man.

With three separate, swift kicks to the loins (and further threats of castration), Bruno was again an immigrant. This time en route to that Lucky, Sunburnt Country where he felt sure to forge his fortune. The land of Opportunity. He arrived by boat with lice and no luggage, hands thrust deep into empty pockets. Leaving behind a legacy of Roman(ian) noses, on three fatherless bastards.

It took him only three shunted steps on busy Sydney paving (two forward, one back) to realise he was a tourist. It didn't matter how he swaggered, or how much street respect he had garnered back there. It meant as much as his name. Meant as much as the language that scurried from his mouth and made People squint. He bore the indelible scent of someplace else. He was a wog, a ding, a dago. A foreskin at a bar mitzvah. It stung. He found no work and slept shivering on the banks of the harbour. Had his head kicked in and his huge nose broken. His Capone hat was stolen.

After a week with no food, Bruno reluctantly mugged a bookie outside the Randwick races and hitched his way west in the cabs of roadtrains. With relief, he found a familiar smell in Fremantle. It was like a smaller Naples, with less threat and more limestone. And no volcanoes.

He stayed. Found work driving taxis. Sold drugs from the glovebox. He was cautious with his dick. He learnt English and proudly retained his Italian vernacular. He drank redwine and smoked heavily. Told tall tales of ol' Napoli.

He invented a quaint Italian upbringing in a quaint Italian village outside Rome. With a hardworking father called Rocco who ran a farm of Llamas. With three sweet sisters and a beautiful, beautiful mother. He clung to the warmth of this spurious background, and the community that seemed to accept it.

He courted and married. Paid cash for a slice of vacant land in the middle of a quiet street. High up. And in the cool of that evening, alone with the signed papers in his hand, he pissed resolutely on the grey sandy dirt.

Bruno built a house and an adjoining (corner)store.

Months later, he climbed a rickety wooden ladder. Almost strained a hamstring as his foot drove through the fourth step. He clambered on to the thin corrugation of his verandah rooftop and stood looking East. Surveying everything below him. Studying its geography. The seventies spread of brick and tile across the escarpment. The reach of the river. The hazy fur of drygrass along the hills, quilted with dull granite and foliage.

Bruno clenched a brush (left hand) and a tin of paint (right hand). And with his back to them all, he smeared his name in capitals across the gabled wall facing the street. If his grammar had been more advanced he would have relished the apostrophe. The bold, bright red letters bled into the timber, darkening instantly to the hue of stewed rhubarb.

In chapter seven, Bruno will explain the weaknesses and virtues of Embracing Technology. His latest investment has been the internet, with his intention being to pillage the stock market. He mainly uses it to trawl for free porn and collect bad blind jokes that he stockpiles for Eleanor. He has one ready for every time they meet.

Bruno leans forward and speaks loudly (so she can hear).

Hey, Hallynor, you know aye haff a new joke for you. You will luff this one, aye promise you. Are you ready? Yes?

Eleanor sighs. Okay Bruno. Hit me.

Okay? Okay. You ready? Here it comes: Why doan Bliynd People skydive?

Bruno, you've already told me that one. It's old material.

Oh, okay. You heard it then?

I did.

Warren sniffs at a strip of beef jerky, looks guiltily at Eleanor. Bruno furrows.

Okay, okay. Ah! Aye haff another one. Aye always haff something uppa my sleeve, eh? Okay. Here it comes.

Eleanor does her best to transmit impatience.

You will luff this one, is a true story, yes? You see, there was a Bliynd Man, this morning in fact, who walked straight into this shop, yes? And he walked right up here in front of me, and you know, aye was just about to hask him if he needed any help, yes? Anyway, right there before my very eyes, he starts to swing his dog; rownd and *around* and *around* his head. And aye say: Excuse me sir! But wot on herth are you doing? And Hallynor, this man he turns to me and he says: Wot? Aye am just having a look arownd! Aha! Ha ha! Is a good one, eh? Is a good one.

He guffaws and snorts. A deepbellied laugh that he leans back to accommodate. He calms down, wheezing.

You like it? Is funny eh? Is a good one.

About as funny as a pap smear Bruno, thanks.

Ah, well. You know Bruno, hiss always godda joke for you.

Eleanor does not like Bruno. She thinks he is a repulsive, odorous shit with the social finesse of an amoeba. She is rarely excited to be anywhere near him.

Just as Eleanor was about to ask, Althea, Bruno's diminutive wife, wanders in from the kitchen. She is plump, with short thinning hair and varicose veins. She carries a fresh tray of sausage rolls. Despite her size, Bruno takes every opportunity to belittle her in public. He likes to say that if she dies first, he's going to have her stuffed and glazed and put in the front garden with a pipe and a red hat.

Eleanor likes Althea. She is the sole reason she frequents BRUNOS Famly Cornerstore. Althea helps her with the shopping and bitches openly about Bruno. They have coffee sometimes. Althea likes to say that if *he* dies first, she's going to boil him up and start a soap factory. She blames him, above all, for the early exodus of their three boys. Their twins, Dino and Pino, left home in their teens to work on an orchard in Tasmania. And their eldest, Bruno jr, is a barrister in Melbourne. He has told Althea that having had more family disputes than a book of Greek mythology held him in good stead for the courtroom. Bruno calls his first son his Superannuation.

Most of the work is incumbent on Althea, largely due to her ability to fit between the aisles. She is not allowed to handle money, with the exception of Eleanor's.

Hullo Eleanor! she chirps brightly.

Morning Althea. Gorr, what have you got there?

Sausage rolls, dear. And please be telling my husband that

these are for *customers*. She waves a pair of threatening tongs at Bruno and flakes of pastry dive at him. They are *not* for his monstrous belly. I cook for him enough for him, I think.

You heard the lady, Bruno.

Warren stares with passion at the goldbrown rows of sausage rolls. He dribbles.

Bruno shakes his head. His spare scrotum flaps. Aye am like a slave to this woman, aye tell you now. My wife, she treats you better than she sees to her own husband. Is a sad state off affairs. Doan you lissen to her, Hallynor. She is feeding me things that aye cannot taste and she is telling me: (he inflects croakily to an alto) Bruno, this is *healthy* for you. Is what the doctor says you must be eating. Bah! And now she brings all this luffly food to dangle under my nozz and she says it is for *customers*. You can't see me Hallynor, but let me tell you, aye am fayding to shadow.

Althea scoffs. Can you hear something, Eleanor?

Very faintly. I can't make it out though.

Fayding to a shadow, Bruno repeats solemnly, glancing at his wife.

Eleanor, let *me* tell *you*. My husband is fading to the size of a *barn*. Besides, he knows where the kitchen is. Take no notice of his nonsense. Althea moves up beside her. What can I get you today?

Um, what do I need? Paper. Eggs. Tea. Couscous. Bananas. And tampons.

Bruno reddens, shuffles with discomfort. Hands his wife a paper bag. They slip down the aisles, chatting softly. Warren follows.

At that moment, Bruno glances left, again hearing the softslap of a customer entering.

Ewan Dempsey shuffles in, dishevelled and bowed slightly. He squints awkwardly in the sudden dimness. He'll bring in four blowflies and homicidal intentions. Brought here by the plangent lovemaking of two prurient possums. And he has decided to drill them, once and for all. They have thieved his sleep, stolen his pattern. He is irrationally angry, furious even. More than he should be. And his inhumane Last Option is in the back corner of this cornerstore, grinning bluntly, next to the Taiwanese fireworks.

An eager plastic strip stays matily lazed over his shoulder. Like a limp, lecherous tentacle. He wipes it off.

Bruno swells suddenly with recognition. He wags a chubby finger. Ewan pauses.

The whale bellows: Althea! You woulden belieff who has just come into my store!

What?

This! This man here! The whale beckons with a clammy pectoral fin. This hiss the man who lives across the road, you know, from Alan and Greta's house! You know, this is the strange one who is wayking me up in the morning!

Bruno *what* are you talking about?

Ewan feels himself shrinking back towards the entrance. Bruno turns to him.

Yes! You are wayking me up, you see my wiyfe and aye we go to Alan and Greta's house every Sundeye night; is a family thing, you know we haff dinner there anna little bit to drink, yes? So we hallways stay the night, and aye like to sleep in, you know, because we are closed until noon on the Mondeye. And aye yam wayking up! Aye am not sleeping in, you know, because all aye can hear is this farkin lalalala from juss across the road! So loud! My wife, she is snoring next to me and aye yam tossing and turning and tossing and turning. We haff to *drive home* now becozz aye cannot sleep! And it hiss *you!* Aye haff sin you. And you are *playing* something, yes? At such a strange tyme, when aye am trying to sleep!

Althea bursts out of the aisle. Bruno! *Shoosh!* Leave this poor man alone! Do you think he cares if you are getting enough sleep in the morning? Anyway, Greta thinks it is gorgeous, and it is certainly *not* loud. She turns to apologise. He is gone.

Backbackback. The hardslap of a quick exit.

Hey, hey! Come back, you didden buy anythink!

But Ewan is feeling the heat like a cloak. In the middle of the street. Fast steps. Elusive steps.

He hears the hardslap of a quick pursuit. Behind him, he turns. His belly sinks. And there she is, with a trotting dog and inadvertently stolen tampons. She is flushed and coming at him. She looks fierce.

Hello. Didn't see me in there? It's you right?

Ewan walks, feels lost and swallowed. The Blind Girl follows. Warren glances back, lamenting the sausage roll that never was.

Jesus! What's your problem?

Walks faster. She can hear his feet clapping hard. She is losing her bearings, confused.

Hey, would you *stop* walking away from me? Fuck, what *is* this?

They near the corner. To her right, two men scrape shallow trenches in a dry lawn for reticulation. They glance at each other and snigger.

And maybe it's the heat. Maybe it's her bloated belly cramping up like it's viced. Maybe it's because she's tired, so tired. Tired of being tired. Tired of running on empty. But she's working herself up, Eleanor, in the thick of this heat. More worked up than she should be. She's forgotten the sound of footsteps. Her sweaty bum is clenched tight enough to worry a whole cluster of walnuts. And she's yelling into the air.

What the *fuck* is the matter with you? You don't understand do you? You don't get it! Fuckssake, I just want to *listen!* That's all! And I don't *know why*, it just bloody happened. You might be keeping Bruno awake but I

And she stops there. Subdued. Feels naked saying it: *But I need you to get to sleep.* She stands a little dazed. Spent and dizzy and remote. Impossibly small. Warren farts (poofffffft).

The landscapers are giggling now. Eleanor Rigby turns, caustic:

Shut the *fuck* up, she snaps.

They shut the fuck up.

Bruno's manboobs jostle as he trundles out and towards the end of the verandah. A hot wind lifts his hairturban up on its axis, like a kettle lid. He pads it down without shame. Calls out:

Hey! Hallynor! You forgot to pay for those … *things!*

THE BENDS

Maze of open streets. Lost, you are running. Away. Feel
nothing but dense abrasive heat. Hard to breathe, you are
sweating, she is gone. Left the blind behind and sprinting now,
fast. A tall man not so tall. You feel watched. You see your
street name. Faster. Lungs are tight, tight, tight in your chest
and it burns like shame. Gate then steps then door. You leave it
open in your haste. You are staggering stumbling crashing
down your bare hallway. Timber reverb. Heat. She's there, like
always and you hear her, loud. Diving falling into this room
where she lies limbless on her side. Claiming her. She's
wrapped up, you give her limbs. Spooning. Locking her breast
and shoulders and an open string growls. It's a G string, you
don't giggle. Holding, not held. Hunching leaning rocking and
you don't know why. You don't know why. Shake, shudder,
bitemarks on your knuckles. Seized with the exertion of just
holding it in. These are the Bends. You catch bursts from your
core and quell them. Cold varnish Hot cheek. Her neck it is
choked tight in your fist. Vines of arm veins. Curled up safe: a
leg on each side of an endpeg. Head on a Turkish rug; a

replica, the same pattern, pattern, pattern, but this is no Magic Carpet.

Sleep.

***

INTERIOR. DAY. LOUNGEROOM.

An Estellevision station (that *cares*) interrupts David Attenborough and his World of Insects to advertise the Fast Food Experience. ESTELLE releases an evacuative sigh. Close-up shot of her stubbing a cigarette into a curled, ash headed grub (*Discardus fagendus*).

Wide shot of Estelle being swallowed by the lounge. Between her spread legs rests a glass of water with icecubes. It cools her crotch. She aims a remote. Her gaze is welded.

Sound of a door opening (off screen). Estelle hears the scuffle of a callused heel. And paws padding. She does not turn.

ELEANOR and WARREN pace into the loungeroom. Strafe pan to a two shot; Eleanor heading straight down the carpeted hallway with Warren cantering freely alongside, Estelle still and silent.

Door closes (off screen).

***

In 1839, with typical colonial bastardry, the English were persistent in importing opium (processed in British India) into China.

Facing an impending nation of stoners, the Chinese emperor was anxious for a trade cessation. He entrusted his diplomatic imperial commissioner, Lin Zexu, with the task of nipping the British bud. Lin Zexu promptly penned a letter to Queen Victoria, beseeching that she end the opium trade, or else (he warned), The Empire Would Strike Back. He threatened to prevent the return trade of tea and rhubarb; without which the British would surely perish.

All we are saying, reasoned Lin Zexu in sugared summation, *is give peace a chance.*

However, Queen Victoria either never received the letter, or neglected to have it translated. As far as Lin Zexu was concerned, the ball had never left his side of the court.

Thoroughly pissed, Lin Zexu travelled to Canton with the intention of confronting the British merchants. The tumid Brits were uncooperative and unwilling to negotiate. (Eh wotwot? Oh, no, no, that's rather not on, old boy!)

Fuming, Lin Zexu abandoned diplomacy and ordered his officials to seize and destroy all the opium in Canton harbour. He then hijacked the rhubarb supplies of the British army and laughed evilly (bwahahahaha!), citing that the ensuing constipation would drive them back to the Old Blighty. It was a good try, the rhubarb ploy, but ultimately not enough. The brutish British, unappreciative though they were, were ruthless in their immediate plundering of the Chinese.

The Opium War lasted three years and concluded with the Treaty of Nanking, in which the British wasted no time in relentlessly fucking them over. Among other clauses, they nabbed

Hong Kong and opened several new ports of trade; and Lin Zexu was forced to admit that his faith in rhubarb had not worked.

Eleanor Rigby has a letter like Victoria's: unread. It is not written in Chinese, though it may as well be. It was left by her sister, on the night she stole Running. Found when it was too late. Because by then, like Zexu, she'd put her faith in rhubarb.

But he's dead now. Forgotten. He's History.

And she's stuck. With a tourniquet on Time.

On a linenless mattress she sits. The plastic sheet slippery. Discarded clothes litter her bedroom floor. Warren sprawls over her feet.

A page stained by age to the colour of turmeric. A yellow rash. It's in her hands now, held tenderly. She traces a finger along its face. Just to touch it. Its paperness, smooth. She scales its perimeter. She can imagine the light slender scrawl of her sister, but not the words it might form. Her elbows rest on her thighs. She leans forward, revealing two deep dimples between her bum and her back. What she holds is a Certificate of Missed Opportunity. Of what could have been. Of answers.

But she will *not* evince the regret that lurks cold from her bloated belly. The longing and the envy. She won't let it. Won't feel it, won't allow it.

Eleanor wishes she could read her sister's letter. She has to know. But who has there ever been to translate, read it aloud for her? Whom to trust?

Towards the end she had felt her disappearing. When they were midnight clockhands, safe, holding each other there. So thin and stiff and brittle, her sister felt. She could hear the gurglechurn of her fisting stomach under the covers, amid the muffled crackle of the longplayer. A Paul Simon lullaby. The Boy in the Bubble. The Girl under the Blanket, dreaming of Africa.

And then she was gone. On that night. She'd runaway when she needed her most. And then it was too late. Eleanor Rigby, helpless and blind and left behind. The feel of paper and betrayal. And all too sudden you knew it was just you here.

In a child's room, with a child's adornments. Where the walls are a hot lilac. On a pine shelf sits a rack of dusty paperbacks. Enid Blyton, Dr Seuss, May Gibbs, Judy Blume, illustrated fables of Aesop, and a child's favourite: Roald Dahl. After reading *George's Marvellous Medicine*, Eleanor had wished for amnesia so she could read it again and again and again with that same delicious tension and never know what was coming. Her favourite book, though, was always *Matilda*. The pages are thumbed grubby and thin. Read over and over and over, the story of that small girl who beat the world and escaped with the power of her eyes.

On a hot wall: a wideopen Mouse that is notquite ticking or tocking (stuck, stuck, stuck, stuck, stuck). Like a bomb.

Eleanor Rigby slips off the bed with a static crackle. Rolls her shoulders. Determined.

The evening is cool and suffused with an apricot afterglow. A fresh breeze breaks. To the east, the moon is out with a herd of early stars. As though they have crept stealthily from the ether to watch the sunset.

Eleanor moves along the pavement among a tedious traffic of diligent pet owners. She knows the way. She can smell barbecues and sprinklerspray. Cars interrupt games of cricket played on warm asphalt. Kids are sent outside to eat watermelon. She walks past a waft of pot and patchouli, a woman calls out and asks if she'd like her tarot read. She declines politely.

Her chest is taut and her breath short. Her period bites sharp. She bumps her dog with a friendly thigh.

What the hell am I going to say, Warren?

He guides her from the low barkless arm of a devious sheoak, which waits patiently to clothesline the blind. The light has aged to a spread of vermilion.

The gate is open. She weaves up the path. Smells bougainvillea and mint.

She is peered at by a bashful gnome, a leaning saffron sunflower, and two inquisitive possums on a verandah beam, still alive. She walks underneath them. Stands on a prickly unwelcome mat.

Eleanor knocks through a slab of air. A door-shaped hole. Warren sniffs. She raps the thick architrave, an inaudible thud that stings her knuckles, taxes some skin.

Silence. Her bare shoulders goosebump with breeze and nerves.

Hello? Hello?

The possums turn around, their eyes wide and glassy, their tails intertwined.

Ello?

She hears a scuffle and a sniff. Doesn't see the tall figure that emerges slowly. Ewan squints, groggy and stiff. Puzzled by his slumber, the open door, the red twilight sky, her. Dazed he traces the path of her long shadow that reaches down his hallway to touch his toes.

Hello?

Warren doesn't like the smell of this place. He backs up, warily watching the man down the hall. He tries to look thuggish.

You're there, I know. I can hear you. Door was already open.

Still. Silence.

Eleanor feels her pulse thumping. Almost hears it bashing against her sternum. A rash of heat across her face.

Look: I was just, well, I just wanted to sort of atone, okay? I'm sure it must be unnerving being stalked by the blind, but I'm quite safe, really. And I'm sorry that, you know ...

She tails off. A pause, thick with discomfort.

This is going well isn't it?

Ewan is very still and very quiet. He does not blink. She tries again:

My name's Eleanor anyway. This is my warren, Dog. She flushes. This is my *dog, Warren*. And it's just, that, whatever it is you play, like, your instrument, it's just ...

Silence.

Still.

There is weight on her instep. Whatever it was she wanted, she didn't come here to make an arse of herself. She lingers for one more breath. Swivels. Warren responds with enthusiasm. The sky is stark crimson. She turns back. Sharp. Fuck it.

She steps inside, feels smooth cool floorboards. The smell of stale air and mothballs. Heaves it in.

For my birthday this year I baked myself a sponge cake and I whacked a candle in it and got food poisoning because the eggs were off and I had a flu so my nose was blocked and so I didn't know. I gave it to Warren. Whatever. You want statistics? I'm a twenty-one-year-old virgin and I go for days without sleep because I have bad dreams that wake me up just in time to piss myself. My surname is *Rigby* for fuckssake and I have a mother who is addicted to television and I'm tired of minding my *own* business. No. I'm just *tired*. And do you have any idea why I would want to like, come to your house and tell you this? No, of course you don't, and neither do I. Neither do I. Jesus, I mean, I just don't *do* this. And I don't know *why* whatever it is you play here helps me to sleep, I don't know, *soundly*, but it does and I don't know why. I really don't. But, you know, I know it must be hard, but you really don't have to avoid me okay? I'm blind so I don't really respond to body language too well. If you want me to piss off just say so. Trust me, I'm resilient, I'll be okay.

She feels strangely lucid. Out of breath. Delirious.

Silence.

What are you, bloody *mute*?

The sky is a sheet of fading mauve. She opens her mouth again. She's interrupted.

Cello.

She swallows. His voice is baritone, soft and all of a sudden. Young.

It's what I play. The cello.

Cello. Chellow. Well, it's nice. It's really nice.

Silence again. She feels her slim momentum slipping.

So, wots your name?

Pause.

Ewan, he says, even softer.

Ewan. Well, it's nice to meet you, Ewan. She smiles. Ewan. Yoowen. Sounds like something you'd do to a sheep, doesn't it. Doin the Ewan.

Pause.

Sorry. She rubs a palm into her forehead. My *God*, I sound like Bruno. Sorry. She laughs nervously.

In the dark, neither of them can see. Eleanor takes up Warren's harness and she's suddenly bold. Her voice is resonant down the hall.

You know what, Ewan? Nobody has ever taken me out to dinner. I think you should. Yeah. I think you should. She smiles, chirpy. What do you think? Tomorrow then? Good. Good. So I'll be round, what, seven thirty?

Silence.

Still.

Good answer. Okay, well, I'll see you then. Bye.

And she's strolling back down the path; quick, before it catches up with her. She just leaves it there, hanging. And Ewan does not interject, hasn't the time.

Two possums watch her leave with four wide eyes. They are smiling.

Ewan slowly flicks a light to make sure she has gone.

THE LIFE OF BRIAN

Back here:

They're in a coldblue Volvo streaming through a bleak puce desert at dusk, heading west. A red screwdriver rolls and clatters under a seat. Brian used it recently to pick open the toilet door after his son locked himself inside.

Ewan is very quiet and very still. There is no music.

Denise is not in the car. Right now, she's in the Maldives. Nude. Tossing back her moaning head as she writhes on a clean, cream beach; straddling a man she has just met (Fuck! Oh! Fuck! *Oh, fuck!*). His name is Ron, or Rod, or Rob; a clerk or a sales rep on long service leave. (Later, she will abort the resultant pregnancy by swallowing the powdered root of rhubarb *officinale*, given to her by a native herbal apothecary. The cathartic will purge her stomach and womb in a shower of shit and blood.)

Ewan and his father stare straight ahead. Loss sits in the backseat, subdued and silent.

∗∗∗

In 1855, a tall, pale Irish emigrant called Peter Dempsey furrowed his brow and harnessed his elderly horse, Neville. Peter had become greatly concerned by his waning Faith. Since tearing his Protestant roots in Limerick and settling in America, Peter couldn't seem to rejuvenate that warmfeeling of almighty Providence that he had worked so hard to achieve as a younger man. He was unhappy and disillusioned with this new country. And that was why he and his wife, Maeve, were travelling southwest from their hogfarm in hometown Pottersville, Michigan, to Battle Creek. They had heard word of a resident prophetess.

On their light wagon, Peter gripped the leather reigns between thumb and forefinger. He smelled of earth and pigshit. He had a ptotic left eyelid, which slid like a pink patch over his pupil and often hampered his perspective.

In the church of Battle Creek, Peter and his wife sat straight-backed and alert on a hard yew pew, inspired by the wilful exegesis of the Adventist matriarch Ellen White. Sat stunned as she dispensed her tenets of redemption and resurrection and immortal Kingdoms of Glory. She assured him that Christ was indeed coming back for a second crack at it; to restore Man to God, once and for all. With New Heavens and New Earth. She wasn't much to look at, but her sonorous Testimony was irresistible. Peter's hand lifted from his lapsed lap and rubbed his black beard. Maeve nodded and touched his thigh.

He was still stung by the time they arrived back at the hogfarm. Absently, Peter surveyed the property. It was very quiet and very still. A carious stench filled the humid air. Abraham, the genial dipsomaniac he had left in charge of the property, appeared to be gone. And Peter, holding himself upright on a muddy stile, was confronted by thirty acres of dead livestock. As he trudged through the pens, he soon saw why.

Michigan was a leading propagator of perennial garden rhubarb at this time. When it was in season, Peter often purchased the nutritious rhizomes, because they were dirt cheap and good feed for his hogs. It seemed Abraham, on an excursion to surrounding plantations, had inadvertently invested in *whole* plants and fed them to the pigs, poisoning them with the leaves.

Maeve wept, but Peter did not despair, being under the influence of holy spirits. As he surveyed with one eye the gloomy tableau of rotting pork, a sudden, convenient rod of light burst between parting clouds from the ether. He nodded as though he understood. A sign. O yes. A message from the Almighty. He was anointed with a thin drizzle.

Turning, he spoke in his thick, convoluted parlance: Maeve, pack up al yar tengs. I've had an ephipany.

Epiphany, dear.

Yes. That's right. An epipany.

Peter sold the farm and was reborn.

From pens of pork to the sheep and goats. Because in that short moment, Peter decided that God had decided it was his earthly purpose to tend to the Scattered Flock. That *he* was responsible for spreading the hallowed word of the Adventist. He set out to hastily prepare The People for Christ's imminent return.

And where else for a self-ordained missionary to expound the revelations of good, clean, healthy, Christ-directed living than that doomed southern penal colony that had just struck gold and lost God? A whole *continent* of sin, just waiting to be redeemed. Where immigrants were arriving hellbound with pick and shovel, to be led astray from the glorious cloak of His holy omnipotence.

So Peter and his wife travelled southwest to New South Wales, clutching their meagre luggage and earnest propaganda. The pilgrimage was expensive and their savings were slim. Still smelling of burnt pork and raw rhubarb, Peter pondered the problem of financing his Mission. As they hit the harbour, it occurred to him that if the Jews could thrive on usury, then the Seventh Day Adventists were going to *collect*. So in Sydney, he established a small debt collection agency and routed the luckless in the goldfields. It was busy work. He became particularly successful with the opium-addicted Chinese, who despite working the hardest were often left destitute by pillaging Diggers. And while Peter cheerfully seized their assets, he often preached to them about the use of narcotics. And while he preached to them about the use of narcotics, they often exploited his forbidden passion for a punt, playing a game they called *fan-tan*. And as they exploited his forbidden passion for a punt, they almost always seized their assets back, for Peter was an uncannily luckless gambler.

Nevertheless, with such a high rate of thwarted investment in the madness of the gold rush, Peter's business expanded steadily, as did the blessed message of the Seventh Day Adventist. (So much so, that in 1891, Ellen White herself hit out to the Lucky Country, to give counsel on its denominational development. Peter gushed and had her sign his favourite softleather bible.)

With the church and business prospering, Peter and Maeve

slipped into an entirely different Missionary position in order to do some Creation of their own. They soon begat children; who begat children; who begat children. And who each inherited the blurry Dempsey lifemould; an intertwined path, paved by the Prophet and the Profit. Spliced between the family business and the Lord's enterprise. A working week with a tithed income and a Saturday Sabbath. And blessed, white, spitshine purity through rigorous, righteous abstinence. Three baptised generations of pale children who had never danced, seen a film or munched a sausage. Primed for eternal lives of religion and repossession. Amen.

On the 6th August, 1945, God's Earth shook as a small twig emerged at the lower end of the Dempsey Family Tree. A blunt twig they called Brian. And the Earth shook that day, because the world's first atomic weapon had exploded over the town of Hiroshima.

***

Denise was tired of the shit she had married into. Tired of bleak, regimented housewifery and sex only on Special Occasions. Tired of dour, subjugated Healthy Living. Tired of the spurious face she wore before her threadbare faith. Tired of having that hypocrisy reflected by her husband. All the Make Believe. She was tired through a lack of iron. She needed meat.

One day, after burning her finger while ironing, she had shaken her hand and hissed the word *fuck*. It made her stop. She giggled. The pain subsided. She said it again, quietly to herself: *fuck*. It felt good. *Fuck*.

Fuck!

Soon enough, Denise was sneaking excursions to steakhouses and cafes and smoky bars. These small liberties were initial bliss, but they barely touched the sides. Neither did daytime movie sessions or the casual perfidy for a starved libido. They simply served to remind her of all the things she was missing.

She got out.

Of course Denise regretted leaving her son, but he was culled in favour of a clean slate. It was far easier to pretend she'd never had one.

On the day Brian was preparing to tell her about moving west, Denise already had her bags packed, the money withdrawn, the ticket and the taxi waiting.

Lord! Didn't think you'd be this excited about it, he had said, arriving home. Who told you anyway?

I'm leaving, Brian.

No, we're leaving next week. We'll take the car over. Save some money. So they told you about the promotion?

I'm leaving, Brian. The cab honked.

And she left as a red Renault pulled in. With no turning, no waving, no goodbyeing.

It was a Tuesday afternoon.

***

Brian worked hard to appear crap at his job. He also worked hard to appear to be a solid, devoted Adventist. In the eyes of his family, Brian prayed well but was a pisspoor collector of debts.

His siblings constantly urged him to embrace a more ecclesiastic role, but he smiled and assured them that his rightful place was with the firm. They nodded weakly.

Being a part owner made Brian very difficult to fire, so his brothers contrived instead to promote him. To promote him all the way to the other side of the country. A sort of enforced nepotism. A relocation; so he could be crap at his job somewhere else.

Brian had sat in subordinate silence as his brothers explained:

Look: *Brian*. We're expanding. And quickly. It's tough to keep up. And it's all kudos to the diligence of employees like *you*, Brian. At the end of the day, we have to look at what's best for the firm. Don't we? And that (he leaned closer) is why we need a good man to establish our name as we press into new territory. Not unlike a missionary, Brian. A responsible, dedicated man. We need *you*, Brian: over *there*.

Brian nodded in docile affirmation. Like a hapless dickhead. A twig in the breeze.

And, as he rose, he couldn't conceal a small knowing smirk that curled his lip.

God smote him good.

And that was why she left. It wasn't an act of frustrated volition that led to his wife's desertion. He would have known, would have sensed it. No. It was an act of God. O yes. The Lord's almighty wrath.

He was a sinner and a thief and he was punished.

The reason Brian appeared never to win the Collector of the Month Award was because he had (rightly) assumed that no one would suspect such ineptitude of embezzling the thousands and thousands of dollars that he filtered out of the place. Brian liked to balance the books *his* way. Though he never held his silent surfeit for long, because on Tuesday afternoons, Brian liked to share the forbidden thrill of his late grandfather ...

The casino (*chaching!*). A heady place for a heathen. Hard to get more secular than a spinning roulette wheel. But in all those bright, heavenly lights, breathing all that pumped purified oxygen, Brian believed he had found his true Kingdom of Glory. His faith allayed for Chance. This was his church. Where Time stood still. He prayed for numbers, for suits, for dice. Shifty dealer dialogue was his sermon.

The casino: where you left either smelling of shit, or roses.

Brian always left smelling of shit. And guilt. And disappointment. He was an incredibly consistent loser. An impossible exception to the Law of Averages. Regulars recognised him as the resident Jonah, an unlucky charm, and often clung to him for their advantage like opportune parasites. If Brian had fifty on red, they would slyly slide a hundred on black, and grin unctuously as they raked in their chips.

But Brian even lost on the rare times he was ahead, because he knew he could always be *more* ahead. And why leave when you're more ahead when you can be *even more* ahead?

So he left with nothing every time. But he always came back. With other people's money.

And nobody ever knew. Except him. And Him.

And that's why she left.

Despite appearances, Brian had loved his wife. And the loss of her sucked at the meat of him. Left him jaded and humourless. And alone.

But Brian did not learn his godly lesson. Not even that could cut deep enough to quell his surging urgings.

As he had expected, the isolation of Perth made for easier embezzlement. Gambling recommenced in earnest. He stole more and bet more. And away from the scrutiny of his family, he was also able to spend more and more time at the casino. He needed it. He laid bets with a new determination, as though he were trying to win her back. He shifted chips and chewed steaks wrapped in bacon. Ordered bourbon and other assorted drinks shaded by tiny pink umbrellas. Chewed on thick cigars. And on bad nights, he got a room and some paid fellatio (one of the few investments for which he ever got a return).

And Brian left emptier than he arrived.

Smelling of shit and stale spirits, he would walk quickly back through the casino carpark. With his Shame like a rod of gravity pressing down from the firmament. He kept his head bowed, chastened; because like any serial sinner, the only thing Brian had faith in was the Lord's censure. He felt that weighty loom. He was well aware that he already been Celestially Warned, and he knew the Almighty would not take any more of this shit. He expected it. Awaited that holy bolt of vengeful lightning to crack down and sting his nuts. Brian knew he was the only Adventist in history to dread the Second Coming. He had debts to God, and his tall bearded messenger was on his way soon to collect. And he wouldn't be so serene and forgiving this time.

But he was slippery and sullen with Greed and Loss. He just couldn't stop. He stole even more. Bet even more. And every evening and every Sabbath and every Sunday he spent with Chance and lost. He thieved from the insolvent. He gambled. He drank liquor like a Russian and smoked tobacco like a Texan. He bought blowjobs. And outside the casino he shuffled like a hunchback, stinking of impurity, grimacing, daring not look up. His contrition truly shook him. He could not eat, could not sleep.

Despairing, Brian devised a convenient way to devolve his responsibilities as both a single parent and a sinner. He grafted his guilt, handballed it. Simple. Washed his hands of it, like his wife, like Pilate. Brian believed that if he could extol the virtues of the Lord unto his son, make *him* believe, then he would come out somehow distilled by it. Sanctified and satisfied. Unburdened, with a vacuous conscience. And so this was the man who passed his reserved, reticent son a signed softleather bible. And locked him in the backseat of a coldblue Volvo with it. Parked in a casino carpark. So he could lose with peace of mind.

***

Back here, alone in Mt Pleasant, Ewan lives for the heady feeling of mail in the letterbox. He likes to snatch letters and rush upstairs to his room and touch them, their paperness. Smooth.

Sent by Jim. They arrive on Tuesday afternoons. Lessons in ink, condensed, abridged and sealed and stamped with his name on them. Jim encloses a letter and new pieces and the scent of Sydney. And scribbled diagrams on the back of manuscript paper that tell him what to practise and where his fingers should be. Jim remarks on his intonation from the other side of the country.

It makes Here bearable, but never ever as good as Back There.

Ewan likes to hold these letters for a long time before he puts them away. He keeps them in a shoebox he sheathes with a thick jumper and then hides in the base of an ageing set of drawers. Kamahl guards the fort. Cased up in his celloshaped suit of armour.

On Saturdays and Sundays and some weeknights, Ewan sits in the backseat of the Volvo. Parked in a casino carpark.

On his knees, he peers out the back window and waits until his father is swallowed by rigid swing doors. Then he puts his bible down, next to his water flask and lunchbox, and sometimes his schoolbag. He undoes one, two, three buttons of his shirt and pulls out sheets of Secret Hidden Treasure. Lays them out smooth over his lap. They crackle like electricity.

Looks left and right. Rightandleft. And back again at those rigid swing doors.

Then he puts the palm of his right hand under his chin. And he plays Mozart on his forearm. Or Vivaldi. Or Haydn. Or his very favourite, Bach. He follows crotchets and minims and quivering quavers all the way down to his elbow, humming them as he plays. Four invisible strings on a fleshy celloneck. Pressing skin and sinew with agile fingers. His thin arms long and perfect. An audience of dancing dustmotes. And when he knows the piece, he sometimes closes his eyes and he is justabout *there*. Bringing it back, with every note. Almost there in a musty room with a Magic Carpet. Because he finds that nothing holds memory like music. It's like a sack you can sift through, to pull things out and hold and keep.

He plays until his right arm is numb and his lips are tingly. Stuffs his Secret back into his shirt. Then he tents his fingers and waits.

Sometimes he wakes to the sound of footsteps and car keys. Sometimes he doesn't wake until his father shakes his shoulders. Then he asks him, urgently, if he has read his bible. And Ewan whispers *Yes* every time. And his father disperses a sigh and says: Good. Like it was a reprieve. A relief.

Some days he comes back early after losing quickly, and Ewan has to quickly hide his Secret. These are the worst days. These days he takes away the softleather bible and asks for quotes, verses, anything. Just to hear him recite them. And with warm throat and tingly lips, Ewan learns to just make it up. He knows the characters and the style of text. And his father didn't know otherwise; he'd believe Leviticus was the Greek God of Lust if it sounded authoritative.

Both exonerated, they would head home. Silent and subdued.

As time elapsed, Ewan felt hungry for more correspondence. Once a week wasn't enough. He sent a letter back every day: to Sydney, from Mt Unpleasant.

Jim began packing envelopes with more pieces and less advice. More time and less effort. His handwriting began to suffer too. It fell over. Became a shaky, messy scrawl that was barely legible. Not even their frequency endured. Though Ewan's hope did. He wrote two letters a day. Asked for help and advice. Told him that he was getting so tall, Kamahl's endpeg came nowhere near the floor. He was growing up fast. He boasted he could play Brahms on his arms.

The other end laughed and ached with too many things.

Once a week became once a fortnight became once a month became far too long to wait for the boy with dappled bruises on his arm. He played Angry music. He played loud and sharp and fast music.

And then there was nothing. It felt like betrayal.

When Ewan was fifteen, a brown paper package appeared in his bedroom. It was celloshaped. And hard, like his chest. He felt its paperness. Smooth.

Ewan tore it softly. Revealed a mahogany hardcase. Deepdark red, the colour of a bloodclot. It had a silver lining. He opened it slowly, the hinges squealed. She was nestled in a velvet inlay and she was beautiful. Shaking, he lifted her easily to his knees. She smelled of him.

In a covered cavity of the case, Ewan found scattered dry ganja seeds, some rhubarbroot balm and a canary yellow firecracker. A small note said:

> *Shit, Zoltan! Where did the Time go?*
>   *Be well,*
>   *— Voolfgung*

A hole burst open in his belly. His fingers traced her thin welted grain; touched the coarse bumps and bubbles in her skin, followed her shoulders and round hips. Her gut strings were grotty and out of tune. Her neck smudged by a million notes ground out by four fingertips. Fluid, nimble fingers that had made air move and pain disappear. Like Magic. He slid her between his knees. She fit. Like nothingelse ever had. She whispered to him. Only he could hear. He held her there, and it was not the end of the world.

Ewan did not cry.

***

Soon after, beyond belief and expectation, Brian ended a tremendous losing streak and won up big. On a warm Tuesday afternoon, he found himself with a winning second division lottery ticket (left hand) and a victory slip for a Melbourne Cup trifecta (right hand). He shook with ecstatic happiness. And because this was his lucky day, because he could always be *more* ahead, he withdrew his savings and his son from school. He drove straight to the casino, ran to the roulette wheel and put everything he had on the number six.

It came up three times in a row.

Brian stopped because he fainted. He woke in a delirious daze, grinning. At last, he was the winner; the gambolling gambler. That night he ate lobster, drank himself stupid and overpaid a prostitute for a night of sordid celebration.

He emerged the following dawn, still under the influence of vodka, scotch and other spirits. Still absorbing the fact that after a life of Loss, he had finally killed the pig. Hell, he'd killed a whole *farm* of pigs. Brian pulled open the rigid swing doors to embrace the new day. He squinted. And walked stiffly down the adjoining steps, straight into a waiting sea of saffron. He stopped. Confused, he was suddenly beset by a posse of Hare Krishnas (who were currently targeting Houses of Sin for rigorous recruitment). And as he listened carefully, engulfed, a convenient rod of light burst from the ether. It was Brian sized. Full of weight.

Brian closely surveyed the excitable group. His eyes were wide. His wallet burned. Sobering, he nodded as though he understood. And it all somehow felt like augury.

He was stung. Stunned. On the grassed banks of the nearby river, Brian talked with them until dusk. In a cold blue Volvo, his son slept, hot and hungry.

Krishna, Brian thought. Blue and pure as sky. Vishnu's avatar, a child of God, someone who had already *been*. Someone who had visited once and was *not coming back*. Brian smiled, imagining a broad, clean slate. He was forgiven. He was theirs.

The next day, Brian cashed his chips and bought a plane ticket and a swathe of saffron. He bequeathed all his earthly possessions to his only child and flew direct to the North of India. With no luggage, no hair, no name. At the foot of the Himalayas he renounced the Four Pillars Of Sinful Life (meat, illicit sex, intoxication, gambling) and began racking up transcendental soul points for his reincarnation. Priming his spirit for his own second crack at it. In the chill air he chanted devotional service and tended vegetables in the moist arable land. And he took great delight in a rich, darkgreen patch of rhubarb that he bolstered constantly with the fresh, holy shit of sacred bovines.

***

And now it's Tomorrow Night. Around six thirty.

Ewan sits shitscared in the frontseat of a Volvo he has started but never driven. Thick with dust. He catches a sneeze in his hand. Wipes it on his father's shirt that he inherited and wears.

He looks in the RearView mirror. On the backseat he sees the waved pages of a signed, softleather bible. Above which he notices a gaping exit wound in the upholstery where two promiscuous possums have sought soft foam to luxuriate their lovepit. Depositing two curled turds as downpayment.

He sees too many things.

Ewan touches his arm.

THE OLD SHANGHAI

Thick steam rises in the shower. It has the sweet taste of tin as she breathes it in.

Eleanor twists taps, Hot and Cold, slides a curtain, sniffs. And that shaft of humidity follows her out like a creeping fog.

The bathroom is an ugly spread of lemon and lime and white tiling. The cream grout is stained umber in parts. There are two mirrors. One in front of her, one behind. But being blind means she can't see her body on reflection. Front or back. So she doesn't see the fresh sheen of her skin, or the colour of the crusty towel she is reaching for (grey). She doesn't see the whiteness of her small pert breasts against her nutbrown arms. Doesn't see the two jutting bonebumps on her shoulders. Or the tuft of arrowed hair that she's touched but never seen. Or behind her, the corrugated arc of her spine, the deep dimples between her bum and her back.

Dry, she tortillas herself in the towel and opens the bathroom door. Leaves wet prints down the carpeted hall. Foot shadows; a record of pigeontoed steps.

In her room, she dresses quickly in clothes she has already

laid out. Fast and systematic. In front of another pointless mirror. It's where she has always got changed.

Nervous and restless. She works her skirt a little lower on girlish hips. Makes sure her top is on the right way round and her tits are organised. Worms into her Peasant Birkenstocks. Moves back into the damp bathroom. Smells grapefruit bodywash and Estelle's talcum powder and pods of lavender soap. She feels about for her toothbrush.

It's Tomorrow Night. Around six. And Eleanor Rigby is squeezing toothpaste embarrassingly early. Ready, with an hour and a half to kill. And still rushing. Maybe even smiling as she brushes. Going too fast to get to thinking about the night ahead. Her empty belly roils and folds and cramps with tedious eggdispensing.

She spits foamy minty froth. It splats and gurgles. Rubs her face with a balding handtowel. Glosses her lips with lipgloss. Pats her pockets. Smoothes her bumcheeks with her palms.

Keeps moving.

***

Ewan is still in a coldblue Volvo when she knocks. His head turns sharp. His gut sinks.

He waits. Eyes closed.

She knocks again.

Ewan staggers sapless from the garage into his adjoining kitchen. His hair is dust tipped from the interior lining.

He can't do this. He stands at the foot of the hall. She knocks again. His hairs stand on end. The fan carves languid, like the shit's already hit it. Vertigo, that's what he feels. Heavy dread and the gnaw of nausea. The passage ahead is dim and turbid and hot. The air hard to breathe. He is basted in sweat. Lilian is clear and garrulous to his left. Only he can hear. He glances and his feet lust to push her way. To pick her up, to have her there like armour, like a shield. A sturdy abdomen.

She bangs the door. It rings down the hall.

Slowly, he wades forward. One step. Two, three, four steps. Shuffles. He takes harried, fragmented glances at his Options. From that room, to that door. And back again. And back again. And back again. Why can't she just leave? Just fuck off and leave him be, leave him alone.

She thumps the door. Hello? You there, Chellowboy?

He is. Standing. Barnacled to the floorboards. His head, back and forth and back and forth. Forth. Forth. Like he has a choice. Where to run now? Out of his skin? In a circle? Up and down this dimly lit vestibule? No. He can't, he's mired in this, ineluctably, he knows.

All of a sudden he wants to sleep. To lie down and cup his skull and sleep.

She belts the door. He sees it bow concave. He can reach it, pull it, but he can't.

Hel-low!

Ewan folds and hobbles back a step. Head pounding.

Hey! I know you're there. Hurry up. This is just rude!

Bile is wedged solid in his gullet. And it's forward he moves as two horny possums scratch and wrestle and squeal to climax above him. His thumb snaps a latch. Fingers meagrely meet a doorknob, greasy with sweat, shaking. A shudder gusts from his spine.

He opens the door to a Blind Girl and the breeze she brings. To light and unsteadiness.

***

Bruno emerges dripping from the shower. Showerfog tumbles out kneehigh. Sucking in his mountainous belly, he admires himself on reflection.

You're a goodlooking man, Bruno. A stallion, yes?

(More like a fat baboon, says Althea to herself as she passes outside.)

Nude, Bruno blowdries and combs his greasy sidemullet. He preps his scalp with a blast of hairspray and coils the strip round and round and round. He pats it down and sprays again. He coughs. Observes.

Ah, yes, he says.

***

Estellevision reaches a moment of tension.

Lock it in! Lock it in! Estelle insists to the twice divorced mother of five who is chewing her nails.

Estelle knows that the Price Is Right. She's absorbed enough advertising to recognise the Value of things. She leans forward:

Lock. It. In!

She rolls her eyes as the woman asks a smiling wellgroomed android to swap the dining suite for the jetski. *Idiot*, Estelle scowls.

She would have been a winner.

***

Frank wakes from his afternoon nap to a late wicket in the One Day Cricket. Steve Waugh, caught behind off an outside edge.

Serves him right, Frank mutters to himself, watching the replay. Doesn't move his feet.

He scratches idle balls well past their use-by date and struggles to his feet to take a piss. His thongs shuffle and click, echoing loud in his empty house.

***

The first thing Ewan notices are her eyes. Bright blue and dead set. They crinkle a little at the edges to make room for the width of her smile, the second thing he notices. Her lips are lacquered and thick, parting for a burst of sudden white teeth. She has a tiny nosestud. Her hair is short and indecisive, sometimes tamped and sometimes scruffy, sometimes tawny sometimes blonde. Her long ears give an elfin look to her face.

She wears a thickstitched navy denim skirt that somehow hangs from her thin hipbones, breaking into a fray just past her knees. Thin shoulderstraps cling to her cowlneck top, its deep henna red augmenting her tan. Tight enough to suggest her bra-less breasts, loose enough to conceal her ladder of ribs. A tag flaps at the nape of her neck.

A slab of her stomach is deep brown, with a thin white strip below. She has nutty, nubby toes with crustyskinned edges. Her feet are slightly inverted.

How long did you take in there? God, you're like a woman. Hope you didn't make yourself too beautiful. I must confess, I was a bit early. I have been sitting on your verandah for the last half-hour. So: you ready then?

Silence.

He can't do this. He wants to scream at her: No! I'm not ready! I'm not fucking ready! The farthest he has strayed from here in six years is Bruno's, and that was only yesterday. On his boldest days, he opens his bedroom window three inches. The rest are rusted shut. And shuttered. No. He can't.

But being blind means she can't see the stricken expression that is just *there*, or the blatant weight of his feet pushing back, back, back. Can't see the fear in his wide eyes, in his poise.

No, he says quietly, I'm not ready.

You're not? How come? Her smile eases.

Silence.

Two postcoital possums take their afterglow for a stroll onto the verandah beam. The breeze swoops in.

Shoes, Ewan says. I need shoes.

Well put some on! God! Are you *sure* you're not a woman?

Ewan scuffles stiffly back down the hallway. Looks for shoes. Or red ruby slippers. Eleanor follows, inviting herself in with the dog at her heels.

Shit, how tall *are* you anyway? Sounds like, what, six-seven? Six-eight?

Silence.

Well, let's just say tall then. You're a tall man, Ewan.

Ewan finds his shoes. He kneels dizzily.

He feels surreal and emptied. Stoned, almost. Strangely separate from his senses, as though his vision, his hearing, his flesh is orbiting distantly around him. Far far away. Hazy and incongruent.

Shoelaces. He concentrates on shoelaces. Eleanor breathes in deep.

Your house smells like mothballs. And pot, she says. You should air it out.

He doesn't appear to hear. The dog is sniffing the length of his shin, eyeing him carefully. The hallway is lucent and clearing with the breeze she brought. Fine dust shifts. There is someone else in his house! A girl, and a dog, and the door is gaping wideopen! His jaw clenches. He can't do this.

Pull. Loop. Tie. Pull. He sneezes. The dog flinches and backs up.

Bless you, she says.

Thankyou.

You're welcome.

He stands, feels like retching. Looks at her. Why are you here? he asks. Soft. Almost a whisper.

Her head tilts up. Because you're taking me to dinner. You ready now? It's all right, I'm paying. You just have to *take* me. Can you do that?

Silence. He pleads with a look of unease.

Good. She nods and slips back down the hall, her steps perfectly linear. Her small calico bag swings. Ewan is hesitating. Warren is sniffing a skirting board. He licks it. Eleanor waits as patiently as she can at the threshold. Still inabighurry so she doesn't give ground to doubt.

Ewan grapples with faintness. Implosion. His head is aching and his chest compressed. He exhales. Absently he grabs a nugget of rosin. Pockets it.

Walks. He's level with her now. The horizon is garish with melty hues. The possums are peering from above. Eleanor drops the harness, ushers Warren inside.

It's all right if I leave him here, yeah?

Sorry?

Warren. He'll be all right here won't he? She feels a pause of complaint. He should be fine, really. He's very well behaved, aren't you, Warren?

Warren sits and looks confused.

Ewan is very still, and very quiet.

Let's be off then, she says. They stand on a prickly unwelcome mat. You going to close your door?

Ewan slowly closes the door. There is piercing noise in his head. Now, don't be alarmed, he hears her say, but I'm gunnahafta grab your arm, okay?

She clasps his arm just above the elbow. He feels the heat through his shirt. Touching.

Thankyou, she says.

They turn. Careful down the steep steps. And their legs are brushed by squat unkempt shrubs as they edge through the centre path together.

***

Furry radars pivot and collapse. They've gone.

Warren cases the joint.

He pads and clacks down the hall with idle inhalations. It's hot in here. The coolness from the sea and sunfall doesn't permeate. He wishes he were tethered to the verandah.

Warren works his way through the stubborn atmosphere. The air is soupy and still and stuffy. He sidles into the kitchen and scours the floor, working his snout like a metal detector. The hardwood floor offers hors d'oeuvres of hard cheese, crumbs, fluff and scummy mildew. All fall mercy to his throbbing pink tongue. He has several flavoursome pressings at an aged glob of congealed gravy.

A sickly fridge sees him and starts to groan and splutter. Warren inspects a stiff moth. Feet up. Wings down. A tiny, flipped jet. He leaves it be.

Warren suddenly lunges into himself to nibble his loins and then swipe them with his tongue. When he emerges he hears a rustling at the other end of the kitchen. His ears rise and scan. He's on to it.

Head angled and low, Warren stalks his crackling prey. Softly, softly, softly.

Warren confronts two possums on a rubbish raid.

One stands, giving weight to the pedal of the bin. The other scrounges inside, rising occasionally to drop pilfered goods over the side.

Warren crouches, tail fanning. Then he barks and bounds and snaps and dives. The pedalweight possum reacts first and scampers out a side door. The bin lid slaps shut and the scrounging possum is trapped. The bin squeals and shudders. But Warren's brakes are frictionless. He slides and skids, knocking the bin to its side with a spill of rubbish and marsupial. The possum bolts towards the hallway. Ears pinned. A smear of yellowed hommus streaking its backbone. Warren gathers his limbs and gives chase. Somehow in the mess of legs the bin finds its way back upright. His harness claps his hips. The possum veers left into an adjoining room and Warren scrambles after it, arriving just in time to see it dart victoriously between the wall and a bookcase. It squeezes through a narrow gap in the floorboards. A wellworn possum thoroughfare, softedged with tufts of collected fur.

Warren's snout arrives late. The pursuit ends. He barks furtively at the gap.

He retreats, backing back. Turns and impales his head on the sharpish endpeg of a cello called Lilian. His yelp drowns out her hollow rebuke. Warren looks at her. His nose cranks up again. He sniffs liberally at her bum, minding the sharp jutting rod. His twitching snout follows the curve of her hips, her recessed waist, her shoulders. Her sweatsmelling neck. Confused, he pads back.

Yawns. Tongue curling, then unfurling. Whining as he keeps his front paws planted and his arse aloft. Warren opens his eyes and sees a dog. With its front paws planted and its arse aloft. There, just there, in the deep varnish of a rounded back. He sees a dog. A brother.

He peers closer. So does the other dog. Warren tilts his head and frowns. So does the other dog! They sniff at each other, their noses almost touching.

The two dogs sigh and circle and circle and circle and lie down together.

She tugs him level.

It's the blind leading the blind really, innit? she smiles.

Ewan has to stoop a little to narrow their Height Gap. He is conscious of her grip, her proximity. Conscious of being held. His belly threshes. His mouth is pasty. Glued. He's forfeiting the familiar with every step. It's true. He feels led. On lead legs. By the blind.

They approach a townhouse that he could smell downwind as they first turned into the street. He sees a loud group sucking at the tentacles of a hookah pipe set on a makeshift table, made from an old snapped Malibu. He hears a dobro twang from inside.

Like a toke, people? someone proffers a clear tube. Ewan averts his eyes.

Eleanor turns: No thanks, I'm already blind.

They laugh.

***

Credits roll.

They march up, up, up and disappear to trumpeting exit music. An announcer politely tells Estelle not to move. Estelle obliges in loyal obeisance.

She lifts her bible. Her wrinkly armflab hammocks as she flaps at a touchlamp. She seeks out pink strips with a squint and a chubby finger. Where to go now. She hisses, wincing at a Time

Clash. Two linear highlights. The One Day Cricket, or This Is Your Life?

She sighs and aims the remote.

***

Bruno oozes out of his Babyshit Ochre Mercedes. An inflatable whale through a manhole. Coiffure rising. Althea's stubby box heels are already clacking down the driveway. She leaves a trailing cloud of perfume.

Bruno is sweating beneath his stiffstarched dinnershirt, beneath his (good) red braces, beneath his Mission Brown dinner jacket. He schmacks his lips. Good Lord! He can smell Greta's cooking from here. Can almost see the dish of steamy, creamy pasta. The glazed, pebble bed of olives. The spread of antipasto. The moist slabs of spinach pie. The juicy, juicy lamb shanks. The crusty pecorino bread. Can almost taste the tart redwine that will stain his wet lips and render him unbearably raucous and antagonising. And surrounded by family and no friends, his little lady sitting uneasily by his side, he will bullshit mawkishly about farms and fathers and Llamas and go close to suggesting a lingering Oedipus Complex with the mother he never had. And during dessert (Althea's Rhubarb Fool, with double cream), he'll display brilliant political sagacity with whomever he can trap into interlocution (an so you see, you heffa the right wing an you heffa the leff wing, an you know, is no good. Is becozz with only one wing, the bird he will only fly in a *circle* ah? Won't he? Iss just an halbatross arownd our neck. What you need, what you *haff* to do is

amalgamamate the two. Rightanleff. Meet in the very *heart* off the
bird. A balance, ah? That is goot politics. *That,* hiss how you run
a country.) Bruno will roll up his shirtsleeves and display his
Napoli arm scar like a trophy. Big and Loud. And when he has
eaten enough, drunk enough, he'll pull a wheezy concertina from
the boot of his car and sit at the table to gargle with it, driving
everybody into the other room.

Bruno straightens his tie and jostles hungrily down the steep
driveway to meet his wife.

***

Frank sets down his reeking white bucket, blotted with recent
squid ink. After wrestling the door of his barfridge, he presses
a pack of mulies into the clutter. They aren't the best bait, but
what does he care? What he doesn't give away he throws back.
Except the blowfish. He takes great delight in grinding them
to a pulpy expiration with his thongsole. Weeks ago, somehow,
he snared a three-pound snapper from that mole sheltering the
yacht club. But why cart home what you can't cook? To the
consternation of onlookers, he fed it back to the tide.

Helen cooked the best fish. She'd plunder his good beer for
the crispest of batters that crackled as you peeled flakes off the
fillet. She'd fight you for the leftover beer, too. Their slick fingers
would smudge greasy residue over the glass.

Though Frank doesn't drink too much any more. And
having culinary skills that range from toaster to can-opener has
left him a true connoisseur of the service station bain-marie. He

also retains his rotund figure with the religious Friday pub steak, though he nurses only softies. Maybe a light beer if he's coaxed into it. For breakfast, Frank sifts Metamucil and slops stewed rhubarb over a bowl of All Bran so he can crap without wincing.

Frank lifts his bucket and a bowed rod and leaves his empty house unlocked. The slap of his thongs is muffled by the spongy lawn. He pushes his invisible wheelbarrow on to the pavement, smiling at houses shrouded by bright Christmas lights and decoration.

Frank enjoys surveying the glowing wharf from the other side of the harbour. Twenty years shifting sea containers was enough for any man. Frank is one in a remnant line of retired wharfies who convene at the mole and look back over their previous employer with a mix of fondness and disdain. There's plenty of fat chewing and dirty laughs. They'll talk cricket. Politics. The politics of cricket. Pull at warm port if it's cold enough, grip and cast their titanium virility and all have a whinge about their wives.

***

The sun ekes lower in the sky and Ewan finds himself breathing. Fresh air. Gutly sediments are settling, though his head is still loud. He is defrosting by degrees. Attached almost gratefully to this Blind Girl, who is now the very last of his familiarity. She smells disarmingly good. He steals a glance. So brazen she is, so sure and aware. How she absorbs and attunes and judges contours. How she knows her environment, the topography of things. She doesn't fumble or grope like he would expect. He feels like waving his hand in front of her straight stare, to make sure. She charges. Takes charge. He knows it's *her* taking *him* to dinner. He sees the slope of her shoulders, their determined bend, and how it ages her.

They near a bustling intersection.

Ever play the game Frogger? she asks.

Ewan nods, and immediately sees the futility in that gesture. She forces him to speak:

Yeah, actually. He remembers well. Jim had sneaked him into an arcade one sinful Tuesday afternoon with a heap of change. It was after a movie. His eyes were wide.

Ever play it with your eyes closed? she smiles. And so does Ewan, almost. He hasn't seen this much traffic for years. He shrinks back. Behind her.

Are we right right?

Ewan does not respond.

Are we right right? she repeats with force.

No.

Okay, now?

Yeah.

Walk me up the banked, slopey part of the median strip, okay? she instructs. It's so I don't trip, is all.

He does. They wait again.

Right left?

Yes, he says. Firmer. And they blaze across. Buildings loom closer, tinted by the faltering sunset. Ewan watches warily.

People become more frequent. Going, leaving, coupled, clustered. It gets busy.

His bicep is flexed tight, as though he is holding her back.

***

Warren tentatively paws the pedal of the bin and receives a swift swipe to the snout. His eyes water. Dipping inside, he sifts through for stuff he can loot. He clasps a brown apple core between his teeth. Warren trundles back into the room and offers it to his friend, who is growing fainter with the dark. He nudges it closer, and finds the other dog offering him one in return! They chew happily in concert.

***

Australia are bowling in the second innings, a good position in the current One Day climate. Estelle knows it's always harder to chase.

She eats microwaved ratatouille and suggests field placements for a fierce defence.

***

Bruno drinks quickly, encouraged by salty feta on peppered crackers. He belches, getting louder and hungrier.

***

Frank parks his wheelbarrow and settles in. Chats idly about the heat whilst descunging his reel with a skewed pocketknife. He is berated for his choice of bait as he threads his hook, grinning.

***

A brownvested busker finds his place on South Terrace. He sets his weak boxy amp in a corner and takes a tired and tinny six-string from its case. He tunes with detachment, a little awed by the swelling swarms of people that pass blindly by.

***

In the soft sulphur glow of streetlights they round corners together. Eleanor holds on tighter, lacking the firm trust of Warren. She can feel the clamour and flux of people around her, filling up the space she knows. She is bumped and brushed.

A pimply weed in a powerful car streams past, dangerously close to the kerb. Eleanor jolts back into Ewan. Surprised by his warmth as she sprawls and steps on his left foot.

Wankers, she hisses. The hostile prick drives on. Doof. Doof. Doof. They pause for a moment and untangle.

You know, Ewan, I submit that we adopt India's stance on birth control, except we'll offer car stereos for vasectomies. And I can tell you, I will personally volunteer for the task of snipping vas deferenses. And I'll come equipped with my own pair of rusted hedge shears.

Ewan laughs, almost. Stops, when he realises what it is bubbling up his throat. A strange urge when you haven't had it for years. Half a laugh escapes though; stuttering through his nostrils. And he smiles. Says nothing. Looks at her.

Easy there, Big Fella, she says. You almost did something human.

They hack uneasily through the crowds. The strip is lit bright and decorated. Eleanor pulls in closer. They are side by side. She frowns. Ewan senses her assurance waning. It causes a dim panic to lodge in his belly.

I don't spose you know where you're taking me? she says.

He answers No, but it is stolen by the crowd. Ewan sidesteps a woman charging past in stilettos. His pulse is belting.

How bout Asian, yeah? she says loudly. The Old Shanghai? It's like a food hall, but it's good. It should be coming up yeah? Just across from the markets. Should be on our right.

They near a paved area where tightpacked People watch two longhaired performers twirl firesticks. Ewan is pale. Silent.

Is that where we are, Ewan? her voice rising. I'm sorry but you'll have to help me. This crowd is fucking my orientation. God, I can't believe the *people* out tonight. I hope we can get a table. Can you see it Ewan?

Yes, he says somehow.

They edge down the side wall of a noisy pub. People balk and brush past them, into them. Close, so close. Eleanor's nails dig crescent moons into his arm. His nausea returns. He can't do this. The air is thick with cologne and pheromones. They halt and shuffle. Ewan clenches his pocketed rosin, so hard it cracks in two.

Away from the ring of spectators, they near the Old Shanghai. The place is packed, the sprawl of open tables occupied. Inside, the queue for food is four deep throughout. Ewan cannot breathe. Hard to move. Does not notice Eleanor pressed close against him.

Don't let go, all right? she tells him. Loud. Her eyes are wide.

Ewan is dizzy. Very quiet. Very still.

Impatient People stand impassive, ordering, pondering overhead menus. The smell of curry and coriander and ginger and soy. A herd of milling and surging. A woman bursts through with steaming plates. Ewan flinches. Mixed in the thick of it. He is touched on all sides. So close all of them. Shaking. Cold all over. People. Throbbing disjointed volume, amplified as he pushes in, in, in on himself. An insular retreat. A probe of noise pounding strong and intransigent. Boring at him, into him. Bordering, blocking. Acid on the back of his tongue. Louder. Louder now. Drown. A distant shove. Slipping. People, fractured fragmented images. Gushing in spires. Strobing. His head a fat pulse. Livid with noise now. Pecking at him. They do not remit. Fever. Hot hot panic.

Breaking. You are gasping falling bending now. Sting on your arm. They grant space, parting as you bellow. Push. Turning flailing. Your arms they are grabbed at but you have momentum. Hear a porcelain crash. Fire on your legs. Look down, wet. And shoes; red ruby glow. There'snoplacelike. Mayhem. Writhing loose through stern walls of people. Feel frisked by stares. The sheer quantity of People looking. Hipped table. Clatter. Yell. Runaway, sprint. Ushered by wind. Feet urgent and light. And then: stabbed. Behind you, back, back, back; the terrified shrapnel screams of a blind girl groping nowhere inside a broiling sea of strangers.

IRON

Back here:

Back against a slammed shut bathroom door. Heaving jagged fear. Because insects crawl inside the base of her belly and the tips of the lips of her vagina. Hot thick sticky gunk dribbling. Feel it slipping out sliding out molten. Caked in congealed smears on the insides of thighs, pinching fine hairs. Door is locked. Disgust and shame tear at clothes and reveal a body skinny and hairless. And stained. Legs and arms meet and tighten with cold. Fume of salt and iron.

There are two mirrors. Front and back. But being blind means she can't see her naked body on reflection. Can't see the febrile shiver of pink pluckedchicken skin. Can't see dimples or bonebumps. Or sloped shoulders. Or a whisper of arrowed hair; pointing, pointing at the imbrued hue of your thighs. The red.

Flaccid cotton underpants are warmwet in her fingers. Sticky. A viscous droplet drips on to a shaking calf, scalds, she flinches violently. Wipes at it. Shaking, touches the source softly: blister tender. Fear. Sodarksodarksodark. Just ragged panic in this bathroom. And heat. A glutinous discharge that came without warning and will not taper. Streak on the floor. Lemon. Lime. White. Darkred. It will stain and dry to umber. Glues to her heel. She backs back and gropes and pulls a ribbon of toilet paper. Clamps it between her legs. Just breathing scared. Questions. Everyone is gone to her. She is alone and dying surely? What to do? What to do? What to do? Notknowing.

Look at the helpless hopeless rummaging through drawers and cupboards for something she can't see, something she doesn't know. Clattering useless clutter. Watch her backing away. Bentover. Clenching a clouding makeshift pad between her legs. Squatting sitting smearing claret the toilet seat. Legs crossed tight. Arms crossed tight. Head and body bowed. Folded. She bites into her bottom lip and just cries, throat burning raw and lumpy. Long straight hair sprawled gold and messy over shoulders that pump with her lungs. Sobbing she fumbles to the shower and twists a tap, Cold, and she shakes and washes herself of it. Scratching and rubbing. Palms and nails. She scrubs her knickers. Soaks her jeans. Just in case. Her wedged pad slips and rafts with the flow to block the drain. Water a puddle of light pink. Sound of rain. Back here; back against a tiled wall. Sliding, down. Cold jets gushing and spitting. Knees to her chest and just shuddering. Cold. And just hating. *Hating* him. Her. Everything. Mouth frozen in an ugly wordless bawl. Face concealed by hands. Sodarksodarksodark. Side to side to side.

Spent, she crawls out. Second drawer down: scissors. Poised with a fist of hair, she cuts it. Schnickety shnick. Short. She is *hard* and Grown Up and right here, in Dark Ness, right now, she

decides this will never happen again (*rhubarbrhubarbrhubarb*).
She can't be touched. She has Control. She is made of mettle
and coated in teflon.

THE PIANO MAN

It's like pressing an open wound. These people bending to help her up, to calm her down; they just make her wilder with the touching. She screams and thrashes mad.

And there he is. Cutting a furrow through the bedlam, and saying her name over and over. He seizes thin wrists and hoists. She is on her feet.

You fucking *prick!* Her neck is stemmed with veins. You fucking *arsehole!*

People stare, or steer away averting eyes. Some point, laugh into their hands. Some offer useful commentary. Some stop to crowd this space, wearing sympathy on shaking heads. The whole place is silent with spectators.

You *stupid* fucking bastard!

I'm sorry I'm sorry I'm sorry I'm sorry, he is rasping. He means it.

Her wrists are still held together, so Eleanor can't belt the shit out of him the way she wants to. She struggles. Face red and strained. But Ewan bridles her effort, absorbs her roar and her energy. Her eyes are fierce. She slips a hand free, winds back and puts everything into a fist between his ribs. A table cheers. It sobers her. She has to leave. Pulls at him. There is a band of white ringing her wrists. They move out. She burns, feeling that field of stares. In the open, Ewan tries to take her with the breeze, back the way they came. Eleanor stops.

No. *No.* We are *not* going home.

***

They stride fast past Norfolk Island pines, on to warm harbour decking peppered with gobs of guano. Past the broad paper spread of fishandchips. Above, winged vermin hang and harangue.

They do not speak. Just walk. Away. She treads a path she knows.

Ewan bends. I'm sorry. I'm so sorry.

He is cautious as they charge towards a flight of wooden steps, ready to steady her should she slip. She streams up them. Ewan can't shirk the image of her; fallen, fending, screaming down there. He is truly shaken. Side by side they near asphalt. One listens, one looks, and they cross quickly without speaking, on to coarse sand and rubble. Over piled chunks of limestone and granite, Ewan takes an endless gaze of wharflit water, the sunlight since snuffed by horizon. Hard to get a broader space than the Indian Ocean. And he takes a small comfort in not being able to see the edge of the world. The air has a smooth salty taste.

To his left, moored skeletal yachts hang thin angles and no canvas. He lengthens his step to match her impatience. She suddenly stops. Breaks away. He watches her running her hands along the rockwall. Dipping in cavities and loose joins. Ewan frowns.

What ... are we fishing? he asks.

No, she says caustic, without turning. We're hunting deer.

She searches impatiently. Edging further away. Ewan squints and sees a still row of fatly perched figures, casting and winding.

You could help, you know, she says. Then adds softly: If you're still there.

What are you looking for? He turns absently, then worries about his wording.

Oh, a twelve-inch dildo and a Shetland pony, Ewan. What do you think? Look for a handline and a tacklebox. Oh, hang on. This is it. It's here.

She emerges with her hands full metres away. Holding a thick green hoop and a plastic container, both scuffed and sandy.

He walks up to join her.

Look: I'm so sorry. I don't

Well so am I. I mean, like, why? *Why?* Why the fuck would you do that? You've got no idea, do you? No idea. She shakes her head. That, *that there*, was so *fucking humiliating*. And I would have killed you by now if I wasn't aware that it was probably mostly my own fault.

Eleanor lifts her foot into a crevice. She means to go on, but is interrupted mid hoist.

Elly love? Sthat you, eh? Further down the mole, Frank picks up the pace with his invisible wheelbarrow. His thongs flick sand into his reel. He wears short shorts and a widecollar polyester shirt.

Evening Franklin. She smiles against herself.

Owv you been then? asks Frank, pulling up. Haven't see you for a bit. Missed a run with the herring and all. Who's yer friend then, come on, come on.

Frank, this is, among other things, Ewan. Ewan, Frank.

Ewan has his hand shaken. Ewan, eh. Frank tests the name in his mouth. Yoow'n. Sounds like somming you'd do to a sheep. Frank laughs. Eleanor smiles again, shakes her head and bites her lip.

Christ, son, Frank exclaims, taking a step back. You a ruckman?

Ewan is taciturn.

Sorry? says Frank, after a pause. Dint hear you.

No, says Ewan. No, no I'm not.

Oh, so it's basketball then.

Anything tonight Frank? Eleanor interjects.

No, love. Must have seen you coming.

You got any bait left?

Frank steps back, grins. Come again? *Bait?* Are you sure? You do know that bait will give you some chance of attracting something near the end of your hook. You want to be careful with it, now, I hear it's very effective. Here yar, son. Frank slaps a slippery packet into Ewan's hand. Some orready cut up for you.

Thanks, Frank.

No problem. Trust you'll have better luck than me. I'll be singin to the missus for my supper tonight.

Cook it yourself, you lazy bugger.

Elly, you're talking to the man who once tried cooking a steak in a toaster. Besides, she likes to hear me grovel.

How is she, Frank?

Yairs, good good. Still busy and all, what with the Christmas at ours this year. Anyway, leave you two alone, eh? Frank winks at Ewan. Merry Christmas, the both of you. Nice to meet ye Yoow'n.

Merry Christmas, Frankfurt.

Bye, says Ewan, watching him trundle away. When he turns, Eleanor is scaling agile over the rocks. He follows slowly and is greeted by a cool bluster as he reaches the top. It feels fresh on his skin. His shirt puffs, collecting it. He slips behind the sure crawl of the blind girl. Goes where she goes. A cautious arm extended, just in case.

Eleanor nestles in on her slab of jutting limestone. It is still toasted warm from the day's heat. She sits legscrossed. There is room for two. Ewan sits with his elbows on his knees. He tents his hands and pushes back cuticles, watching the water lap gently against the darker rocks below. Its indelible rhythm soothes. The tacklebox clicks and yawns open.

His wife is dead, you know, Eleanor says. Poor old bugger.

Ewan frowns. She answers his question for him.

Because I don't think anyone here really knows him well enough to know about it. So, I don't know, maybe it's his way of keeping her alive or something. Pretty sad, eh?

Ewan stares at her rigging up. Her dead gaze straight; she ties in the sinker and threads the hook first go, fastens it patiently. Adroit and controlled.

How did she die? he asks.

Not sure. I don't think it was quick though, I'm afraid. Bait?

Ewan passes the greasy packet.

Mulies, she says. No wonder he didn't catch anything.

She stands and shuffles to the edge of the rock. Tells him to move. Waits. Then windmills the line. Flings it deep from a beggar's hand. The line grows tight in her fingers. She sits down.

The saddest thing, though, she says, is thinking about how his Christmas is going to be. It's just really, really sad. But what do you do? What *can* you do? That's the ten-thousand-dollar question.

Eleanor retrieves slowly. Ewan leans back. Feels safer here. Her face is soft in the wharflight. He unties his shoelaces, removes his shoes which are dim now. Toehairs rise like hackles then settle.

I don't know, he admits.

Neither do I, she shrugs.

They share silence.

***

A brownvested busker lingers on a messy F chord and looks around. His soulful ritardando draws eighty cents and light applause from a pair of five-year-old twins.

He has surrendered to three requests (American Pie; Khe Sahn; Brown-Eyed Girl) and declined two (Eye of the Tiger; Back in Black). In his guitar case, he has collected roughly twelve dollars, four cigarettes, and a Free Entry voucher for a club nearby. Tough crowd.

The busker twiddles the nipples of his knackered amp, bends into a Rolling Stones tune and doesn't care.

***

Eleanor shuffles, wriggles, leans and fiddles with her posture. Folds her legs. Unfolds her legs. She reels in, restless, grimacing, and cups her bellicose belly.

Want a pair of ovaries, Ewan? I've got a set going very very cheap right here.

No, thanks.

God was a man, Ewan. I am convinced. Menstruation, menopause, menarebastards. A man for sure. Had a hand on His rod all right.

You've probly got a point.

She wags a finger. Don't think you can exonerate yourself that easily. You're still a prick. You still run away from blind people in crowded places. What do you do for a hobby? Torture furry animals? Here hold this.

Eleanor passes the handline. He is surprised by the strength that's in it. He sits up. Chokes the hoop. Finger hooking the line like pizzicato, feeling the buried weight of undercurrent. He collects the gossamer thread slowly, wrapping it on to the spool.

I am sorry, you know. For before. Really, I am.

She is silent. Her head might shake.

Ewan watches the ruffled tide. He breathes in, fresh air,

intended to come back as words, better yet; an explanation. But he bottles the impulse. And the breath is breathed as any other, suppressed of its possibility. The breeze eases.

Well. Whatever, she says. Let's just say that we both fucked dinner. Which is a shame, because they do awesome curry.

Behind them, two aged anglers head home emptyhanded. They listen to the cricket broadcast on a small radio.

Here now, Eleanor feels calmer by far. Here on the snug ergonomics of her rock. Despite holding neither leash nor line. Despite crampy eggdispensing. Despite the lingering sear of embarrassment; of being saved when she should not have had to be saved. Her anger in panicking.

Ewan shifts. It feels like there's tugging or something, he says. On the line. Kind of jerking.

Well, they'll do that, fish. They're nibbling the bait.

Ewan is silent.

What, you didn't *know* that? Don't tell me you've never been fishing.

Silence.

Are you *serious*? This is your first time, like, ever?

Yes.

God, where are you *from*? You don't get out much do you, Chellowboy? She shakes her head, turns. Like, not even when you were a kid?

No, says Ewan. See, my father would only ever take me out deer hunting. He'd saddle me up on a Shetland pony and I'd have to chase them down and thrash them to death with a twelve-inch dildo.

Eleanor laughs suddenly. Well, that came out of nowhere. If I didn't believe you I'd think you were trying to be funny.

Ewan keeps creeping the line in.

What is it you *do* anyway? For money and stuff.

Not much. Squander an inheritance. What about you?

Me? Two brief careers. One in aromatherapy that lasted a week, before I revealed a complete paucity of interest. It's a pile of shit, let me tell you. I even told them their job stinks. What a way to go. And then there were six months as a telephonist; selling insurance of all things. Nothing now though, but I get by.

Ewan sees a hook gleam at the pressing wateredge. Didn't realise he had reeled in so far. He pulls it up. Bait's gone, he says.

Here. Put some more on.

Ewan pinches and smoothes on the sticky flesh. Doubles it over, like he had seen her do it. He offers her the handline by resting it on her lap.

No, no, she says. You cast it.

Well, I don't really know how, remember.

Snot hard. Just wind it up and let it go. Easy. But make sure you hold it; like this, so it can spool out. Eleanor hands it back.

Okay.

Hang on, hang on, she says, shifting. Just lemme get out of the way. This could go anywhere.

Ewan stands and swings and wheels. Awkward. He extends his arm, but in his preparation to release his angle suffers and he buries the hook into the back of his calf.

Ah, fuck! he says, falling back and pulling it out quickly. The barb does some damage as it exits.

What happened, what happened? she asks quickly from another rock.

Hooked myself, Ewan mutters and rubs his leg. Eleanor laughs loud, openmouthed. Almost delighted. He turns. Here, you do it.

Still laughing, she says, No no no, this is great. You keep going.

Ewan sighs. Turns back. Tentatively, he swings and wheels again. Careful. He lets go quickly. There is a soft snap and a faroff splash.

Broke the line, didn't you.

Maybe, he says.

Give it here, Chellowboy. She sits back down, opens the tacklebox. Nicely done.

He sees her wincing again. Shuffling. Swears under her breath.

Are you on painkillers?

Why? Concerned are you? She threads the hook on her third attempt. No, I'm allergic to them, lucky me. Sometimes a whole box seems viable though.

You should try dark chocolate, he says softly.

What?

Dark chocolate.

She looks sceptical.

Really. Dark chocolate. It's a good remedy apparently. Hormones, or something.

I can't believe you know more about alleviating menstrual pain than fishing. You're a strange man, Ewan.

Well, I *was* carved in God's own image.

Very true.

No, my mother used to secretly binge on it once every month. I caught her once, and she let me eat some if I didn't tell. That's how I know.

Eleanor holds up the handline, rigged and baited. Okay, stuff this one up and we're buggered. So remember to hold the handline right, or you're going in after it.

Are you sure you don't want to do it?

I'm very sure. Here. Knock yourself out. Mind your legs though, she smiles and scuttles off the rock.

It doesn't go far, but he feels taut line and weight in his fingers. He sits relieved. The air is breezeless now. Eleanor joins him. The stubborn remainder of the fishermen retire and amble home to watch the end of the cricket. Seagulls follow them, circling slackly for airshafts. They are alone together on this rockwall.

How's your leg?

Well, I think I'll live, which should disappoint you.

She laughs through her nose.

So, Ewan: you think the world's going to blow up? she asks.

The millennium do you mean?

Yeah. The numerologists' nightmare.

I don't think so. He pauses. No, I had enough of the Judgement Hour when I was a kid.

Shit, you weren't a Witness were you?

No, Adventist. Well, I was always told to be, but I was never a spirited member of that superstition. I was baptised, but that's as far as it ever got between me and the Man with the Rod. Ewan halts there. Swallows hard. Chest tight.

That's lucky, she says. Thought you were an anchorite or something for a second there. Would've explained a few things.

He is almost relieved to see the hook snagged in a thin recess in the granite below. He must have been trawling rapidly. He stands to coax it out, like a puppeteer. It jags loose. Still baited. Eleanor slips off the granite platform. Ewan concentrates on casting. Watches the line peel off the ratty reel with satisfaction. Like an extension of him, a translucent vein. He hears a splash, feels weight, sits down.

How about you? Oblivion?

Well, not quite. But, shit, we've earned it. We aren't very good tenants. If it happens, it won't be numeric coincidence making us go the big kaboom; it'll be fairly and squarely our own fault. We don't really *need* the wrath of the Rod, we're quite sufficient at crapping in our own nests, thankyou very much. Actually we're pretty much an autonomy when it comes to fucking things up. We did it all to ourselves. And it would be nice and comforting to look at all those zeros as a lovely brandspanking new Clean Slate, but they just don't happen. No such thing. There's too much shit to sift through. Just too much shit. She turns and sighs. It's okay, I'm off the soapbox now.

It has left her feeling suddenly open. She pulls her knees to her chest, folds over her arms. In the silence, Ewan surveys a distant ship sliding into the harbour. Eleanor fiddles with the fray of her skirt.

What *is* a ruckman anyway? Ewan asks suddenly.

Eleanor groans immediately. She slaps her forehead. Please. Ewan. Look: just give up now, in the interest of humanity, go back into reclusion and ease your head back up your arse. You are way, way, way beyond rehabilitation. Honestly. What is a *ruckman*?

It's a fair question.

You don't get out at *all* do you?

Do you?

God, it's all I *do* do.

Must be hard. Ewan pauses, recalling the sureness of her feet, her pace and precision. Though you conceal it pretty well.

I don't conceal anything, she says, with force. I just get on with it. I still have legs. Not everyone likes to wallow in self-indulgent pity, you know.

What you can't see can't hurt you, right?

That stung, almost, but for reasons he doesn't know. She is still. Doesn't reply. Ewan is left wondering where those crass, careless words came from, where any of these words have come from. The boldness attached to them. And he's somehow forgetting to prefix his impulses with fear; he's blurting things out, asking, talking. Forgetting to be pensive. Retentive. He stops reeling.

What's wrong with your eyes? he asks.

I can't see through them.

Why?

Well, the myth is true Ewan. I masturbated far too much as a child. So be warned.

He smiles weakly. Waits. Watches as she bundles her knees

closer to her chest; the slope of her shoulders severe. Her nostrils sough and she'll swallow sea air and she'll offer a practised pretext. A reprisal. A recital. Like always.

Glaucoma, she says. Well, actually, acute glaucoma, which kind of does the job quickly. And painfully. It's a fast, severe flood of eye fluid. It came as like, a sudden, *intense* attack. I could barely open my eyes. But when it happened, I just thought I had a really bad migraine or something. I was only a kid. I spewed, fainted. Came round. The pain was shocking, I was squinting. My eyes were on fire. Everything was fuzzing. I was at home by myself. For some reason I stole some sleeping tablets from my mother's cabinet and crashed, woke up the next day with the worst hangover ever and no sight. I'd blacked out. Completely. I saw a doctor, but the damage was all done. My optic nerves had been destroyed totally by intraocular pressure. Scarred. Still are. And that's all it took.

So do you see anything?

No.

Treatment?

Nope.

But how could it happen? Just like that?

Not sure. They seemed to think I was a freak case; even despite the stupid way I dealt with it. Acute glaucoma is supposed to be congenital, but I don't think my family has a history of it. Just one of those things, I think.

Ewan exhales a heavy breath and it deflates him. He resumes reeling. Wants to keep pressing, but leaves it be.

Eleanor leans back, soothed by the tone of her bullshit.

Almost even believes it. So convenient; so much easier to entertain the thought that a disease did it all. It wards off that evergreen, unbearable urge to undo things. And on this low stack of lime and granite, deeply she knows she is no better than the fibbing widower with the invisible wheelbarrow.

She keeps it going.

But at least I *could* see. Like, before it happened. At least I have that. Some things to *go* on, so I know what things look like, so I have some concept of spatial relations. I can't imagine, well I can, sort of, but it must be terrible to never see anything at all.

Ewan nods. Eleanor doesn't, because not even she can believe that.

She is restless now. She plucks at a loose thread on her cheap sandals. Bites at the skin on the inside of her mouth, lips puckered. Ewan feels like passing her back the handline, but he doesn't think he can. It's a strange feeling of connection, powerful in a way. And he feels strangely lucid out here now. It's like it's not even him. Like he's forgotten what exactly that *is*. And there's the fleeting, floating urge to talk back, to tell her things. But it fades as quickly as it emerges.

Eleanor tears and flings a grinning toenail into the lapping water. She looks to be grappling with a thought.

You know, it's not like I can just get in a car and drive off into the sunset, is it? Not even if the road was like, really straight and the car had good alignment. Her smile is wan and quick. And I can't catch no freight train to Frisco either. Ewan, I know *exactly* where I am. And as comforting as that is, it's just, I don't know. I'm really not getting on with anything, you know. She pauses, smiles to herself. And you, you'd be bloody useless to escape with. Who knows where you'd leave me. She laughs, adds: However, Bruno did say once he's going to take me to Venice, so I could be a Venetian Blind.

Ewan smirks. Then says: Well, I can't drive anyway.

I am astounded. A hermit with no mode of transport, who would've thought?

Ewan's reply is rising as he is pulled sharply by the wrist towards the water. Tugged frenetically. He almost loses the line. Leaps to his feet.

Shitshitshitshitshit, he is saying. I've got a fish on here. There's a fish on here!

What?

I've got one! I've got one on here!

Bullshit.

No, really!

Well don't make love to it. Reel it in!

What?

Reel it in! Reel it in! she shrieks.

Ewan winds the line madly back on to the spool, like he's frantically turning a winch. Eleanor, standing too, senses his movement.

Are you winding it back up? Don't wrap it up! Just get it in! Just get the line in! Pull! Quick!

Ewan drops the spool and the line is strong and resistant. Fighting him with frenzied jerks. He pulls back in long, fast, sweeping strokes with the full length of his arm, minding the girl beside him. Feels a flurry of weight and life streaming into his callused fingertips. And suddenly this is all that matters, just this action, this method. The rhythm that's in it. Pulling, pulling, pulling, pulling.

Hurry up! she barks at him.

It's still on here! His arms are pumping. The line collects in a tangled tumble at his bare feet.

And then a footlong herring, slick and flapping, breaks and bursts through the inky waterskin. It's so sudden he keeps pulling. And the fish swings like a pendulum on Ewan's higher axis, and with its momentum slaps Eleanor hard and wet on the left cheek. The perfect reply. She yelps and staggers back. Almost stacks it between a cleft in the rocks. The fish wrests and wriggles and kicks, gleaming enamel. Gills slowly blinking. Eleanor hoots with laughter.

The fish finally retires. Unlucky, hooked by the eye. It settles to a languid twist.

Ewan holds the line above him and stares at it grinning. It is swung by a sudden shaft of cool breeze. Eleanor rubs her cheek, still laughing.

There's dinner, Chellowboy!

***

The streets are still reaming with People and strobed by headlights. Patient queues natter at the entrances of pubs and clubs and restaurants. They jostle for taxis. Huddle around moneyholes. Walking, weaving, passing without absorption.

Carving through the night air with a laboured image and coordinated accessories.

Leave me here again and I *will* kill you, says Eleanor, as they walk side by side among them all. Ewan (bowed a little to narrow the Height Gap) grips a herring in his left hand and feels safer coming back, though he's still stiff and shitscared. He inadvertently fishsmears a passing red miniskirt, but she doesn't turn around.

They cross the road together, untroubled by Doomed Virgins in powerful cars. Ewan glances and notices a small group point and stare at them with recognition.

On South Terrace they shuffle with the noisy, pulsing tide. Passersby tend to give Ewan a reasonable berth and curious looks as they see his scaled companion. The air smells of waffles and exhaust and garlic and deodorant.

They approach the brownvested busker. He is ringed by a raucous, swaying bucks' party. They are linked together by limp arms thrown across shoulders. And they throb with a disjointed, seasick rhythm; inandout, inandout like an emphysemic lung. A tired and tinny six-string strums into a tune and they cheer. One of them, the groom-to-be, stumbles with a shove into the circle to begin spanking the skin off a tambourine. He too is cheered.

Ewan is wary, but Eleanor Rigby stops just outside as they start the verse:

Oh it's nine o'clock on a Sattaday!

She laughs. Claps her hands and whistles. The tuneless, drunken drawl of them is thick with accent. The brownvested busker keeps them in time. The tambourine man does his best to take them out. They lean back:

E says son canya play me a memorree!

A solid Maori with a beautiful tenor breaks from the circle with an outstretched arm, pulling them both firmly into the ring. They are sucked and swallowed into the group. Eleanor laughs, the Maori's meaty arm across her shoulder. Ewan is wide-eyed, his arm suddenly slung over the shoulders of a thin skinhead who doesn't seem to notice the herring dangling across his shirt. Eleanor's arms are suddenly around his waist.

But it's sad annit's sweet
And aye knew it com-plete
When aye wore a yunga man's clothes!

Ewan is tense. Stiff and resistant. He moves with their languorous, swollen sway and watches from his incongruous, higher-up view. All somehow united, even the pale, mulleted creature on the other side, who sings between two cigarette tusks.

The busker climbs that fretboard, redfaced as he puffs his harmonica. They swoon into the chorus line. The circle compressing as they throw back their heads and sing to the sky:

Oh … Oh … Oh
Singus a song yatha Pyano Maaaan!
Singus a song tonight!

Outside of them, People stop to watch and laugh and clap. Couples start to waltz. Ewan looks down at Eleanor, wailing, and can't help smiling. His hand somehow on her hip. The volume in this space is palpable. Ewan turns back to watch the busker.

> *Well I'm sure aye could be a movie star*
> *If aye could gettoutta this place!*

Eleanor's cheeks are a roseate flush from effort. Feels a tingling rash of gooseflesh up her spine. Like electricity. Her neckhairs bristle and she doesn't mind being touched right now, or even the odour emitted by a nearby armpit. Wedged between a Maori and a Hermit, she competes with them for loudness. Can't remember the last time she has sung.

> *Ya diddy da diddy daaa!*
> *Yaya diddy daaa dadaaaa!*

The group begins dropping donations into the busker's case as they sing through verses. Coins, notes, lipstick, a shower of tossed condoms. The stakes slowly get higher. The man under the mullet drops in a pack of cigarettes, gives the busker a matey rub to the head. Then there's a plastic baggie of something tamped and khaki, proffered by a tubby bogan, and the crowd cheers.

> *Yes they're sharing a drink they call loneliness*
> *But it's better than drinkin alone!*

The tambourine man puts the tambourine in. Cheers. A quarter bottle of Jack Daniels. Louder cheers. It's a competition now. The busker's smile is broad as his hoarse voice soars. The ring is a glutinous pulsing. Inandout. Inandout. The air is thick. A pair of shoes is suddenly added to the busker's spate of possessions. There are cheers and laughs. A black bra is lobbed from outside the ring. Whoops and whistles.

The group swoops in with anticipation for the last chorus, and Ewan just watches the busker, who is dipping and skipping and strumming and just loving it. Loving it.

> *Ah, singus a song yatha buskerman!*
> *Singus a song tonight!*
> *Coz we're all in the mood forra melodeee!*
> *An you've goddus feelin orright!*

The song ends and the busker bows to a thick applause. A shower of coins shimmers, catching the light. A small, suited man breaks in from the crowd and fans out three hundred dollars in the gaping jaw of the case. He is cheered as he leaves. The busker stares. Then Ewan walks slowly and tentatively, into the ring, holding Eleanor's hand. Feels dizzy in the sudden silence. Bending, he lays a footlong silver herring atop the pile. Stands, and the force of the cheering pushes them backwards. He smiles nervously. Hands are thrown into the air. He feels his back slapped as he slips away with Eleanor.

They leave them to sing That's Amore to a much smaller audience.

And it's only when they are away from town that Ewan realises he left his shoes back at the seawall. He does not notice their clasped hands; held and holding.

***

Warren is curled asleep on a comfortable Turkish rug. Lilian dozes beside him.

Above them, two possums scurry about preparing a lovepit with carfoam and roof insulation.

Ewan opens his front door to a dark hallway and relief. His bare feet shuffle inside. He turns, doesn't know what to think. Eleanor waits at the door.

Can I lose your ewe quickly?

Sorry?

She flushes. Can I *use* your *loo* quickly.

Pause.

Okay, yeah. It's down here. She steps in, takes his arm. He leads her down the hall, flicking switches.

The footsteps wake her guide dog, who bursts out of the room with confusion. He sniffs aggressively at Ewan's shins, and the smear of congealed blood on his calf. He follows them to the toilet.

Okay, it's just here.

Right, thanks. *Warren!* Bugger off will you?

Warren backs out of the toilet, eyebrows high.

Ewan moves towards the kitchen. Frowns at the damp tongueprints on his floor. Hisses as he sees the scattered debris around his bin. Looks at the dog, then hatefully to the ceiling, as though they're watching.

He is warming up the espresso machine when she emerges.

Something stinks, she says.

Possums raided my bin again.

Well, you should feed them.

Feed them? They aren't my pets, they're my enemies.

So you *do* torture furry animals?

I'd like to.

You better not. Possums are nice. You know, in Aboriginal folklore, possums are seen as fateful creatures.

Really?

No. But it would be convenient if you thought so. Eleanor takes up Warren's harness. Starts to move back towards the hallway, smiles. Well, Ewan, I think I've seen enough for one night.

He follows her out on to the verandah. It's a different silence to the one that escorted them home, which was punctuated only by Eleanor's directions. However, it is broken quickly as they hear the obnoxious bellow of an inflatable whale across the road; pissed on wine and maraschino and wheezing a concertina.

My god, is that *Bruno*?

Fraid so. Every Sunday, remember.

That's *right*. Is why he iss clozzed on the Mondeye till noon.

Ewan smiles. He's even louder than you are.

She shakes her head, shudders. He is such an *arsehole*. And sleazy. Oozy. I can feel him looking at me, it's horrible.

Warren kickstarts at his belly with a hindleg. He struggles for balance. They listen to Bruno sing to himself.

Eleanor is suddenly excited.

Hey, is his car outside?

Sorry?

Is his car parked outside their house? It's a Mercedes, he's always talking about the fucking thing. Is it there?

Ewan peers. Yeah. It's just across the street. Why?

Her smile gleams. Her eyes narrow.

Ewan, do you have potatoes?

What?

Potatoes. Do you have any?

Well. Yes.

Go get one, she whispers. Get a big one.

A potato.

Yes.

A potato.

Yes!

What? *Why?*

They're both whispering now. Just go get one!

Ewan finds himself in the kitchen, reaching for a big gnarly spud in a dark corner of his cupboard. It looks angry.

Here, he says and slaps it into her palm.

She grabs his hand. His fingertips are hard, like they've been dipped in wax.

Come on.

What?

Warren, *sit!* Stay there, okay?

Warren sits confused.

They are watched by a bashful gnome, a leaning sunflower, and a row of cardboard reindeer on a roof across the street.

What are we doing? Ewan hisses as they slip on to the road, treading like terrorists.

Shhhh! She holds the potato to her lips. Take me to his car.

The road is warm underfoot. Bruno's big, boxish Mercedes leers with ugly regality.

Okay. What now?

The back of it. Take me to the back of it. To the exhaust pipe.

The exhaust pipe?

The exhaust pipe! A giggle escapes. She fights to restrain it.

Ducking, they creep around the body of the car and kneel. They can hear Bruno, clutching at a high note. Ewan guides her hand and the potato to the exhaust.

Here, he whispers.

Where?

Here!

Where?

It's here! It's just here! he hisses as she quells paroxysms. Her eyes are wet. She snorts. The spud shakes in her hand, can't help it. Ewan looks around, worried. He clamps a hand over her mouth, makes her laugh louder.

Hnmer grnu drn gid, she says.

What? he removes his hand.

You do it.

No! *You* do it.

You do it!

No!

So they both end up smacking that soft potato up Bruno's exhaust shaft. It makes a hollow thudding sound. And a crunching noise as they drive it in further.

They slide slickly back across the street. Heads still ducked like they're under fire. They rush up the centre path and inside. Warren follows. Ewan closes the door quickly as Eleanor folds into laughter. Leans on the back door. She shakes her fist with drama: Well, there's one for the Little People!

What's going to happen?

Well, the world may not explode, Ewan, but I know a certain Mercedes that is definitely going to go kaboom.

The streets will never be the same, Spud Girl.

She laughs. So does Ewan, almost.

Silence looms on them again.

Right. I should get going, she concedes. I've definitely done enough now. I can't believe we just did that. Anyway, you've got possums to feed. And your Shetland, of course.

Eleanor feels for her dog, opens the door. Okay, then. Goodnight Ewan.

Goodnight.

Merry Christmas.

Yeah, he says quietly. Merry Christmas.

He watches her leave with the door ajar. There is silence in his house.

***

He rouses once in his sleep to a gunshot blast just outside his window. He hears scuffling, slamming, ranting, hissing, the thud of a car being kicked. Ewan peers cautiously out of his window, and laughs softly, observing the tantrum unfold. He wonders how to describe it to Eleanor.

When it's over, he falls back into bed and sleeps deeply, unaware of the scuttling above.

THEOLOGY

On the morning of your Great Aunty May's eightieth birthday, your heels were stinging from the chafe of yellowrubber flippers. They were two sizes too big. Lifting your little legs high and hinged, you marched to the lazy ripple of the shoreline. Tried wading through the shallows forwards, while everybody else was reversing in. The flippers dragged and tripped you up. Your hands were swamped by huge, frayed welding gloves. They held two bags blue. For mussels.

You could smell the toothpaste that Jenny had lathered inside your mask to stop it fogging up. And hear your tubed, mechanical breathing through the snorkel. You lagged behind. Your two cousins, Darren and Darryl, were already streaming up the plane of jetty shade, shafting white bursts of spray. They had wetsuits. You were thighdeep, standing, trying to tip the water from your mask. Your long hair had invaded your vacuum and salty water had seeped in to sting your eyes.

To make matters worse, your wet violet onepiecer was crawling between your bumcheeks; impossible to adjust with gloved hands holding a mask and two catchbags. You jiggled your legs, tried to dance it out.

You finally got going. The two bags were blue fins. You kicked hard, watching corduroy ribs ream past below. You dodged a flotilla of stingers. You weren't scared. Urgent schools of whitebait spilled past surging thiswayandthat. The water felt good on your skin. Prickled your hairs as you flew with two bags blue. Alate. It sounded like Jenny's belly under here. A traffic of rumbles and gurgles and clicks.

You reached the last pylons where the water was clearer and colder. Jenny, Darren and Darryl were already waiting with gloved handfuls. They half filled one of the bags. Darryl was your age. He called you retard for taking so long and frisbeed a starfish at your head. Jenny grabbed his mask, pulled the elastic back and let go. He almost cried. Everyone else laughed.

You were the Carrier of Bags because you couldn't dive. You had best of intentions but no motion. You duckdived and flapped yellowrubber flippers in the air like a synchronised swimmer and went nowhere. But you told everyone that you carried the bags because you were the toughest. Made of the sternest stuff.

Jenny could hold her breath the longest. And you knew it was because she had a heart like a horse. You watched her slide down fluid and precise to tear huge mussels from the base of the jettylegs. Taking her time, choosing the best ones. Then gliding vertical, whipping her body like she was made for it. Belonged to it. You held the catchbags ready.

Darren and Darryl attacked the water. Fought it in flurries of legs and bubbles and froth. Shunting down until the water thieved their breath, then they panicked and bolted roughly to the surface, emerging with small weedy clusters they dropped into the bags quickly. They were the size that you could collect from just under the surface.

Pedalling water you could look up and see through the slats in the jetty. Snippets of still hamstrings, footsoles, eskies, mugs, newspaper. A dust of sand and burley sometimes showered between the cracks.

Your arms ached as the catchbags filled. It was harder not to sink. On the way back, Jenny offered to take your bloated blue fins. You wouldn't let her because you were the Carrier of Bags. The toughest. She shrugged.

Underwater, she tapped at your shoulder and you watched her in the penumbral dimness as she swooped down and tugged at the end of dangled lines. Above the water, you watched them reel in their anticlimax, one by one, and the two of you giggled with tingling lips.

On the beach, you dragged the heavywet catchbags backwards, carving a trail in the sand. Shoulders burning raw. Darren tipped them into one big mound. They clacked and spilled and the four of you sorted them. A greasy, effete squid slithered from the pile. You were the only one who would touch it. You said it felt like snot.

You rubbed the mussels against each other to clean them of weed and barnacles. Backscratching. Then pinched and pulled out their beards, which resembled the tip of a mascara brush. You smelled of salt and suncream and toothpaste. Your hair was drying in clumps. Jenny had been stung on the neck twice. Darren said they looked like hickeys. He was seventeen and pimply and spoke to Jenny's breasts. She swaddled her towel tighter around her bonethin body and rolled her eyes at you.

On the way back to the car, you were the Carrier of Bags again. Stooping. Your steps were short and fast. The sand was collecting heat. Darryl ran out in front and gave you a two-handed nipplecripple. It stung. You dropped the bags, but you didn't cry. Darren punched him in the arm. Darryl protested, said it couldn't have hurt because you didn't have tits anyway.

Jenny moved fast.

And a beach full of people seemed to turn and watch united as she whipped his shorts down to his ankles. She pushed him over too. He sprawled chubbily, hairless and shrivelled and pale. He wrenched his shorts up and launched a hissy fit. He threw a spray of sand at Jenny and ranaway. Darren laughed and yelled out that he couldn't be embarrassed because he didn't have a dick anyway.

Your sister was a bestfriend then. More. She was a constant and precious thing. Always. An ally. You could feel protected and never be ashamed of it.

And you could see her disappearing right there in front of you, but never did you believe she'd leave.

Darren drove a Kingswood station wagon called Charlene. Her dinged and dented panels were all in varying shades of brown. She had a whitish roof, with a rash of rust the colour of earwax. Her chrome roofracks rattled loose and her windscreen was a galaxy of cracks. She had a faded beertowel for a dashmat.

Darren said she was beautiful.

Opening the door to the backseat, you rubbed at your nipples and let the trapped sultry air filter out. Darryl was sulking. You layered the hot vinyl seats with wet towels as Darren poured coolant into the radiator.

Charlene didn't want to turn over. Darren coaxed her gently. She spat and gurgled to life on the sixth go, but Darren stalled it reversing. Then he flooded it. And you waited, sweating. You wound the window down. It wouldn't come back up.

Finally you shuddered on to the road. You adjusted your seatbelt and narrowed your eyes against the carwind. Singing the Beach Boys and Van Morrison to passing pedestrians. Locking eyes with your sister in the side mirror. A smile for just the two of you.

***

On the night of your Great Aunty May's eightieth birthday, a herd of mussels steamed under a wet teatowel on the barbecue. A cauldron of chilli tomato broth simmered beside. Your Uncle Dave perspired and watched his watch. He wore an apron with rubbermoulded breasts. There was a black mark where he had singed a nipple. It could have been one of yours.

A piled platter of crayfish medallions and crabflesh sat like a monument in the centre of the table. Curledup prawns looked stunned in a cavernous glass bowl. Beside it, a big silver tray bearing black pudding and your grandmother's stovies steamed the scents of Drumnadrochit.

On the floodlit backlawn, stagnant men held stubbies and carefully monitored your Uncle Victor's homemade spitroast. A skewered pig dribbled fat and twirled slowly. It hovered above a glowing pit of coals that filled the halved shell of a forty-four-gallon drum. The shadows of darting insects had a mirrorball effect. Your Uncle Victor (who had a colossal nose that everyone called Vic's Inhaler) was boasting about his welding and expounding the genius of his Makeshift Rotational Device (a bikewheel and a fanbelt). He wanted to know where his welding gloves were.

Darryl plucked Cape gooseberries from their crispy scrotums and threw them at you. He missed and hit your Uncle Bob in the ear. He was Warned.

Your Aunty Eve; old, squat and cantankerous, burst out of the kitchen screeching. She snatched her Good Teatowel from the barbecue. A plume of steam billowed like she was unveiling a magic trick. The mussels grinned.

She slapped your Uncle Dave across his rubber-moulded breast.

That's my good linen, Dan!

Dave.

Dave!

Eve, that teatowel is older than you are.

But she had charged back inside. Slid the sliding-door with rigour. Dave scooped the mussels into the broth. He gave you one to try. It was hot and juicy and seasalty.

Good eh?

You nodded.

The women segregated themselves in the kitchen. They talked and cackled loudly. Except your mum, who was pouring melted chocolate over profiteroles. Her hair was tied back, revealing streaks of creeping grey. She was half listening to your Aunty Gwen talk shit about Feng Shooey and Chinese Herbal Medicine.

Your lilac-haired grandmother shuffled between them, muttering, bossing around invisible people with the nine-iron she used as a walking stick. The Real People ignored her.

Your Great Aunty May sat quietly on a kitchen stool, sedately getting pissed on the brandy that would never make it into the pudding. She farted occasionally (poofffft).

Eve whinged about the teatowel. Nobody cared. Your Aunt Madeleine was pregnant and narky. She exuded the scent of a women's magazine.

Estelle was reserved and reticent behind caked makeup. When she slipped silently to the bathroom, the women swooped and huddled around the pavlova together with greedy concern. Gwen said she was worried. Said something was awry. Said she had changed. And you hid behind the liberally sagging bottom of your Great Aunty May, holding your nose and listening hard. They spoke more quietly as they discussed him. You didn't hear much, although your grandmother, in a rare lucid moment, pronounced that she had never liked the Cut Of His Jib. Her accent was still thick and lyrical. They nattered and bickered. Madeleine scowled. Eve wrung out her teatowel and said she couldn't remember her ever being so distant, so aloof.

Then your mum came back and the kitchen hushed.

Outside, you had asked Jenny what a Loof was. She said it was something you used in the shower with soap to wash yourself. Like a sponge. You squinted. It didn't make sense.

Jenny was sitting reluctantly with your cousin Sally, a divorced gothic vegan who was allergic to nuts and had bad skin. Darryl called her Sallymander. She was surly and sulky. Nobody cared.

He sat alone. Sat cloistered eating oysters, nursing a tall glass of black stout, with small caged eyes. Throwing his head back and racking the shells. Just as reticent and reserved as his wife. You looked away and he wasn't there any more.

Darryl was torturing the cat. You watched your Great Uncle Lester play absently with the bottom row of his teeth (you had always been convinced that he was chewing on something, until you asked what he was eating).

Chaos erupted when the spit cradle caved and the crackling sow bellyflopped the embers. Fizzing sparks darted and rose in a dispersing cloud. The oily porker burst into flame. There was a moment of silent shock. It teetered, considered a victory roll. The fanbelted bikewheel churned on.

Uncle Victor hurdled the fiery pig and bolted into the kitchen. The rest of the stubby-holding Pig Monitors stepped back from the bonfire. And watched.

The pig burned on.

Victor sprinted back with an oven-mitt and a wet teatowel that he had snatched out of Eve's hands. Dave rushed to assist with a pair of tongs and jiggling rubberbreasts. Eve shrieked.

Victor! That's my good teatowel!

Nobody cared.

You and Jenny looked at each other and laughed openmouthed. Everyone rushed to the edge of the backlawn. Except him. And Sally, who was spewing over the hydrangeas.

Darryl prodded the pig with a cricket stump.

Dave (teatowelled) and Victor (oven-mitted) grabbed the searing rod ends and shoved the blazing pig off the spread of coals. The sunken cradle groaned. They rolled it across the dewy lawn. Smoke stung their eyes and Dave singed his other nipple. They had the sow barely smouldering when Darren emerged triumphantly from the shed with an oily tarpaulin. He cast it over the pig to smother the flame.

There was a few moments' silence before the tarpaulin was alive with a roar of combustion. Everyone leapt back again. The shouting resurged. Darren looked for somewhere to hide.

Gwen turned the sprinklers on. Everyone racked beneath the patio. Dave peeled the tarp off using Darryl's cricket stump, guarding his face with his forearm. Victor was seething, though his expression was that of surprise, because his eyebrows had been singed away.

Gwen! Turn the bloody sprinklers off!

Gwen turned the bloody sprinklers off.

The air was still. And quiet.

The pig lay like a giant burnt kebab. Charred and wet and spiced with lawn clippings. Its thick blanket blazed alongside. Everyone gathered around in a cautious huddle, like a procession of mourners. They looked on, wary and silent. Your

Uncle Dave snuffed his nipple as curlicues of smoke trailed upwards. There wasn't much lawn left.

Someone murmured from the back:

Yairs, nice welding, Vic. Built to last, mate. Top job.

And everyone laughed. Victor was kneeling now, carving doggedly to salvage some dry flesh and pride.

Oh, come on. Look: it's still good. It's still good. Good meat in there. Just look at that. He held aloft a hard, grainy nugget of flesh.

Vic, it's cremated.

The table filled up. Chairs scraped. Eve clucked over her teatowel. Nobody cared. Darryl was caught harpooning the smoking pig with the pointed stump. Gwen slapped him and led him inside. He didn't come back out. You smiled indulgently.

And that was when your Uncle Theo arrived. Late like always. You leapt from the Little People's Table and tumbled into him clasping. Next to Jenny, Theo was your favourite person in the world. He felt warm. You waggled noses.

I haven't seen you for ages! Where were you at Christmas? I had a present for you.

I was sick, Ellybelly.

Sick? How come?

Tell you later. How'd you be?

Good. The pig just fell in the spit!

Gawd. It did too. Lucky Snapper, eh?

(Snapper, Eve's vomitstreaked cat, had been freed from its ligature and was now gorging itself on pork. Uncle Victor speared a plastic fork at it. The cat loped away insolently, displaying its puckered arsehole.)

Theo was yet to be noticed. And no one would all night, if they could help it.

Theo was the family skeleton, an implicit taboo. You just didn't *talk* about Theo. He was a half-brother; the result of a quick highland fling. Deemed only as The Mistress's Bastard, Theo had lived with his mother (The Filthy Whore) and was largely forgotten until the family sold the Guest House and decided to emigrate. He came over with them. Initially, he was tolerated begrudgingly by his half-siblings, but after their father passed away he was simply ignored. Now at family gatherings such as these, Theo often arrived to bask in their discomfort as they pretended he wasn't there.

Tonight, though, he had come to say Goodbye. To announce his departure. He was going back. (And hearing it, Estelle would push her plate away and clutch her belly, feeling that chill flush. That bloom of envy and longing. And you would clench your jaw with the force of restraining hot angry tears.)

But now you hugged him hard. Theo was fey and funny and perspicacious. He had a nice, wily smile. And when he talked he was always the same size as you. He had sparkling fizzy eyes that smiled with his mouth. He was tall with spindly legs. You noticed he was bald on top, with a curtain of hair around the sides.

You've gone bald, Theo!

I know. I look like an egg with a scarf.

And if you looked closely, the egg had a thin red crack at the back.

I thort you weren't going to come tonight.

No way! And miss all this burnt pork? Theo smiled.

Uncle Victor snarled into his plate and tried to pretend he hadn't heard.

Come on. Let's dig in.

Together you filed along and loaded up your plates, which said Happy Birthday in tilted gilt letters. There was a big empty space in front of your mum, where the pig would have been. Theo greeted everybody and was effortfully ignored; except for Jenny, who said Hello.

Theo followed you back to keep you company at the Little People's Table. He sat in Darryl's chair. His knees were almost under his armpits as he wrangled with bendy plastic cutlery. He nabbed things from your plate. The air smelled of charcoal and chilli and citronella.

Let's just eat with our hands, eh?

I helped catch those mussels.

Really?

Yep. I had to carry both of the bags.

Ah. Important job. You need muscles for mussels.

Theo leaned back and belched, then blamed it on you. The two of you giggled. You talked about school and football and music and people you didn't like. Then Theo told you he was getting married soon.

Is she pretty?

Oh yes.

Rich?

Definitely not.

Funny?

For sure.

Did you bring her here?

Absolutely. But I've got her locked in the car.

What?

It's okay. I wound the windows down.

What?

I'm joking, schmuck, he laughed. She couldn't come tonight.

Oh. Wot's her name?

Nigel.

Nigel! No it *isn't!*

True! It's French though. Pronounced: *Nye-jelle*.

No it isn't!

It's true!

Crap!

You both laughed and chewed. Theo burped again.

What's her name really?

Kate.

Kate's a nice name.

It is. So do I have your blessing ma'am?

You're not allowed to forget about me.

No way, Jose. I'm only marrying her to make you jealous.

During dessert, you stacked a plate with profiteroles while he smuggled you a coffee. He spoke loudly:

Here. Is. Your. Nice. Warm. Cup. Of. Hot. Choc. O. Late. Ell. A. Nor. En. Joy.

Thank. You. Un. Cle. Thee. Yo.

You clinked your mugs and winked, but no one was listening anyway. After munching a profiterole, he took a scalding sip and leaned forward.

Show you something, he said.

What? You leaned forward too.

Look: Watch my eyes, he said. And you did.

You watching? he asked.

Yep.

Okay, concentrate. Look hard. You ready?

Yep.

He looked back at you sternly. Then he said it: *Rhubarb*. And his pupils dilated. Wide. Scary. Like sudden spilled pools of ink. Like magic. It made you shiver. He said it again and they constricted. To two beady little dots, like they'd been pulled from the inside. They slowly regressed back to normal. Theo smiled.

Do it again, do it again, you said. And you made Theo do it another ten times.

How do you do it? That's like *magic!* you said, excited. You wanted him to teach you.

He breathed out slowly, puffing his cheeks. Leaned back. Looked around. Like a frog with folded legs. He watched you. Took a long, cautious sip, squinting when his lips met the mug.

In a whisper he explained that it was a Big Secret. And that Big Secrets were a Big Responsibility. They were heavy things to carry around. Like a sack on your back. That followed you wherever you went.

But you promised him. He whistled.

Okay. I'll talk, I'll talk.

You both sipped at coffee. It was bitter, but pleasantly hot inside. Theo cleared his throat. Patted his thighs.

Well, Jellybelly, when I really was sick recently I had to go to hospital. I was there for quite a long time.

Hospital! No one ever even told me!

That's no surprise. I'm invisible, don't you know? I could probably stand up right now and do the cancan and nobody would even notice.

Go on, you said.

So he did. And they didn't (although Jenny lifted a curious eyebrow).

So wot was wrong with you?

My malady, milady, was a jolly spot of cancer smack bang inside my head. Like a big ugly bomb.

Really?

Really. Anyway, in hospital there wasn't very much to do. I was very bored and in pain; it was sort of like talking to your Aunty Gwen. Also I was very tired with all the therapy and everything. Then one day, the doctors came in and told me that they were pretty sure I wasn't going to last for very much longer.

Really? you stalled chewing.

Really. It put a downer on my day, I can tell you. I was quite disappointed. Depressed even. So: one night when I was bored and sad, I got really serious all of a sudden. I picked up a little shaving mirror by my bed, and I started to look at myself, you know, because I'm so ruggedly handsome. I was tired, so my eyelids kept dozing over and then opening quickly. And I noticed how my pupils reacted to the light, how they got smaller when they opened. I became very immersed. Kind of fascinated. So I borrows me some matches from this guy with toiminal lung cancer besides me, and I starts playing around with the light. Watching my pupils do funny things like this: (and Theo iterated *rhubarb* fast and soft under his breath, his pupils bursting like fireworks).

You smiled, wide eyed.

And I remember thinking that this whole dying business was really not on. I didn't want to buy the farm and kick the bucket just yet. I was still sprightly, you know, still hip with the buzzin cuzzin. So I told myself, then and there, that I was going to thrash the pants off this bugger with the scythe right? So what I did was, when I flicked a match and watched my pupils go small, I said *rhubarb* at the same time. Then I blew it out and said it again. Rhubarb. I don't know *why* I said rhubarb, it was just a funny word that came into my head. But I did it again, and again, and again, and again. I did it for days and days, concentrating fiercely. Crazy. I went through a zillion and one matches. They were scattered all over the place. Everyone thought I was a nutter. It was all I did. And then, suddenly, I could do it. Without any matches. I could just say it and it would happen.

You absorbed it, staring blankly. Astounded, but still a little deflated.

So it's not exackly magic, *exackly*?

Oh, but it is! It is! It *is* magic. And he tapped the side of his head. *This* is magic. This here. They don't call this the Temple for nothing, right? This is the single most magical thing in the world!

You stared up at him.

You can do *anything* with this thing here. Anything you want, anything you can think of. It's the most powerfullest thing you've got. And you're lucky. You've got a good one. It's all in here, Elly. You've just got to really really really want it. And I just really really really didn't want to cark it yet. Not me. So what I did was, I trained myself not to hurt any more, not to feel pain. And I believed I could do it, I just had to be fierce. So I said rhubarb to all my sore bits, especially my head. Concentrated hard. Like a spell. Zap, zap, zap, Kazamm! I said rhubarb to everything. I was the Zenmaster, baby. And I believed it. Truly. Of course, everyone on my ward was convinced that I was a freak. A loony. I could see them looking at me, weird, kind of expectant. Like I was going to burst out of bed at any moment and do the cancan or something. But I showed em. Look at me! Do I look dead?

No sir!

Exactly. So remember, nothing can get you in there. He tapped your forehead. Nothing can touch you. And you can do anything if you want it bad enough.

You sipped warmish coffee and tingled allover.

Hey, you know who my nurse was?

Who?

Her name was Kate.

Really?

Yep.

Then the Big People's Table shuffled and murmured as Gwen carried the cake out. She hadn't wanted to waste eighty candles, so she had frugally formed the two numerals using only thirteen.

Great Aunty May didn't mind. She was shickered on brandy and making a rapid transition to rum. She grinned wetlipped and swayed in a circular motion.

Gwen cut the lights and stunned the swarm of loitering insects. The cluster of candles cast barely enough light to see the edge of the cake. Your grandmother was conversing delightedly to a hanging basket.

Everyone sang and hippipped with Great Aunty May rocking in time. She craned forward slowly, and blew out ten candles with a breath that was almost flammable. And in the dim light, everyone watched as a fine rain of misty spittle snuffed out the remaining three. May grinned proudly. Lester stopped chewing his dentures.

And you and Jenny and Theo giggled yourselves out of breath in the sudden cover of dark. Like a cloak it was. A thick, deep, touchable thing. Felt safe. Felt good. And it crossed your mind that this must be what Jenny felt in the water. Coated and buoyed. And somehow you attributed this warmfeeling to the lack of light, as though *it* was responsible for the safeness and rightness and preciousness of this moment; not the link of fingers nor the heat of bodies.

Dark Ness, you thought all to yourself, and smiled with the memory.

POCKET MONEY

Eleanor Rigby weaves uneasily through a thickening atmosphere. Everything seems to have gathered intensity for the Eve of Christmas. Heat. Volume. People. She feels grimy sweat between her toes as she moves out of the meandering congestion of the malls. Drifting past glorious bursts of airconditioning. And out further, beneath the solid shade of those Moreton Bay fig trees. Warren sniffs and licks at the sticky seeded fruit pressed flat into the pavement. He pauses to paw away the tartness.

Broad leaves skid and tumble in a hot breeze, amid warbling native doves who nod among themselves like lunatics. Seagulls cark and whistle in a bleached sky. Warren's hackles blare at the sound.

She wastes no time today. Change jangles loose in her big pockets.

Estelle's Christmas present swings in a plastic bag at her side. Cheap perfume, same as every year. Something nice to smell so Eleanor knows she's still there. And there's also a bottle of cheap bubblywine, whose taste isn't necessary (though she'd had to wrangle for it. The man at the bottle shop had asked her for ID. Eleanor Rigby said she didn't have any). And tomorrow, she'll leave the two gifts unwrapped on the coffee table, murmur Merry Christmas, and Estelle will be sleeping by noon and smelling of roses; same as every year.

But she's gleaned her meagre savings to buy something else this Christmas. And it's there in her pocket, just burning away at her thigh.

Tickets. Two of them. To the orchestra. And she's even got good seats.

She hooks a thumb inside occasionally. To touch them. Their paperness, smooth. Gets a charge from it.

Eleanor hurries under desolate scaffolding that smells of lime and fresh concrete. Past the greasy waft of a lunchbar. The scent of second-hand clothing. The nattering buzz of a tattoo shop. Warren pants, lumbering. His tongue is a hot pink dangling slab, dribbling a dotted trail. He isn't sure where they are headed.

Eleanor pauses to readjust the bag. Breathes deep, grimacing. Considers performing home surgery on her uterus. Heat undulates. She hears heavy, approaching footsteps.

Scuse me? Hello?

Yes?

The footsteps stop. She interrupts a tall, wide biker with a plaited mullet who is lusting for an armful of ink. He smells of stale tobacco and festering sweat. Eleanor leans on one leg.

Is there a petshop on this street, do you know?

A wot?

A petshop.

Er, yairs akshully, love. There is. Round the corner here. Just passed it. Here, I'll show yer.

She takes a handful of leather. The man nudges away the sniffing dog. They discuss the weather and the cruel heat absorption of black leather.

He steers her to the store door.

Cheers. Thanks very much. Merry Christmas.

No problem. Merry Christmas, love. He grins through a dense beard. Turns away scratching his arse. The back of his studded jacket is branded with insignia. Above which it says: If You Can Read This, The Bitch Fell Off.

Eleanor confronts the door of the petshop. There is a white sign in front of her that says Pull. She Pushes. Then Pushes harder. Then Pulls. A small bell tingles, and the powerful, acerbic reek of stale urine stops her at the entrance. Warren's nostrils flare. He surveys the store of caged animals with trepidation. Puppies, kittens, guinea pigs. Birds bickering at suspended mirrors. The rumble and burr of aquariums, with lucent goldfish gliding ignorant with enviable memories.

Eleanor aligns Warren in front and lets him lead. They shuffle past tight shelves of birdseed and fishflakes and worming tablets. He looks moisteyed at a studded collar. Sniffs at a stack of gnarled chewy things. Licks one.

An elderly woman behind the counter sings Good Morning. Eleanor waves genially to the sound. Face screwed in the pungent, pressing fug. The old woman leans forward.

And how can I help, dear?

Eleanor touches the counter. Leans.

Dyou have crabs?

***

Ewan grits teeth and grapples with Vivaldi. Frowns finishing the piece. Twists a stubborn bownut. He feels indolent today. Disengaged. Holding her haunch and slender neck, he lowers her down gently and places her on her side. He rubs at the soreness of a recently punched sternum, where Lilian's heel has bitten into him.

Ewan stirs and rises. Steps over his cello and into the hallway.

It's just after noon. And there's a clear idea in his head that he's held all day. It surprises him.

Keys and nuggety change jangle loose in his pockets. He opens his front door to a waiting wall of sultry heat. Squinting, he hesitates. Closes the door behind him.

The pavement is like a hotplate under his naked feet. Ewan skips on to grassy bits, slows for glorious bursts of shade.

The street is quiet and expectant, like the main strip of a Western. He glances with unease, but keeps moving. Sees a strip of mashed potato across the road. Smiles to himself. The heat is thick and parched. It bears weight and wards him back. He keeps going. He can hear his footsteps slapping in the shadows of fences and shabby hedges. Hands deep inside his pockets, fondling change.

Con's (real) Cornerstore has closed its doors to conserve the cool. A green sign says Open. A white sign says Push. Ewan Pulls. Pulls harder. Then Pushes. And the door Opens. His sweat chills. Four ceiling fans wobble perilously. An airconditioner idles.

Another small fan pivots behind the counter, shaking its muzzled head slowly at Con, who is pouring generous slush puppies for two patient kids. Con glances up. Winks.

Ewan skirts the aisles, evaporating. Finds what he is looking for. Con scatters slippery coins into the till.

Afternoon sir, Con calls. Bit warm out there?

Ewan emerges and slides three slabs of dark chocolate on the counter.

You could say that.

Got a craving mate?

It's not for me, he says softly.

Ah, I see, I see. Bit late for you, innit? You're usually my early bird.

Ewan is silent. Reaches into his pocket. Con leans forward.

Listen, howd you go getting them traps orf that Ayetalian bastard down the road?

No, I didn't get them actually.

Well, son. Ratsak is the go. Aisle four there. Solve all your problems that will.

I might just leave it for now.

Ho ho! Con straightens and smiles. You've changed your tune! Bloody hippy now is it?

Ewan forces a smile.

Jest pullin yer leg mate.

Ewan nudges the blocks closer. I'll just take these then, thanks.

Na na na na, Con waves him away. Forgeddit. S'on me today, son. Got to look after my loyal custom, eh?

Ewan pauses. Looks up. Oh. Well. Thanks very much.

Doan mention it. Hey, you be careful with that stuff. It's an afro-dizzy-yak you know. Or maybe you do, eh? He winks and grins.

Ewan takes the chocolate. Her chocolate. Thanks again, he says.

Mary Chrestmas, mate.

Merry Christmas.

Ewan closes the door gingerly and it's like stepping into an oven. He squints in the glare. He's got a sudden melody in his head. And a brownvested busker. And conceived by that memory is another idea that grips him. He's slipping home fast now; because he's got something to rush home for. He's forgotten his exposure, forgotten the heat, as he charges back with change rattling. And he's thinking about tomorrow. Like he's abandoned its trajectory already. Like it's something to look forward to. And maybe he's hoping she'll be in it.

***

Is my fayvorite Blind Midgit! Buongiorno Hallynor!

Hello Hello.

Bruno rings up the till (chaching!) and stubs the nub of his cigar in an empty change compartment. He looks at Eleanor strangely.

An wot is this you haff here?

This?

Eleanor raises the plastic carrybox hooked by her right hand.

Inside it on a bed of coarse sand is a hollowed rock, seasponge, two small orange bowls and a conical shell.

It's a Christmas present.

Wot is it?

It's a hermit crab.

A wot?

A hermit crab.

A hairmet creb? An where is it? Is no creb in there? They haff done you a deal, Hallynor. There hiss no creb in there.

It's inside the shell, Bruno.

Bruno narrows his eyes.

Insiyde it? So is like a snail, yes?

Yes Bruno. Like a snail. He's a cranky little bastard, nipped my finger twice already. Perfect for its recipient though, I think.

On cue, the surly crustacean emerges and drags its pearl caravan into the rock cave, reversing in. It pulls the ball of seasponge behind it to conceal the entrance.

I'm going to call it Ewan. What do you think?

Hyoown? Hyoown the Hairmet Creb? No, no, no you need a goot Italian name, like Bruno, yes?

He straightens, manboobs widening with his repulsive smile.

Is Althea here?

No, not today. She hass the Day Off today. She hiss cooking for tomorrow. Cooking, cooking, cooking.

Sounds like a day off. Well then, if you would be so kind as to assist me, my good man, I am in dire need of a turkey. And some vegies too. Oh, and zum zecret urbs an spices.

A turkey. Okay, okay.

Not too big though, Bruno.

Bruno descends from his counter pedestal and ambles importantly to the Meat Section. He reaches into a bin freezer, basking in a glorious burst of chilled air. He removes a frosted, fair-sized chicken and glances across to the Seasonally Adjusted price of the turkeys. He wipes away the furry frost. Small Turkey, Big Chicken. It's all the same to Blind People. After all:

1. Profit Obtained is Profit Justefied.

How bout thiss, yes?

He handballs the stiff bird and Eleanor gauges the weight in her hands. Runs her fingers over it. Warren scans it with a critical snout.

Bruno, this is a chicken. You've given me a chicken.

Wot? Bruno reddens, waxes falsetto. Nononono, is wrong, is wrong, this hiss a small turkey. You say, Bruno: not too big not too big, and I giff you a small turkey. Is wot aye giff you. Is not a chicken.

Bruno, the word *chicken* is fucking embossed on the packaging. I can read it. Here. Look: *Chicken.*

Bruno pauses, concedes, mumbles and snatches back the bird.

Now, could you be percipient enough to get me a *turkey* please? No gourmet quail or duck or *chicken*. I just require a *turkey*, if you could.

Bruno mutters in an incoherent vernacular. He blames his staff (Althea). He slams a freezer door and waddles. He finally rummages through a pink-piled stack. Pulls out a sickly, puckered bird that appears to have died of old age (after a long battle with malnutrition). Its wingtips are cobalt.

Okay?

Dyou have another one? It feels kind of weird.

Bruno inspects the frozen flock of twelve. No, no, this hiss hit. Is the last one. It has bin bizzy yes? For the Christmas, Bruno offers his explanation to her crisp nipples.

Okay, well, I need some vegies too. But it's all right, it's *all right*. I know where they are. I don't want to push you too hard.

She leaves the bird with Bruno. Warren works her through the shop, his tail sweeping her shins.

Eleanor bags potatoes and resists the smile that pulls at her lips.

She has high hopes that his Mercedes kaboomed into showering shards of sparking tin. With him in it. Glittering and glinting as they fell like confetti around Althea, who watched in astonishment by the roadside, and then began clapping and cheering and punching the air. Then jigging. Clicking her heels. Eleanor imagined her cradling the spud, stroking it. Glancing gratefully towards the heavens, while *Dingdong the Witch is Dead* played somehow in the background.

She doesn't ask him, though. She'd rather hear it all from someone else. Tomorrow. She smirks all the way to the counter, to be ripped off knowingly by dodgy scales. She touches two thick strips of paper in her pocket, on her way to the change that's in them.

***

Estelle is leaving.

On Christmas Eve. During an Estée Lauder commercial.

Estelle is leaving now, and if she hadn't pruned her neurons or snipped synapses, if she wasn't dead already, she might know. Might feel it. Sense this sliding. Struck by this very last Stroke.

But that has always been her tradeoff. Ever since she learned that the best way not to feel nervous was to scrape out her nerves. With a grim resignation. And cold conviction.

She stumbled into Numb Ness. And stayed.

She found it lying displaced beyond the shuddering shivering shaking weight of fear. And she huddled hidden and safe in that thick cloak of anaesthesia. Convinced herself that she couldn't be touched there. But he found a way. And he stole the only lasting thing that mattered. He opened the door. Light poured in. *Light* came out. With her sister. And saw, watched, were made to. And it tore through that dead leather skin and shattered her like nothing else. And that was when she died, on that night, and now she is leaving.

Just the solemn, silent passing over of the rest of her.

She's leaving now, but not the way she should have done Back There: with packed bags and volition and two children those two clockhands you should have should have should have

Leaving now with a bloated chin falling to a bloated chest, with no one here to see you off. No turning, no waving, no goodbyeing. Leaving with empty pockets. Leaving to unite with a womb and a spine, the bits that beat you to it.

Leaving with a slack cigarette still smouldering between passive mauve lipstick. With a perfect airbrushed model in front of you smiling a perfect bleached smile. Another person's smile. Another to borrow, to wear like it's yours. To save face. Efface. Estelle, you're leaving now and you don't even get Exit Music through the warm pulse of Estellevision. They're trying to sell you Jesus now, but it seems a little late in the day for all that. *Ah men*. A cloak, a cloak, you're slipping now. But there's no pain here, just Loss, just forfeit. No fear, but never fearless. Esteelle: you too, mocked by your name, but you mocked it back. Estelle: Latin for *Star*. And from you: the parturition of *Light*, born in a shock of shared blood. You held that glimmer for a time and then lost it. Distance. Remote, Glad Wrapped. Estellevision. Estelle. Television. Flashing flittering flickering telefission. Juiceless withered cord. A sad disappointed slack slump. You'll die with a sigh and leave no vestige of your departure, no absence. Leaving behind only two boxes of images that were never yours.

It will be hard to notice you've gone.

THE GLASS SPINE

Back here:

His caged eyes watch the Arrivals arrive and Departures depart. From the customs Exit they either scan for family or charge blindly. Met or unmet. Greeted or ignored. They queue for luggage as announcers announce flights, destination, time. People listen or surge or wait or embrace. Sometimes they come to his counter and he smiles with compliance. Patient. And he accepts their yen their pounds their guilders their rupees their lire their deutschmarks their greenbacks or their cards; and hands back an equivalent with a trained smile and they stare through him. Currency. Exchange. He could be anyone.

It started small: an argument, a quarrel, a rhubarb, a shove.

Tonight is Friday and his mouth is dry as he rides the escalator. At the bar, he presents cash and a Staff Card for a murky muddy pint and a small shot of a clear spirit. In a silent corner seat, he watches the tavern fill quickly. Someone gestures to an empty chair, he shakes his head, it's taken. Loud gibberish murmur. Tight groups, big laughs and gossip. Friday night football. Complimentary nuts. The first smooth mouthful he bares his teeth and appreciates the bitter taste. Saws at lipfroth with the back of his hand and tongues his palate. Sucks his teeth. And it's easy to think of all that yeast swelling inside. A chemical reaction, cold blood calescent, like a cloak. Now, pint glass white veined and empty, thumb and forefinger squeeze the shotglass. Lips the meniscus. Fumes. Head back, medicinal taste, heat in the belly. Rising, chair sliding back against converging walls. At the bar again he stands among a press of People. Presents Cash and a Staff Card. *Why did the Mexican throw his wife off the cliff?* he hears the barman ask someone else. *Tequila.* He leaves with the punchline in his hands.

Sits down. Same again. And again. And again. And a small man gets taller and bigger and begins to stare. Cool sips then a burning shot. Weaves a clear path to the bar. A rhythm. He slides empty pints under the table to shift attention from his tally. The dry shotglasses, though, he stacks up on each other on the table, high and clear, with a slight bend. A glass spine. A transparent spine. He stares at it, through it.

Then he leaves. Down the escalator, mouth without thirst. Sliding doors open as he approaches.

***

Picture her:

Picture dim suburban lighting, picture cheap furniture and fading beige upholstery. Picture coordinated curtains. The trapped scent of grilled chops and gravy. Stale cigarettes, a caged red beam inside a ticking heater. The sound of rain. Picture a hard, resistant mattress, Kingsize, picture her sitting picking lint with trembling fingers and waiting. She will lose her womb tonight.

It all started small.

Picture a prescient pack of frozen peas in the bathroom. Something to stop the swelling when she retreats to Recover. It's the same bathroom she miscarried in, the same bathroom she hears her eldest daughter retching in in the shower. And inversely, the same bathroom in which her eldest daughter watched her vomiting over the sink, months ago. Daughter: wide-eyed and gaunt in the doorway, in lavender pyjamas, legs like rhubarb stalks. Her mother was naked. Fat sagging on a gourd shaped body. Bruising across her breasts and her arms and her legs and her belly. Nipples like ugly wrinkled snouts. A spill of peas, a viscous dribble of bile. Her eyes farfaraway. Her daughter's eyes, they held Hate, staring at the bent, defeated woman who glanced and shook her head slowly at her, held a crooked trembling finger to her lips, then pointed, mouthing the word *Out*. The word *Sister*. The word *Please*.

Go back further. Picture Estelle discovering Numb Ness the evening she swallowed a trembling handful of sleeping pills. There was no waiting, no trembling, no lintpicking, she was dead to the world by the time he came home. When she woke the next day there were fresh contusions and her vagina was torn and throbbing and glued to the sheet. Household hegemony had been bashed routinely into her body, but she, triumphantly, had felt *nothing*, seen *nothing*, and all she had to do was heal.

ReCover. Tonight is Friday and her collarbone will fracture when he seizes her neckgristle and drives her backbackback and she falls limp, distantly hearing his bleated belligerent rhetoric. But she won't feel it.

Maybe, maybe it happened by degrees, by attrition. With every truculent, measured swing, with every fleshy packing sound a little dimmer, a little duller, a little further away. Maybe too many blows to the solar plexus. Maybe it compounded that way; this paralysis. Or maybe she decided, defeated. Gave it up and survived. Got by. With a cold conviction. With nothing left to lose. She resigned her spine, blissfully enervated. A Loof then, a sponge. With Fear as her cloak, her insulation.

Picture a *Holiday!* beachtowel laid across the gap of a closed bedroom door, smothering light and sound for her daughters two. Protecting them, the only thing left that matters. There is soft music inside, issuing from a brass snout. Please be sleeping.

And this, please listen, is how it unfolds: it is tonight that her clockhands will part. After they have seen what they should never have borne witness to. The youngest will escape first, but toolatetoolatetoolate; the eldest will shepherd her to the front door before being grabbed, pulled, screaming. But the youngest will break out and run for miles, for Distance, so there is hope. The eldest will stay until the end, after he has gone, for good, and she'll kneel beside the splayed, the spayed, and help her to her bedroom where she'll lay her down, apply peas and balm and calm words. Scared and alone, watching the door. Then she will collect her things in that quiet house and leave that letter, just in case. And she'll run. To where she is *sure* her sister will be.

But the youngest will come back to an empty house (toolate-toolatetoolate) heaving and confused and looking for an ally, a bestfriend, and she'll never leave. The eldest will never, ever come back. Both will feel betrayed.

Picture the springtrap swivel of her head as she hears the keys rattle the doorlock. Please, please be sleeping.

For him, there was nothing quenched in the distance, the absence of those eyes. It was like bashing a hanging carcass. The slack, sluggish, muted, cadaver response of her flesh. Not enough. It started small and got. And this invidious cunt knew how to send a shimmer up a dead spine. How to rouse her. He knew.

Tonight is Friday and he will kick and she will rear. Blood and visceral cold. She'll die inside. And they'll see it.

Please: picture them.

The door will open. To light and sound, to *Light* and her sister.

HAPPY BIRTHDAY JESUS

Out here in the pallid predawn, she straddles her dog and clamps his wet squirming hindlegs between her knees, a flowing hose under her arm. The cold water slaps Warren's shoulders. He squints and flinches in protest.

Eleanor unscrews the sticky cap of Martha Gardener's Wool Mix. Warren, ears pinned, whiffs the potent odour of eucalyptus and Dread. He struggles and whines.

Stand *still* Warren, you dickhead!

Eleanor pours liberally along his back. Rubs in the creamy foamy soap.

A bleary sunhaze spreads bolder over the hills now. An audience of wattle, gerbera, bottlebrush, and next door's olive trees cast their scent into the air. Sometimes glistening are the hastily scrawled webs of pudgy Christmas spiders, perching proud in their temporary accommodation. They gaze fatly with eight greedy eyes at a buffet breakfast. At white ephemeral butterflies that flit and flirt midair in hope of a quick shag. At meandering bees, pollenshopping with twin carrybags. At the messy cluster of flies that hover in the damp.

Warren! *Fuckssake!* Stand *still!*

Warren hates baths. And if he ever sees Martha Gardener, he has vowed to maul her good and proper. Eleanor tugs at his collar. He resists, mulish, dragging away from her, quelling the itchy urge to shake the weight of water from his back. He leans forward, slippery and insolent. Snapping at a passing dragonfly because it's there.

Warren! *Fuck!* Eleanor aims the jetting hose to where his head should be and digs her knees in. Don't make me get punitive, mister! Aw ah'll buss a cap in yo ass, unnerstand me? So *behave.*

Warren yawns. Tongue curling, then unfurling.

She works the soap into his ribs and shoulders. Embedded fleas surface. Warren is mildly, reluctantly obedient. She slips around to wash his chest.

There, look, she says. See, this isn't too

And he's off.

Eleanor Rigby preheats the oven and peels a banana for breakfast. Warren, dried and fluffy, sniffs at her hands. She prods at the soft, defrosted turkey. Leaves dents. The skin is loose and rubbery in places, wrinkled and gelatinous in others. Her disgust is audible. She entertains an unwelcome vision of kneading one of Great Aunty May's eighty-year-old breasts. She shudders away the thought, plucks out a series of slimy feathers from between its legs.

Eleanor tucks the mushy wings around to its back, so the turkey appears to be reclining. Lazing naked. Sunbaking. On a grassy knoll, gazing listlessly (headlessly) upwards.

I'm terribly sorry about this old dear, Eleanor consoles softly, paring open a cold slippery cavity, but this may cause some discomfort. And a blind chef stuffs a gaping arse with soggy breadcrumbs and fresh spices and a raw egg. Egg! she thinks, and giggles at the irony.

She bastes the bird with a sheen of olive oil. Sorts through her spices using her nose. Sprinkles a generous layer of basil, marjoram, rosemary, oregano and paprika. She has never liked thyme. She adds salt and pepper and some potent, stringy stuff that Althea offered.

Eleanor can hear the television, though she doubts Estelle has risen. She won't wake until late morning, after which she'll shuffle to the toilet, then to her glass cabinet for a mailorder crystal wineglass. Then she'll toast herself and down a bottle of warm champagne in less than an hour. Christmas: the nadir of the year. She'll sleep deep through it, clinging to an empty bottle, adenoids grunting.

Eleanor tries anyway: Morning Stella. Merry Christmas!

No answer.

But Eleanor doesn't care. She has big plans for this bird.

She lifts and lowers it into a roasting dish quarterfilled with dissolved chicken stock. Covers, and lays it in the oven.

Rinsing her hands to peel the vegies, Eleanor feels a bandaid slip from her index finger. She checks the other three are still there and not inside the turkey. Reminded of that surly crustacean, she sloshes and retrieves the bandaid, empties the sinkwater, dries her hands and decides to check on it.

***

The crab has been finding it hard to sleep.

It is kept awake by an incessant reminder of Home, because every time it retires into its shell, it is beset by the sound of the ocean. It has decided to escape.

So during the warm, still night of Christmas Eve, Little Ewan the Surly Crustacean gently prised open the seasponge entrance of its rock cave. Carved the air with its eyestalks. It scanned. It waited. The coast was clear.

Slowly it emerged from its limestone garage, dragging its pearl caravan (and the sound of the ocean). It edged to the perimeter, tipped the water from one of its orange bowls and began bunting it towards a corner. It tottered back with caution. Did the same with the other bowl, placing it next to the first. The crab hurried. Dragged its ball of seasponge and heaved it atop the corner bowl. The effort rolled the crab on to its back. It was able to push off the adjacent wall and back upright. It took a brief nibble of some dried apple. Sustenance for the Journey Ahead.

Eyestalks erect, Little Ewan confronted its makeshift stairway. It was time.

It climbed doggedly, trudging up the steep seasponge. At the top, the crab levered the lid with ease. Its hairthin antennae twitched, tasting Freedom.

Suddenly, the seasponge fell away and rolled, but the crab latched the recessed edge and dangled. Struggling, it clambered over, tumbling on to Eleanor's desk with a nutty crack.

It scrambled away, casting a long conical shadow.

***

She finds the lid loose.

She dips her hand into the clear carrybox; shakes the spongeball, ploughs the coarse sand, uproots the cave. No crab.

Shit, she says. Shit, shit, shit.

How the fuck did it get out? Eleanor thinks as she gropes around the desk, lifting things, scattering things. She drops to her knees and sweeps her arm across the carpet. Under the bed. In the bed. No crab. Shit. *Shit.*

She crawls into the hallway, padding the floor like she's lost a contact lens. Warren shambles down, fluffy and sweetsmelling. He curiously presses a wet snout to her forehead. She pauses. Addresses him:

You're a retriever, Warren. *Retrieve.* Start sniffing, my boy. For crabs. Remember that crab, Warren? Remember that fucking *fucker* of a hermit crab? Here, look, and she takes the crabless carrybox and holds it under his snout, so he can pick up the scent.

Warren looks confused. She grabs his loose cheeks and implores.

Okay, Warren? *Warren?* Are you ready? This is very important. It's time to do your stuff. Listen, *listen* to me. Warren's lips wobble. This is it, Warren. Your Moment of Glory. This is the true call of your ancestors. Forget the guide dog crap. *Retrieve.* Find the crab, Warren: *find the crab.*

Eleanor ushers him into the bathroom. He waddles bemused, wondering if there is anything to eat. He is quickly distracted by the cool water in the toilet bowl. Eleanor trawls the ugly tiling (lemon, lime, white, sometimes umber) collecting dust and dry pubes and fallen cobwebs. She searches the shower recess, under the sink, through cabinets. She shakes towels like a matador. No crab. *Shit.*

Warren is bored. He blinks hard, thinks about the kitchen. Thinks about the turkey. He trundles out into the loungeroom. The blaring flickerbox makes him flinch. He recognises Estelle sleeping on the couch. Still.

And Warren sees the crab. There, in the gap between the lounge and the wall. He frowns. Shifts forward for an olfactory analysis. Closer.

He sniffs.

Closer. Warren's snout smears the shell.

The crustacean and the dog regard each other for a moment.

Then the crab lashes out with a deft right nipper, latching to the skin of Warren's top lip. He yelps highpitched and wheels. Shakes his head in a manic flurry. Tries to scrape it off with a paw. Growling. Whining hysteric dogbabble. Warren shakes again, ears slapping the side of his head. The crab's cling is slipping as Eleanor jogs down the hallway.

Warren? What's the matter? What's the matter?

She hears a dull crack against a near wall. Then a muffled carpet thud.

What was that?

Warren pounces. She hears his teeth grappling with something hard. Like an iceblock. Or a rock. Or a crab.

Warren, no! She dives forward. Hauls him back. The crab stays locked in Warren's jaw. Drop it! Drop. It. *Now.*

Warren resists the strong, vengeful urge to Crunch. Down. *Hard*.

Drop, Warren! *Drop!*

His jaw slowly, reluctantly opens. The crab dribbles out and rolls. Eleanor rescues the shell, slimy in her fingers. Little Ewan is huddled deep inside his caravan.

Shit Warren, I hope you didn't kill it.

Warren doesn't care. He licks his throbbing lip and feels sorry for himself. He pads off to watch the turkey. To coax it out with a persistent wistful gaze.

Eleanor rattles the shell. It's still there. Cupping it in her palm, she carries it back to her room. The crab, sensing Defeat, emerges quickly and spitefully pinches her lifeline like a bad omen. She yelps and pulls the crab away. Shoves it into its enclosure.

Little *fucker*, she hisses and slams the lid with venom.

The crab watches her leave, shakes a livid nipper.

Eleanor returns with a roll of masking tape, two phonebooks and a bandaid. She had considered a nutcracker, but thought better of it.

The crab watches, beady and indignant.

***

Frank wakes stiffly on Christmas morning. His back feels like a barbed plank. It doesn't tempt him to rise, but the grill of heat denies him further sleep.

He props on an elbow and swings himself to sitting on his side of the bed. The joins groan. He lets the task of waking sink like syrup into his muggy head. Hawks back a chunk of overnight phlegm and transports it to the en suite. He dribbles it into the sink.

Frank scratches wiry chesthair and yawns. Over the toilet bowl, he pulls out his depressing pink mollusc and aims. Tries to shake some life into it while he's there. It wobbles ridiculously; like a wizened, epileptic gecko. It does not stir.

At the soapless sink he rinses his hands and downs a series of colourful tablets. The cool bathroom still bears the fading scent of potpourri, held in terracotta pinchpots that Helen had made. He pads his hair down with water and spends no time in front of any mirror.

Frank scours the floor for underpants. Locates a wrinkled pair and turns them inside out. Sits on the edge of the bed to heave them up. He breathes heavily and dresses slowly, feeling tired.

He slides into the wellworn comfort of his Inside thongs, and loads his Invisible Wheelbarrow with a heavy mix of age, fatigue, arthritis, impotence, bereavement and other assorted aching. He shuffles to the kitchen.

Frank sits down to sweet milky tea and another mushbowl of All Bran, Metamucil and cold stewed rhubarb (so he can crap without wincing). He munches grimly while he peruses the paper, checking the sport and the forecast. Resolves to throw a line out later on, after the heat has eased from this day.

Be a hot one fersure, he announces to his bowl of sogging twigs.

It is a vague and indolent morning. His thongs scrape and drag without conviction. Like a head without a chook, he thinks. But he keeps busy. Spends a quiet hour beneath the back verandah disassembling his knackered lawnmower. Dusted and rusted beyond revival. Upon further inspection, he finds the carburettor has a small fracture and there is the absence of a sparkplug.

He calls his son, Barry, in Echuca. Says Merry Christmas awkwardly to an answering machine. Wanders aimlessly through the back garden, plucking weeds, flushing his reticulation.

He spends half an hour squatting hunched in the toilet, shitting inconsistent mush that even smells of All Bran. A good slurry is better than shitting bricks, he thinks (a well used Frankism), and does not wince.

He stares without absorption at the calendar on the back of the door. July. 1994.

In the absence of toilet paper, Frank reaches for a stack of old women's magazines. He wipes his arse with a pictorial spread of the royal family, like a true republican.

Hungry, thirsty and sweltering back under the verandah with greaseblack hands, Frank's chest soars upon hearing a clear knock on his front door. His eyes dart for a rag.

Ang on! Ang on! he calls out and surrenders his hanky, peeling open the sliding door. He walks briskly, excited. Covers the brass knob of the front door and opens it to a burst of heat and glare. Insects tick. There is no one there.

But before he's disappointed, he looks to his feet and sees a sixpack of beer and a foilcovered plate, gleaming. He steps over it. Searches the street with a myopic squint. Eager and puzzled.

Hullo? Hullow? he calls out. No one responds. He frowns. Moves to the end of his lawn. Looks left, and right, standing on the tips of his toes. Then he sees her and grins. A pint-sized pixie with an esky and a dog. Walking away fast. She disappears behind draping foliage at the end of the street.

Frank chuckles. He does not call out. Lets her go, leaves her be.

Bending stiffly, he picks up his plate and beer and wishes for a moment she had stayed. For a quick chat, to share his beer. But he understands why she didn't, and why she couldn't. It's his own fault. Frank understands the sweet subtlety of this gesture, and can't stop smiling, although he now knows she knows. And he's not saddened, or even ashamed by it. Just stung by her careful generosity. Besides, he thinks, she's probably off to see that boy of hers. The tall, quiet one with the handshake like an inflated dishrag.

Frank laughs with his belly and it tips some weight from his wheelbarrow. Makes him hungry.

On the table he pares back the foil, and the fragrant steam billows into the grinning chub of his face.

Aw, lookit that. Jesus bloody Christ. Ah, thankyou little love. Thanks very much.

He shicks open a beer, takes a moment to inhale it all.

Moisteyed and smiling, Frank waves his fork and his stubby with a gluttonous gobful of oddlooking poultry. He offers a muffled Merry Christmas to one and all and chews with high delight. His beard traps gravy for his roaming tongue.

The meat is tough but it's sweet tasting. And sitting here, he breathes deep and savours the pleasant shock of this moment. He fills up, fills out. The beer is cold and smooth and perfect.

***

She knows the way, but she's not chasing sound this time. It's something simpler today.

Eleanor Rigby walks a fierce pace. Feels thirsty under the grating noonsun. Her hands are full with a dog and an esky. She bears no empathy for the wedged crab breathing her armpit fumes.

Down these busy streets that are loud with guests and hosts and familyandfriends. The squeals and tantrums and the tinny whine of battery-operated toys. The crunch of cardoors. Highpitched greetings, muffled by embracing. The smell of fried onion, garlic, dandelions and eucalyptus. Suncream. She walks by close games of bocce and continuous cricket. Past tall culms of sugarcane clustering near a ditch. They sway like gospel singers. She distantly hears a Salvo blowing his trumpet on a streetcorner. The hollowpop of a liberated cork. The shrieks and laughs and murmurs of People. Of Christmas. And she's not chasing cadence today, just company.

***

Ewan is in his shed preparing the assembly of a pegbox when he hears her knock. His belly grips and rises. He knows it's her. He lays down his tools, moves out, ducking his head for the Hills hoist. Inside, the fridge spasms and burrs as he enters. She knocks again. He slips down the hall, unlatches and unlocks the door. It's her. And she smiles, standing on a velvety Welcome mat. Tilts her head and holds up the esky.

Wella hah thair! she chirps loudly. Anna Mary Christmiss to y'all! Y'know ah jist thawt, well *heck*, with it bein the festive season an all? Ah jist thawt, hell, wooden it be raht nahce if ah cooked us urp this here turkey fowl an, y'know, breng et over an share, lahk? Sow, anyways, here ah yam, an ahm surely hopin ah gots me the raht howse otherwahs this'd jest be damnwell embarrassing.

No, this is the right one, Ewan smiles. Merry Christmas.

Today she wears a bright white singlet and thick khaki skirt. The tip of her nose is peeling. There are two red clips in her hair. She is sweating. Her dog has a Santa hat strapped awkwardly to his head, covering one ear. Ewan reaches, takes the esky.

Thanks, she laughs.

Come in, he says, and the insane gravity of that gesture presses down upon him. He is *asking* her *inside*.

She has brought a hot breeze which he snuffs with a closed door. They work down the passage together. He sees her drop the leash of her guide dog. The grip on his arm tightens. Warren canters on ahead. Nose down, he searches for water.

Ewan takes her through to the kitchen. He sets the esky down on the table.

It's so bloody *hot* out there, she says, puffing flushed cheeks.

They share a brief silence. Ewan lifts the esky lid and smiles.

You really didn't have to do all this, you know. But thankyou. Very much.

Don't mention it. Thanks for letting me in. You know, if there's one good thing about stalking a hermit, it's that they're usually home.

Have a seat, says Ewan. It's just there in front of you.

Thanks. Eleanor sits, places the crab beside her.

He takes two plates from the dishrack. Lays them on the table. Begins to sift through cutlery. Unsure of what to do.

Dyou mind if we don't eat right now? she asks. It's just, I'm not really hungry yet.

Yeah, sure. Sorry, do you want a drink or something? Coffee? Water? Wine? Juice?

Some water would be nice, ta. And maybe a coffee too.

I'll put this in the oven then.

Ewan hoists the casserole dish from the esky, lays it carefully on the table. Takes a long, hard look at the bird in the centre of the dish, ambushed by vegetables.

Choose this one yourself? he asks.

Choose what?

The turkey. If it is, in fact, a turkey.

I have my own doubts about that. Why? Am I lucky I can't see it?

You could say that, Ewan smiles. It's not pretty.

Well, you know, I'm blind. I could roast anything. I once deep-fried a budgie.

Really?

Absolutely. It tasted like chicken. Like a crunchy chicken.

Of course.

Of course, she smiles.

Ewan heats the oven and slides in the dish.

I noticed you have sacrificed some potatoes too. Must have been hard, wasting valuable munitions like that.

Her face lights up. She slaps the table. That's *right!* Bruno! Tell me what happened! Did it work?

Ewan prepares coffee and tells her what happened. Looking over his shoulder to watch her face, to watch how she listens. Contorting, gathering surprise, laughing, anticipating. He can see her shaping the images in her head.

So he was actually kicking the car? she asks. Like really, actually *kicking* the car?

Yes. And he was screaming at it too. All the dogs in the street went mad. All thanks to you, Spud Girl.

And what did Althea do? His wife, what did she do?

I think she caught a taxi home and left him there.

Ha! Good for her!

Sugar? Milk? he asks.

Sugar please. One. And a half.

Ewan measures and stirs. He edges the mug across the table, to where she's sitting holding her elbows. He watches her, tentative. And then slowly he's reaching. He's reaching out, he's taking her index finger and he's carefully, carefully leading it to the mughandle. She does not flinch, does not pull away. And he's not sure whether he needs to do this. Not sure where the courage to do this is coming from. It's like it isn't him. He lets go.

And the water is just on your right there, he says softly.

Thankyou, Eleanor murmurs. She could be blushing. She could be hot. She gulps thirstily at the water, finger still hooking the mughandle.

Ewan takes a seat on the other side of the table. He watches her lift the mug and blow gently, then sip with caution.

Mmm. Good cawfee, she says.

Ewan's eyes drift now to the clear plastic box on the table. He frowns. It looks like a desolate, waterless, fishless aquarium. There's a strip of paper tied to a shell.

What have you got there anyway? he asks.

What is what?

The box, just here.

Oh! You mean *this* box. Eleanor slides it into the middle of the table, pats the lid. This is your Christmas Present. Hope you don't mind. She smiles, pushing it further. Merry Christmas.

Ewan peers into the box. Eleanor is grinning.

Ewan, meet Ewan. Your metaphorical equivalent.

Sorry? he asks.

What?

I don't think I understand, he says, staring hard.

You don't understand? What do you mean you don't understand?

Look, I don't mean to be rude, but, *what* exactly is it?

You mean it's not in there?

What isn't in there?

The crab! The bloody crab! No! *No!* It can't have! It can't have escaped *again!* It's not possible! No! It's just not possible! She reaches across and shakes the box, it rattles. The crab surfaces languorously.

It's okay! says Ewan. I see it! It's there, it's there.

It is?

Yes.

Oh, thank God. I lost it this morning, you know. It escaped, somehow. I think Warren found it with his lip. I don't think I chose you an alter ego with a very good temperament. Look: crab wounds, and she presents her bandaided hand.

Ewan laughs softly through his nose. Well, thanks very much. I appreciate it. I always wanted a smaller version of myself. He taps the box. So what's this paper? Is it a name tag or something?

Ah, well. I'm glad you ask, Mr Hermit. This is where I get really clever.

I see.

Yes. Now, what you have to do is take Little Ewan the Distempered Crustacean *out of his enclosure* to find out.

You've planned this out very carefully, haven't you.

She laughs. Ewan strips back a thick layer of masking tape and lifts the lid. Smiling, he gingerly pinches the tip of the mottled shell. A small attached envelope rises with it, a phone number scribbled on one side. Hers. The disturbed crab emerges again, begins to unfurl. It regards Ewan with a beady, evil stare, then curls back inside.

I think it likes me.

You see! It recognises a brother.

Ewan removes the two thick cards from the envelope with shaking fingers. Returns the crab. His spine tingles.

These are tickets, he announces softly, slowly. To the Concert Hall.

I know, she says. I bought them. It's a soloist. Chellow. Some Russian up-and-comer that I can't remember the name of. Good seats, too. See how clever I am, Mr Hermit?

Ewan's necknape bristles, he feels a flush of warmth to his cheeks. He stares at them. Feels their paperness, smooth.

God, Eleanor. I didn't expect this. At all. Thankyou very much. Really, I mean it.

So who are you going to take? she interjects, chuffed.

He pauses. Well, I'd have to take the crab, wouldn't I?

I think there's a policy against crabs at concert halls.

Oh, really? Well, you know, there's always Beryl over the back fence. She's been dropping me hints for years.

Ah yes, Beryl. Sounds like she's an experienced woman.

Absolutely. All the boys at Bingo tell me she's easy.

The slut.

They share a laugh. Both a little giddy.

Meanwhile, the hermit crab has sensed a diversion. He has spied an unlidded ether and has decided to go for it. Frantic, he shunts his feed bowl to the corner, casting a chary eye. He grits his mandibles and wears wide grooves of escape into the sand.

Thanks for this, Eleanor. Really.

You're welcome, as long as you take me.

What about Beryl?

Take Beryl and I'll kill you, she says, and lifts her coffee. Feel like that turkey yet?

Sure. But first, Ewan says, as he rises and moves to the fridge, still clutching the two tickets. The cracked seals give easily. And he takes out three blocks of dark chocolate. It's a bit of an anticlimax now, but here: Merry Christmas. He slides the blocks in front of her.

What's this?

A Christmas present. Hope you don't mind.

A present! Really? For me?

Yep.

She smiles, lifts a block and thumbs its square ridges. Chocolate?

Dark chocolate.

Ha! *Now* who's the clever one? She grins. Thankyou, Chellowboy, this is very sweet, you know. Ta very muchly.

Guess we'll find out if it works, eh?

That we will, for the war rages on, so to speak. She shakes her head, smiling. Dark chocolate. You're a funny man, Chellowboy.

They share a short silence.

Got that turkey yet?

It's coming, it's coming. Ewan squats into a rush of heat with floral oven-mitts. Removes the glass dish. Inspects it.

Actually, says Eleanor, I might just have the chocolate. Bugger the turkey.

I think someone's beaten you to that.

Well, I have had my hand up its arse. Close enough?

That's an appetising thought, Eleanor.

Well, it felt wonderful.

Bet you say that to all the turkeys.

She laughs. You know, Ewan, I had no idea you had this kind of propensity to talk shit. You're outcrapping me. I can't believe it.

Neither can I. There's even a leg missing, Ewan goes on. You've bought an amputee.

She laughs.

Warren sits patiently as Ewan hacks roughly at the breast, slicing slabs of whitemeat.

So how much did you want? he asks.

Oh as it comes. Do your worst.

Okay. Did you want some bread? I have bread, I think.

No, no that's fine. Thank you.

Gravy?

Of course.

Ewan lifts the plates. Okay, I think we're set. Did you want some wine or something?

No, thanks. I don't drink.

Fair enough. Ewan refills their water and sits.

Oh, wait! says Eleanor. We have to do the cracker! We can't forget the cracker. It should be in the bottom of the esky.

Ewan fishes it out and they share an end. It's a little moist with condensation.

Okay, ready?

Ready.

It snaps and cracks with a blue wisp of smoke. Eleanor wins. She pulls out the green paper hat, the novelty toy and the bad joke.

Okay, I'll wear this so one of us can see it, she says. And you can have this plastic thing and the crappy joke. She hands them over the table.

It's a tiny grenade full of sherbet, Ewan says.

Oh really? Warren loves sherbet. Give it to him to chew on and he'll love you forever. How about the joke?

Warren chews the toy. Ewan clears his throat. Okay: *What do you call a donkey with three legs?*

What?

Ewan pauses: *Wonky*. And to his complete surprise, she bursts into laughter. Makes him smile.

Oh, that's bad. She lifts her glass, still chuckling. Okay, Ewan, I think a toast would probably work best if I hold my glass still and you do the clinky bit. How does that sound?

All right, here we go.

They toast, and say Happy Birthday Jesus, smiling.

Thanks again for this.

Aint no problem, sir, she says. An ah thaynk you agin fur havin me in yur fahn home.

Warren snuffles the table edge, his snout laced with sherbet. He whines, seeing the bird elude him.

Shoosh, Warren. You'll get some later.

Warren moves to the corner and slumps sloppily. Herrumphs.

Ewan is pressing butter on to a slice of bread when he stops, suddenly fascinated. And he watches as Eleanor acquaints herself with her plate. Sorting out what is what. And where. And how much. He watches her gauging the contours and consistency by using her knife. She starts from the top and works clockwise, greeting her meal with pokes and prods and small tastes.

He stares, amazed. It wrings his chest. Almost hurts to see. It makes him restless. Fills him with impulse. He doesn't know what to feel.

I can't eat all of this! she announces. Did you actually put any on your plate?

More than yours, he says, voice hoarse. He watches her awhile longer.

It's not tender is it, she laughs, chewing.

It'd be a long time before it melted in my mouth, but you've done well.

You think?

For sure. Nice spices.

True. I get all my dry spices from a stall in the markets. It's really good.

The markets?

Yep. Get my coffee there, too.

But it's packed shoulder to shoulder in there isn't it?

So?

Ewan shakes his head, chewing.

It's amazing how you get around, you know. The way you do it, how easily you can navigate. I don't know. It's like you're taking your dog for a walk or something. It's incredible.

Well, Eleanor frowns and swallows heavily. She pushes the crepe paper hat higher on her head, ponders her words. It's not really. It's not hard to get around. And it's not like I climb up poles to braille streetsigns. I've lived here all my life, so I know the streets, like, *really* know them. I know how they network. And I know where things are. You don't need eyes to physically complete the task of walking. Just like you don't need ears. Or a tongue. It's just trust, she says, a little softer. Just trust. In your instinct and your judgement and your surroundings. And Warren, of course.

She takes a sip of water. Her dog's ears lazily respond to his name.

And I trust my dog totally; unless I'm bathing him. It's not all as restrictive as the world thinks, Ewan; not if you don't let it.

She saws at turkey, knuckles white and chest tight. They sit in contemplative silence, cutlery scraping. And she thinks: but that doesn't mean I'm doing any better than you, Mr Hermit. Doesn't mean I'm not immured, like you, like that crab. Just a bigger vicinity. A bigger enclosure. And the thought unsettles her.

Not restrictive. Not if you don't let it. More bullshit, more balm. Thick. It's a carapace she wears, like armour: a stubborn, enduring veneer. An impervious coverup she takes wherever she goes.

Not unlike a cosmetic facade, that saves face and conceals bruising.

But she is *not* her mother.

A small splash.

A kerplink.

Because after raising a defiant nipper, Little Ewan again reached the lip of its box and poised; turned to salute the Homestead, then back again to leap for Freedom. It curled, somersaulted twice, then plummeted into Ewan's glass of water.

It sinks dismally and rests inert at the bottom. Tiny bubblets rise. The attached envelope, a lowperformance parachute, hangs over the side. The crab seethes, looking like a dubious teabag.

Shit! Ewan exclaims, his murky thoughts disturbed.

What? What? Eleanor jolts to attention, also surfacing. What happened?

You won't believe it. The crab just dived into my glass of water!

They laugh.

See, I told you. Can't be trusted.

Ewan lifts out the crab and drops it back. Secures the lid, pressing the tape flat. He empties his glass. The wet crustacean retires to its rock cave, fuming, to brood and plot.

There is the heavy, laboured sound of Warren breathing deeply. Snoozing. He dreams of galloping through a vast verdant meadow, laden with daffodils and prancing roasted turkeys. His backlegs jerk ecstatic and he smiles.

They both prod at cold meals. Neither of them hungry.

I'm done, Eleanor surrenders her cutlery.

Same. I think the turkey won.

Sorry it was a bit chewy. I think I should have marinated it for a few months. Or deep-fried a budgie.

I think you did well. In any case, I blame the turkey, not your culinary skills, says Ewan, rising to clear the table. Warren scrabbles to his feet, sensing the movement of turkey scraps. He is led to the table by a twitching snout.

Need a hand? Eleanor asks.

No, no. I'll be right. Do you want me to give these to your dog?

The leftovers?

Yeah.

Is he giving you a choice?

Not really. I think he might eat me.

Just give him whatever is left.

The carcass too? There's still a heap of leather left on it.

She smiles. Yeah, why not. It's Christmas, let him gorge.

Surely he can't eat it all. Surely this is too much, for any animal.

Surely not, Yoowen, Eleanor proclaims. For this is no ordinary beast.

Warren is dribbling. He whines and squeaks with his neck craned. Eleanor laughs.

Shuttup Warren! You're embarrassing yourself. I bet you he's dribbling. Is he dribbling?

Yes, he is dribbling.

Warren is focused on the traversing feast as he trots outside. Ewan lays the scraps down on the lawn.

He almost devoured my hand, he says, slapping the flywire behind him. He watches the dog in silence, drumming his fingers on the sink.

Eleanor sits at the table, fidgeting. Wears a fond, distant halfsmile and a vacant stare.

Above, two possums breathe evenly together in a postmeal nap.

Lilian rests on her side, quiet, with her back towards an open door.

The Air is settling still. Loitering. If it had thumbs it would twiddle them. A lull gathers and lingers and sighs.

Eleanor wards it away with a rushed, intended question.

So, what's for dessert then?

Dessert? Are you serious?

Of course. It's Christmas, that's the rule. You have to stuff yourself stupid on rich elaborate desserts. Everything else is the entree.

Dessert could be a long, long, long way away from me.

Oh, come on. There must be room for something.

You've got dark chocolate.

Yeah, but that's not elaborate. I'm thinking elaborate.

I don't have much in the way of elaborate. However, I do enjoy a smoke and a coffee after a meal.

Well that's crap, says Eleanor. Then she triggers a sudden index finger. Points and waggles it in the direction to which he should be standing. Ewan, I have just had a perfect idea for dessert.

So they're making muffins. Side by side. And Eleanor is standing sifting the flour that Ewan has measured, trying to recall a recipe. To her left is a half-block of broken dark chocolate.

Ewan has a pair of scissors. Over a chopping board, he is finely mulling a stumpy, resinous bud that he has had drying (among others) on a turnbuckled taut line. He sorts the seeds, keeps them for later.

Chocolate Space Muffins. Her chocolate, his weed. The air sponges the smell of their ingredients.

You realise we're preparing to bake the world's most effective method of menstrual relief, Ewan says.

I disagree.

How so? Ewan asks, piling up the rough flakes on the chopping board. They crumb his fingers.

Well, personally, the most effective method of menstrual relief would be to, say, remove all the eggs from our baskets, so to speak, and hand them generously to you people; then subsequently subject you to some cruel, painful cyclical process that goes for days. That, for me, would be far more satisfying.

I think everyone would be happier with these muffins.

Just as long as you're aware there is a better alternative.

I have a feeling you're going to keep mentioning it.

Eleanor smiles and briskly whisks. Yoghurt! she announces, cracking another egg. Yoghurt is the secret essential ingredient to every good muffin. We need yoghurt. Do we have yoghurt?

Yoghurt? I have yoghurt. Yoghurt I have.

Goodgoodgood. We'll need about, say, half a cup?

Ewan moves to the fridge. Meanwhile, the crab is initiating another breakout atop its spongeball. It heaves and levers at the lid, a clean and jerk motion. A strip of tape gives.

Eleanor is folding the mix with a wooden spoon, making wet slapping sounds. Ewan drops in the chocolate.

Nuffin like a muffin, she says.

You can't get these at the markets. Ewan sprinkles in his secret herbs and spices.

I'm not going to totally lose my marbles am I? I have to get home today, you know.

Tell you the truth, Spud Girl, we're both breaking new ground. I've never had this kind of muffin before.

They really aren't going to make me crazy, are they?

What do you call crazy?

Oh, I don't know, Eleanor smirks. You know, I might declare myself a virgin on your doorstep and then make you take me to dinner. She laughs suddenly. Yeah, that's how I lure all my victims. And *then* I bring out the Shetland and the dildo.

They laugh, together. And their laughs feed each other, swelling. Ewan watches her nostrils flare, her teeth, her tongue buck. He feels lightheaded and replete. Feels good. Feels safe. And with his home as a ballast, without the threat of being seen; she's almost easy to be with.

Warren, hearing the outburst, surrenders his gorging to paw the door open.

Their laugh weakens to a sigh. Eleanor takes the offered tray and spoons dollops of muffinmix. She finds his oven, slides them in. Ewan keeps his smile. Can scarcely believe this day. He thinks of a brownvested busker, knows what to do now.

Stay here, he says, and does not hesitate. I have something else for you.

There is something urgent in his voice that stifles her response. She frowns and sits.

Ewan steps heavily down the hall. Feels nerves swoop, flushing and curdling his belly.

First room on the left, the door is open. Stiffly, he bends, clasps a hip and a neck. She does not protest. Ewan takes the bow, turns.

He's in the kitchen and shaking now. He tugs a chair back with a hooked foot, concentrates on breathing. Watching her. Listen, he says.

He plucks lightly, tuning. Hears her inhale with recognition. He winds a stubborn bownut. He sweats. The hot air is patient.

Horsehair presses gutstring to make sound for someone else. This is what he has practised these last few days, what he has really intended to give her. His chest belts against the cello.

Fingers on the fingerboard. Holding. His eyes are shut, no one can see in this kitchen.

The first note, an open string, is a little soft, a little unsure. He sways into the next. A little flat, but he smothers it with vibrato. (If the note is out, embellish it quickly with lovely bullshit, Jim used to say.)

Eleanor traps air in her lungs. She knows the tune. He sweeps from the opening chords and into the vocal line. The cello stirs her. She listens and absorbs. It's a rich, Ed Vedder baritone; a beautiful earthen growl. And so close. So close. He slips into a higher register.

E says Son, canya play meeya

Memory. She can almost hear the lyrics pronounced. It's sad and it's sweet and it's thick and flowing. Heavy and heady and sonorous in the sharp acoustics of this kitchen. The melody bends, dances, touches her skin and bursts. A tangible, sentient thing. Touching. And it travels differently from what she's heard previously. It resonates stronger, directed and honest. He hits the chorus and the moment is beautiful. The room roars with the crescendo. It's an edifice of air, and it threatens to fill her up. It gushes in spires. And if she's not careful, Eleanor, she's going to lose it. It'll flense her, this sound, this music. Expose her, spilling, spilling. Because it's working its way inside now. And nothing can get inside, for she shepherds out the world. With a tough stubborn veneer. Brittle now. It's picking, pecking at her. And her eyes, her eyes, they're going to betray her again if she's not careful. Her breaths are short. She's swallowing, jaw clamped shut, throat burning raw. Lump of heat. Livid with music.

It does not remit. Hot hot panic.

Ewan slips fluid down the highest string, a stirring soprano. He's wide open now, and she's

Leaving. With slippers rubyred. Running before she breaks. The timber crash of a chair, face taut and hot, and she's gripping a harness, belting down the hall, straight into the front door. It floors her, Warren barks. Her mouth is ugly and downturned. She swallows and it stings her throat. She wrenches the door open.

Estelleanor. Who leaves silently now, and leaves silence. With no breeze. Just heat.

Heaves. Notquite running. Brisk, bent, like her sack has gathered weight. Right now when she could be losing it. She is watched by a bashful gnome, a leaning sunflower and a silent figure at the end of the hallway. She hurries, through the gate, down the street. Her crepe paper crown featherfalls to the ground. And something rises in her chest, but she stops to quell it. To keep it down, keep *it in*, numb it. And at that exact moment, her period stops. She presses a hand to her belly like she's covering a wound, walling in her tripe. And if you look closely you'll see her lips utter like an extra in a midday movie. Over and over and over and she wonders how, how, how to ever let go, how to ever be out of burden.

And she halts her mind; there she conjures a map, an arrow, a place, anything else to cover this space, this screen, to smother these thoughts.

In the kitchen the crab scrabbles and topples backwards. It embeds its shell into the loose sand. It wriggles, stuck. It shakes its nippers, furious and vulnerable.

At the open entrance of a shed, a perusing possum is tearing open a white plastic bag and chewing the moist green leaves inside.

In the slowly dispersing air, a tall man gets smaller, watching her leave. Deflating. And it just reaffirms everything he had almost forgotten, and everything he ever lost.

He grips his cello to stop the shaking.

ASHEN

and the light came in and they came out, were made to amid
screams, they saw her and she saw them and her held ashen
body writhed alive, tried to rise, *gotoyourroomsgotoyourrooms!*
then lying wailing stiff jerk, jerk, jerk, fleshstabbingflesh there
was blood and they watched it   run

RHUBARB

Back here:

Dim dark room. The door is slammed shut then locked and a small girl sits and pants. Long hair. Pink pyjamas. Cold sweat, she's been running and she's come back here and there's no one left. Cheeks smudged and wan, the smear of tears. Throat scoured raw, the taste of snot and acid. Head thumps incoherent.

Behind her, Mickey Mouse exclaims mutely, pointing at his right foot, like he's lost it and found it again.

Small girl sits in front of a mirror, queasy and tense, Despair in this room. And behind her, there's a sheet of paper on her bed that she will never see, left by her sister, who has just runaway with provisions (clothes, cash, creditcards) to the only place she was ever going to go. The paper tells her where she is and what to bring. But it's too late.

Luminous lamp. The small girl switches it on, off, on, off, on, off, on and stares through stares at glazed redrubbed eyes. Reflected. She watches her pupils constrict. Recoil. Bigtosmall. Offandon. Bigtosmall. Darktolight.

Dark. Big.

Light. Small.

If she closes her eyes while the light is On the colour is Red.

Cold, so cold she feels.

For warmth she thinks of haircurtains and artifice and suddenspilled pools of ink and Temples.

There is no volition in this room just inertia just terror. This is a panic panacea, a wayout anywayout, anything, a cover, a cloak to make it stop so it can never, *ever* happen again. This is the dark at the end of the tunnel, crawl in and hide here there is refuge and survival. You can do anything with your mind, do anything with a bodyfull of fear, a bodyfull of hate. There is trauma in this room. You can see it in her eyes.

On. Off. On. Light. Small. Dark. Big.

Off. She's not afraid of the dark. She closes her eyes now. Nothing left to lose. Small girl does not breathe, though she shakes shudders shivers with this undertaking. With fear. She has to make it stop.

She says it. Fear says it. Terror says it. Panic says it:

rhubarb.

First a whisper. Then louder, a sob,

rhubarb.

Rhubarb.

Rhubarb.

It builds it whorls it gathers in this room. Listen, please listen: it's louder and louder and frantic now, with the courage found in clenching, just clenching shut her eyes and screaming it. Its momentum is dangerous and powerful and the force of it is bending her, doubling her over, stalling her chest. Spittle on the mirror, shrieking loudloudloud. Nowhere else to go. Burning hot. It can't happen again, makeitstop, make her not see because you know you know what happened don't you pleaselisten you know he opened that door youknowwhathemadethemwatch. Rhubarb.

Rhubarb.

Rhubarb.

Rhubarb.

A Part of her is leaving.

Rhubarb.

Rhu

Barb.

The light pours out.

Off.

Nothing left. A child's room falls silent. Hard to breathe this thick air dense with dread, because it's gone, like magic. And there are only silence and loss and darkness in its place. She opens clenched eyelids and fumbles the lamp switch On and blinks.

Nothing.

It is three forty-five. Lightyears from midnight. And this is where it all stopped. This is how her sight was cauterized by terror. How it was smothered and stolen and laved in black. And it can't be undone, because she has kept her fear.

Dark Ness. The place where she went. And she didn't travel far.

Dark Ness: an empty, gutted place. Dark Ness was fear sliding a lid over the hole she dug herself. It offered no light.

And now, here, in Dark Ness, a suddenly blind girl panics, quivers horribly afraid. She can hear her breathing. She retches empty, nothing left to purge. She sobs, scared, so scared here and rubs and scratches at her eyes.

A bodyfull of fear. A bodyfull of hate. A bodyfull of hurt. With a lid. And no one left to help her out. How brittle she is, how small.

Nothing in. Nothing out.

A child has lost her sight, but kept the weight.

And so there is still despair in this room. More frantic, more frenzied now. With trauma, with weakness, with what she has done. And she can't run because she can't see. And she turns she turns she turns but there's nowhere to put it down. All this weight. All this weight that she has no right to have.

But a suddenly blind girl has tonight discovered the ability to conceal. To cover and contain. And right here, at three forty-five, she is doing it again. Already. Iterating that magic word, like it holds relief, and she's packing it; all this pain, this hurt, this Memory, shame, fear, hate into a sack that fits them all.

Like she's leaving somehow. Like she's going somewhere.

She draws a drawstring tight.

A Big Secret. A Big Responsibility. A sad sack on her back. That will go where she goes. Towed. And she'll shoulder the load, behind her like a shadow; always, always with her.

Oh, but you didn't know.

You didn't know that you couldn't always keep it at bay. Couldn't always keep it behind you, with the drawstring drawn and the cargo hidden. Didn't know that Everything packed would unpack. And so easily, in Sleep's own inertia. Where a heavy sack would be left unguarded and a child's hoarded images would be left uncovered. You didn't know that Sleep would hold you down, pinion you rigid. And as you slid away sinking, in the wake of heavy breathing, you didn't know that your sack would open up like a wound and spill noise and carve it all into your mind, to make you watch again and again and again.

You didn't know that sleep would be Memory's egress. The place where dreams are bred and shaped and played and replayed; where Everything buried would surface. You didn't know that the weight you carried by day would bloom mutinous as you slept. So vivid. And it just made Everything harder to let go.

So it was Dread that installed your vigil, gagged your vinyl lullabies. And a windup gramophone grew a pelt of dust.

And the tragedy was that outside of here it was never *ever* going to happen again. Because he left that night and never returned. Escaped. Like everyone else except you. Stuck, stuck, stuck. In Dark Ness alone.

You didn't travel far, because you retreated and took Everything with you. Like your mother. And you were anchored, embedded in it. In Time, in space, inside.

You went nowhere, Eleanor. Spent your sight, and all for Nothing. Left here with dead eyes and hindsight, for you could never blind your mind's eye.

Though you would daydream of wringing out your cortex, juicing it. Deleting Memory. The good and the bad. Sweetly effaced, leaving a blessed Blank Ness. A wiped empty headspace the colour of white. But you know: Clean Slates just don't happen.

So you wrestled with fault and regret and shame. You would stagger on, holding yourself culpable, knowing you did this to yourself. And it thieved your hope. Made it harder to get by, to get through days, to see them out and survive.

And to stave away this guilt, Eleanor Rigby did it again. Armed with scissors, schnickety shnick, sobbing helpless in a bathroom, with thick stickiness between her legs. She invented a stern resistance. Decided she was made of mettle and coated in teflon. And it became a costume she clung to and wore everywhere. A sticky stubborn veneer, a coverup. A rind to ward off the world and inure herself to it. Nothing in. Nothing Out. Taking no shit, feeling no pain. Keeping her Distance. She didn't prune her neurons, just choked them. And eluded their electricity. She fooled herself by adopting a strength that was never really there. A ruse. A lie she almost believed. With all that anger, regret, shame buriedhidden by specious posturing and precious bullshit. Layerunderlayerunderlayer. Like panicked weight in a sad sack. Like fearcovered eyes. A cloak.

And she survived. She got by. And that Distance kept her separate and sequestered. Alone and Apart.

And that was her tradeoff.

The Distance was never so broad as between you and your sister; your ally; your bestfriend. Your Close Ness was severed the night she stole Running. The feel of paper and betrayal. But she waited, Eleanor. Do you understand? She waited for you that night until dawn. She was at the seawall, by Bathers Beach, where the both of you fished and swam sometimes. She waited and waited and you didn't come. She couldn't, just couldn't go back, do you understand? So she left. Without you. She had to. With no turning, no waving, no goodbyeing.

Just another Part of you missing.

And every year she sends a letter for your birthday whose postmark you cannot read. You never open them, and hide them before it hurts too much.

You started to fish from the mole (on the rock that used to fit the both of you) because holding the water was like holding her for a time, if only by a thread. And so it was always here you rushed; harried and piss-stinking after every forcefed dream of back there. You held her and let the weight that lurked beneath a calm clear skin soothe you, fill you, settle you. She was never absent. A constant and precious thing. And sometimes, just holding this line in the snug ergonomics of your rock, you might get some vacant, protected sleep. With a soft dog for a pillow.

It became your prayer. Your Faith: a small thing throwing out a line to something Big, for calm and for comfort.

You cradled that line, flung from a beggar's hand and kept it there; holding, with the illusion of being held. And it was enough for you, enough to keep going, to get by. She was here, you felt it, you were sure of it. It was her. Big. She had moods, she behaved. Sometimes she thrashed underneath. Tore, surged, snapped your line, pulled at you. She was sometimes still and tender. Or playful. Always, always changing.

Sometimes, on clear nights, she might beckon you in. To join her, to swim with her, float awhile together. Dive and glide under, with the safesound of her bellyrumble. She promised to hold you up, to give you bearings with her tide. She summoned you, with ribs of water peeling out and away. And your back was goaded with the soft urge of an easterly; The Shit Behind You.

And you fisted the line and shook your head. Because you couldn't, because you knew.

That it was too Big, the water. That you could never control it. You didn't *know* it and so it demanded your trust. And you couldn't, you just couldn't. There was no Distance in water, no separation. It touched you allover. And there was no hiding in its transparence. And all this weight, this brimfilled sack of it that you couldn't ever put down, it would sink you, wouldn't it? Like loaded catchbags, like an anchor. It would drown you, wouldn't it? As you clutched them and clutched them and clutched them descending.

Because you couldn't let them go.

And that's what swimming was, wasn't it? Weightless Ness: a new place. An absence of gravity. An open space outside your vicinity.

And she wills to jump, Eleanor Rigby. She aches with the desire. But Fear holds her back and keeps her here. And she can't. Can't shirk the slim comfort of her boundary, this place she *knows*.

So she'll shake her head. *I'm sorry*, she'll whisper. Then bundle in her line, ashamed. And she'll go back the way she came, through streets she knows, walking in the safety of her cerebral map. Rushed and burdenbent. So she can keep Getting By: that slow, careful, diurnal task. Where she starts where she left off and ends up where she started. Each day with the same trajectory. Of getting around. And around. And around. Moving, moving, moving, and going nowhere.

Here: it's Christmas Day. It's three forty-five.

A blind girl sits and pants. Stares in the direction of a mirror she can't see. After all this time, that hasn't passed.

And look, Eleanor, look: you've done it again. It's History repeating; the stuff your dreams are made of. You've runaway, for Distance. Before that, music could seep in and open you, gut you, uncover you. Before it had you held and spilling. And so you turned for a wayout, anywayout; for safety, sanctuary, somewhere.

And so you ended up here somehow, back where you started. And so lost nothing and kept Everything. Your bones are aching with the strain of weight and hot hot fatigue. You feel empty. And you know, you *know*, that there could have been solace in it. In tearing back fabric, showing old scars and scabs and festered blisters. In paring back skin and offering rawness. And she was so fucking *close*, but she missed it again. Knows that sound could have been carving space in the air for her *own* weight, her own truth.

But isn't that what drove her there? Because she knew that sound, recognised it on an onshore breeze. Because she could hear herself, see herself in its curves and hues and pulses. The tacit, subdued hurt in it. It was the closest she had come to a reflection in years, to illumination. Isn't that what drew her there? Impelling a rare caprice with People, so that she risked proximity, risked Everything, just to wedge herself into his life, like his myoozick had done to hers. Didn't she feel A Part of it?

Gone now, because she couldn't, she just couldn't. The inertia of Fear swaddled her and took her home, back the way she came.

A blind girl sits and extends a cautious, unsteady hand. And she touches that mirror, cold, with a fingertip. With stunted strokes she is tracing the outline of a face she is trying to imagine. An older face. Of what she might look like now. Someone else. Someone different. A face she couldn't recognise.

But there's only long hair. Sallow cheeks. Glazed, redrubbed eyes.

Her hand drops. Her body sighs and folds. Feels a languid and familiar lassitude. So tired she is. And there's that lambent sound, those notes; stuck, stuck, stuck riffing loud in her head. They cradle her malaise like a lullaby.

Vague and vapid and dizzy, she feels. Falls heavily to bed. Lies uncovered and sinks deep.

LOSING IT

Christmas night. Ewan is sprawled and uncovered, his legs jackknifed. He breathes heavily, sniffs, swallows. Paws unconsciously at his stubbled chin and blurts a messy stream of gibberish before slipping away.

And is sitting. On an enormous orange shell. It is hollow, with the sound of the ocean in it. He has a cello, though he has no bow. And the instrument stretches, leans back into him as though yawning. Moulding itself to his curves. It has a strange bodyshape. Thin of shoulder, thin of hip. And a strange pale colour.

He gropes, strains to hold it, to wrap it in his arms, but he can't. And it's right here, within reach, but he can't touch it, can't feel it. It's like trying to hold smoke. A ghost. Like it's not real, not really there. And so he ends up clasping his shoulders as the cello dissolves, making no sound. He is naked. And suddenly cold. The shell shrinks, and he runs. And runs. And runs. Chased by the sound of the ocean, which melds into the urgent beleaguering noise of Peoplepeoplepeople. He runs through dim roofless corridors. There are stars. His legs are full of syrup. Burning. And he is on a beach now, stumbling along the shoreline. He falls to his knees, buries them in wet sand. And there is a silverstreaked herring lying huge and stuck before him. Bucking and kicking and flapping. Its gills gasp. They are both heaving the same rhythm. Its eye is glassy and blue and still.

He touches it, feels it. Soft and warm. Real; like flesh, like skin. Its gillslits pulse faster with despair. It writhes and wrests. It needs him: needs to be saved.

He holds a sudden knife, to gut the fish, but it disappears as a tide spills and climbs and licks him. The fish is clawed at by backwash. It begins to slide, to leave him. He clutches its tail, holds it, drags it back because he knows he needs it, to be saved. It is heavy.

He shakes his head softly. Let me, he says to the fish, let *me*.

And he breathes in salty air and bends to resuscitate it, mouth to mouth. But he is interrupted.

Above him in the starladen nightsky, a onelegged turkey flaps past, bellyup, like it's sculling on its back. Or rowing a boat. It is steaming. And it laughs (*Hee!Hee!Hee!*) a highpitched giggle that echoes loud. And in a booming voice; a voice from Back There, a silly pompous celloteacher's voice, it exclaims headlessly:

Hey, Fishlips! Gobblegobblegobblegobblegobble!

And it glides away with butterfly wings, laughing, laughing.

Ewan screams mute, watching it depart. Still naked he pleads, begs, bends. Then, frowning, he raises his right forearm. With his left hand he holds it in First Position, pressing hardhardhard and feeling his lips tingle. He digs with a four-finger vibrato until he opens up and blood spills, dripping off his elbow on to the convulsing fish.

Hee Hee! Look! yells the bird from a distance, A Red Herring! A Red Herring! The giggling turkey eclipses the moon and then explodes in a burst of fireworks that ratta-tat-tat in glittering sparks. A champagne cascade.

Ewan drops to his knees. Makes no sound. He draws breath, bows his head, bends. But there is no fish.

It's her.

Jerking as she weeps. A strange pale colour. She hugs her chest and holds her shoulders. She is naked. Thin of shoulder, thin of hip. And there is blood on her belly. *His.* And there is blood on her thighs. Rich and gleaming and enamelled. *Hers.*

She dips a finger near her navel and touches his blood. She tastes it. Swallows, and calms. Ewan's blood clots and stops flowing. He caps a finger red on his elbow and holds it to her ear. The finger resonates like a tuning fork and makes sound. A note, an E, rings out. They both hear it. They both shiver and share it.

Blood gouts silently between her legs. She winces, clamps them tight. Afraid, she gasps, blue eyes wide. Ewan reaches, to touch her blood, to feel it, to cup it, to hold it, to taste it. But she senses. She knows somehow. She snatches his hand and holds it and bares her breast. It looks soft and warm. She shakes her head. I'm sorry, she says softly. She bites her lip.

Ewan frowns. In his fist, the one she still holds, is a gnarled potato. Hot and hard.

Slowly, using the sudden taut cellobow that has just appeared in his free hand, he begins to peel its skin. A thin coil that drapes on to his lap in jerks. The peeled potato glows. He offers it to her, throbbing light, and that same note rings out. He places it in her hand.

Here, he says. Let me.

And he draws breath. Bows and bends. And he blows oxygen into her eyes while she breathes staccato whispers into his ear.

And that's when he comes. Not with her, but above and alone.

Ewan groggily surfaces to a molten spread. He feels its warmth distantly. He snorts and sighs and sleeps on, leaving his dream behind.

***

Early on Boxing Day, with thin ruffled sheets cast to one side, Her side, Frank wakes to be greeted by a searing backache, a gutache, a headache, stinging knees and a nodding, bobbing erection.

It pokes stupidly over his domed belly, like a blushing man peering over a sand dune.

Frank flinches, startled. It almost scares him. He almost didn't recognise it. He stares blearily, blinks and stares harder. It beams back proudly. Enthusiastic, like it's excited to see him, glad he's finally awake. Frank sucks in his ivory sand dune for a better view. Jesus *Christ!* It's all there. He prods his resurrected dick. Confused and disbelieving, he nurses it carefully between his fingers like a cigar. He grips it and shivers. Squeezes it, bends it. Feels sudden volts of tingly hotness. It doesn't snap. Or break. Or deflate.

A gruff groan escapes him.

Still holding it, he closes his eyes in this bed with a pleasure he recalls. And it's no surprise She's there.

Younger.

Luminous.

Alive.

Not the gaunt, sallow, fading yellow flesh that left him bit by bit, gram by gram. Not her. He sees her the way she was, outside visiting hours and colostomy bags. The way she used to be, the way he wants her still. Needs her; in this bed, on these sheets. He imagines her for a time. And he keeps her there. Her features embellished a little with absence. Her shape, her colour, her movements.

Frank tightens and starts up cautiously. A slow, steady rhythm. He keeps his eyes shut, holding, holding her there. He sips air through his teeth. Cloaked in a thick spread of sparking nerves. His legs shudder, his toes curl.

She's here. And she's clear and distinct with longing and remembering. His free hand lifts and cups the sad air, but it's her soft warm bum in his mind. And it's almost like it's not his hand, almost like he's inside her now and not making dry desperate love to a memory. And he can almost imagine her holding him back. Clinging, like he is now.

His eyes clench. Hard wrinkles spread across his face. His raw throat croaks softly. The bed creaks onesided, keeping Time with the looseskin yikkayikkayikka of his dick. His teeth grit and his belly wobbles.

A surge builds in him, gathering momentum. He fends it off. His bum vices (tight enough to paste walnuts) and his breathing stalls.

The image of her is so strong now, so intense, he can even hear her. He could break here, explode. Behind his eyes, in his head, it's loudloudloud with his weightless wife riding him writhing moaning. Harder and faster. She locks up. Gasps. Grips him. And he locks up. Gasps. Grips himself.

And that's when he comes. Above and alone.

He cries out. And a shocking choking retching spasm seizes him, pins him while his dick bucks, sighing stale spurts of disappointed air, of nothing. Emptying itself of emptiness.

And there's silence.

He is still.

He breathes. Opens his eyes.

His urethra blinks back indifference. Frank lets go, and his brief resurrection retires without grace. Shrivels and slides back down that heaving, hairy slope.

The rest of his muscles remain taut. Frank has sloughed no tension. He came, but went nowhere. Feels no heady calm, no afterglow. He glances at Her side, and the bed is as empty as he feels.

He shuts his eyes, suddenly relieved she is not there. So she doesn't have to see him. See what he is. A sad, pitiful old bastard. A hollow, hollow vessel. He feels low. Dirty. And is swept gutfirst by hot shame. By grief. By guilt. Such a cheap disrespect of her memory. Wanking on it. Feels like betrayal.

He rolls into her recessed rut. The mattress yields and he buries his burning red face into her pillow. Trembling and humiliated, he shakes his head and whispers his apology.

And then it's just the loss of her he feels. Just conceding it, finally, that terrible absence. Because, he knows, that no matter how slow, how certain it is in coming, you can't be prepared for bereavement. And he knows now that it's just him here, just him. And that means she's gone. And it burns, the knowing, it hurts. But mourning this empty space hurts less than pretending she is still in it.

At his emptiest, his lowest, Frank dozes. Exhausted. His head on her pillow.

He wakes sweating in the late morning. His mouth is dry. And he rises with a strange lightheaded composure. He stretches.

Nude and wobbly, he pads to the bathroom. Pisses. Showers using soap. Finds a clean towel. Smears the rash of steam from the bathroom mirror. Lathers. Shaves. Combs his hair.

Frank endured the laundry yesterday to pass the time. He rummages through a basketful of clothes smelling of sunlight and Omo. Dresses well, slips into his pair of Going Out Thongs. Strides his Invisible Wheelbarrow down the hall. His gut gurgles.

In the kitchen, Frank flicks the kettle switch and shovels coffee into a mug. Fishes through a cupboard and emerges wielding a deep skillet. Sets it on the hotplate. He watches a liberal wad of butter sizzle. Lays bacon, mushrooms, tomato and a bubbling puddle of baked beans. Fat spits and saliva pools in his mouth. He cracks two eggs, toasts bread, pours water into his coffee.

Frank clears the coffee table with a brisk swipe and lays his stacked plate. Sitting, he points the remote control carefully, as though it could detonate his television. He squashes the buttons hard and settles in to watch the second session of the Boxing Day Test.

He regards his fry-up. Briefly considers his impending constipation. But today, right now, he just couldn't stomach that same mushbowl of fibre. The bowel cleansing mix of All Bran, Metamucil and rhubarb. He just can't do it any more.

A dose of rhubarb won't cure a Heart Condition. It's just the exodus of shit for more of the same. It's the diet he has to change.

So this is a Last Meal of sorts (somehow coming *after* the Resurrection). A knife, a fork, and a dozen disciples in white taking drinks in the box before him. This is it for Frank. Because when he gets back he intends to start blundering his way through the kitchen, start eating properly. Like he used to, like he should be.

And there's a lot to nut out, he knows. Like how he's going to get his shit together. And carry on, and on, without her. And *keep* going.

Frank downs the dregs of his coffee. A wicket falls. He leans back a little bloated, closes his eyes. Lingers and sighs.

He brushes crumbs off his knees then switches the telly off for good. And everything gets suddenly real in its silent void. He feels nervy. A little anxious. He rubs his smooth face. Scratches the back of his head.

Frank rises, his weak knees creaking. Lifting his weight and everything in his Invisible Wheelbarrow, the mass of two bodies and too many things. He slaps a flannel hat over his sunburnt tonsure. In his shed, Frank uncovers a rusted trowel and some packets of seeds. He shovels some moist soil from the garden into a real wheelbarrow. Takes some water and moves through the side gate, locking it shut behind him.

Over the road, he stoops to stealthily uproot some flowers from a front garden.

And he carries on. To visit an unkempt grave in the heat and to tend to it. On his knees. Like he should have been all this time. And he'll promise to come back, to maintain its condition. To pray, to talk, to do whatever he needs to do. But he's there to empty his wheelbarrows, visible and invisible, and to straighten his back. To say Goodbye to his wife. To bury her and leave her to rest. Bless her for the time he had, and to let her go.

***

Ewan doesn't wake with an erection.

He rises early; slack and sluggish and a little drained. His groin is crusty. Clumps of wiry hair are glued to his skin. He has strange red marks on his left forearm. One two three four of them, linear.

For breakfast he pulls a dense, cloudy bucket and sips bleakly at black coffee. Both taste bitter.

The morning is fuzzy and slow. He plays badly. The heat picks up where it left off.

Inside, the smell of her has remained. It has diffused into every room. A trapped incense, strong and persistent. He meanders within it, breathes it in, can't help it. And her scent gives her a presence. Like she never left, like she's still here.

But she isn't, and so it only reminds him of her absence. The heat gives it potency, the fan disseminates it. He spends time surveying the other things she bequeathed by leaving. Her vestiges, artifacts, proof she existed. And feels buoyed by the notion that she might return for them soon. Today, maybe. He inspects them closely, as though the objects themselves are interesting. Touches them. The esky. The crepe paper crown he retrieved from the pavement outside. The casserole dish that he's washed and dried. In the same dishrack he sees the plate she used yesterday and recalls the methodical way she introduced herself to her meal. Clockwise. Feels sharp pangs to a tender place.

At the end of his kitchen bench squats his old beige ringdial telephone. Mute and unmoving, its handpiece like a bob cut. And scribbled on an envelope next to it is her telephone number. He looks away, down, to his long bare feet. Sits down at the table, in the thick of the motionless quiet of his house. And it feels incongruous now, the silence. It makes yesterday louder.

He breathes the leftover smell of vanilla of aloe vera of eucalypt of sweat and spices. The charcoal of muffins still in the oven.

He gets up and wanders outside.

Looking across the lawn to the unusually open entrance of his shed, Ewan sees a small duncoloured mound. He walks over and squats. The possum is lying on its side, its dark eyes shut. It is breathing, slowly. He sees the ripped bag and the scatter of leaves and he swears under his breath. Gently he shakes it, prodding its little ribs. It sleeps on. He scans the shed for its mate. It isn't there.

Gingerly he picks it up. Hot. A soft, furry coal. It needs to be saved. He brings it beneath the shade of the back verandah. It is the female. Its tiny head lolls between his fingers, its pink snout chapped and dry. He rests it on a cushion and wonders what to do with it.

From his linen cupboard he takes a pillowslip, then finds some string in the kitchen. Outside, he drenches the fabric under the hose. Pokes a hole in each corner with a piece of wire. In the garden he ties two corners to a loquat tree and the other two to a rosemary bush. A shady possum hammock.

He places the slight marsupial inside. Its weight almost brings it to the ground. He tries to dribble some water into its mouth, then leaves it be.

He finds himself wading languorous through his cramped workshop. His roomful of replicas. The air is hot and inert, suffused with the dense scent of drying buds and the must of timberdust. He potters. Cleans his bench, sorts his tools and his wood and paperwork. Stacks his moulds. Has a brief, halfarsed scrape at the viced scroll. He flushes his airgun. Keeps his hands busy. His mind at bay.

He emerges sweating in the late afternoon. Takes the bags of rhubarb leaves with him, tosses them into the garage. He drinks three jars of water. Checks on the possum: still sleeping.

In the gold evening glow, he overcooks pasta, and sits at the table to look at it. He prods and pushes indolently. A queer queasiness has thieved his appetite. He sips idly at warm wine and observes his eponymous crustacean burrowing furtively in its enclosure.

Hello brother, he says.

The crab's tunnel collapses in the loose sand. Ewan smirks, laughs through his nose. The crab turns its shell on him. Ewan reaches in, lifts it out, and it rattles, because his hand is shaking. He places it carefully on the floor.

Go on then, he enthuses, tapping it. The crab scuttles away.

His meal grows cold. He sits with it in the creeping dark.

Ewan thinks of tickets, two of them. He smells her smell and feels the thickness of silence. And for the first time he can remember, he feels aloneness as the absence of the living.

And like always it's here that your chair grides back and your flat feet pound floorboards one two three four and you're down the hall first room on the left and you're taking her lifting her holding her. Limbless Lilian, and she's all yours. You're tracing her shape with your palm. Fingers on her purfling. Breathing sharp you smear sticky dogsnot and apple from her back on to your father's damp shirt. You're leaning bending and reaching grasping and you're winding a stubborn bownut. With a hand on her shoulder and a hand on her hips you're guiding her and settling her between her your legs. Letting her lean back.

She is a tone out of tune each way, although it's somehow hard to hear. Just like this morning. Strange. You roughly twist ebony pegs and it's close enough, it's close enough, but you need rosin on this bow, can't find it, but you don't give a fuck you just need need need, you can get by without it. And now you're straightening her, aligning, impatient, leaning back, leaning forward, just trying trying trying to slot her into that same wellworn groove, where a recent bruise is yellowing, where she should fit. Where she should fall back like fluid like fabric like flesh like always. She should tessellate, but she doesn't. Doesn't fit, somehow. Feels different, stiff, recalcitrant almost. Presses your flesh with her hardness. Her woodness. Bites and resists. She won't fit, won't fall back, back, back and adjusting the endpiece won't help either.

Limbless Lilian, who can't hold you back. Who now won't be held. It is not a shape you recognise.

But you're punching into Elgar anyway in the dimness of this room. Off by heart. Pulling those first doublestops hard and meaty before settling into the brooding fugue. The plaintive key of E. You suck in air.

But once inside it, you feel no gripping shimmer like always; no flaring up inside that beautiful bittersweet overture. And you grind your way through this first movement and all you feel is slipping, slipping.

The bow is a club. The strings are taut fat cables; thick and heavy and unresponsive. Your fingers are tender and unsure and clumsy and clumsier. You close your eyes, clench them annoyed, and you concentrate. But her sound is distant. Indistinct. It's muffled and farfaraway. You open your eyes, expecting to see a row of four clothespegs set along the bridge, but there are none, and you frown and play harder and louder. You're swaying, bending, whispering to her. Your vibrato a humming blur.

But the harder it gets the harder it gets. This screaming sustained crescendo doesn't register. You play harder still, on edge, disregarding dynamics. Pressing with stern force; forte forte forte forte forte. The bowhair is flattened back against the stem. The frog cuts into your thumb.

But you barely hear. Like you're playing underwater. Stoned. With earmuffs. You grapple with rhythm. The notes feel wrong and disjointed. The pinned strings they vibrate like plucked elastic. A blur. You can feel the body buzzing with volume and exertion, but it's dim in your ears. So soft. And the sound that you get, however faint the timbre, is barely scraping your skin. Not even a meagre flicker up your spine.

This has never happened.

But it can't, it can't, and you panic. Afraid, confused, you play harder. Just sawing, sawing, sawing fierce angles into those strings, but only your breathing now is audible to you. Louder than Lilian, than Elgar and E minor, than Backthere. You pitch and pull her and she chafes against your chest. Aggravating your bruise, rubbing it raw.

Your index finger cramps suddenly with the pressure but you don't stop now you can't you can't. You wince and lay your head flat against her shoulder, just to hear something, anything more so that you might siphon some relief. Like you should be, like you've always done.

You complete Elgar's concerto and stunned and shitscared and without pausing, for air or reflection, you weave into Mozart into Handel into Haydn into Dvorák into Kodaly into Everything you can. An urgent, desperate medley. You just play and play and play and play and grind your teeth against the pain and you are drenched with sweat and you are not giving up. Not giving her up.

You play and play and play and play for hours into this stifling night. Almost deaf. It's just the dull slap of strings you hear. Finally you segue into Johann Sebastian, your very favourite, rocking her, holding her tightly. You play the six Bach suites (bach to bach to bach to) and rub hot the fingerboard.

You play and play and play on until your hand spasms and cramps and locks up stuck. And you cry out loud, bursting hard and frustrated into an open D just to keep the sound, the momentum going, only to snap the silverwound string. It flails and whips your wrist. And the force of it all has her slipping from between you, has her falling stiffly to the hard bare floor at your feet. And the loud jolting echoing thud of her is the only sound to ring garrulous in your ears. You keep rocking in your chair, nursing your hand, and you realise she is a hollow vessel.

You are shaking. You close your eyes.

And even here. Even in *this* room, it smells like she's been here. Eleanor Rigby. The blind girl who stole your music; and left you no counterfeit. Who bequeathed you silence and the memory of her noise.

***

A vigil has slipped. On and on and on she sinks.

The window is shut, the trapped air hot. Dry and stifled.

On the wall is Mickey Mouse, redshorted and ringed by numbers. His arms frozen wide open. Splayed, like he's ready to be dissected. The thin red secondhand doesn't move or tick or tock. It just offers a determined, stunted flicker (stuck, stuck, stuck).

Mickey grins a plastic grin and points gleefully at the numbers Three and Nine.

It's three forty-five. Lightyears from midnight.

There is music.

Her breathing is long and slow. Her heartbeat rationed. She does not welter, does not move, does not wake.

She is kept under by a constant series of singing notes that occupy the midst of her headspace. Random and plangent and unbroken. A remix. A thick weave of patterns and rhythms and harmonies. And dissonance. Always changing, always blending. A cerebral jam.

And softly, gently, it holds her, under the cusp of mares. Like a spell, like magic. And it lets her sleep, further and deeper than she ever has. Breaks her vigil with a coma.

It keeps her there by displacing those endless images that still play themselves out, that would otherwise wake her. It defies them with its Bigness. Keeps her out of their reach with the strength of its cadence, and the presence of a player somewhere, of solidarity in her slumber. Gives her the strength to see them through.

Sometimes at the height of a crescendo she might tap Time into the air with a listing foot. You might hear her hum inadvertent.

On and on she is sleeping. Her chest slowly filling to collapse again. And outside of here, days and nights and dawns and dusks all pass without her.

***

It is three days past Christmas, three days to the New Year, century, millennium, the-end-of-the-world, when Bruno embraces the dawn with a yawn under his store verandah. He scratches a slack sloping boob.

He is Prepared.

He rummages through his pockets. His red elastic braces stretch with the loose slide of his pants. And his hand emerges with a jangling ring of shiny new keys.

Shiny new keys for his shiny new deadlock and his shiny new array of padlocks and slidebolts and chains. Eagerly, he shuffles forward to confront them all. Fumbling. And fifteen fiddly minutes later, Bruno bursts through the open door breathlessly to apply his new six digit code (666-666) to disarm his shiny new alarm.

Bruno sighs, switches lights and heads for the counter, now even higher up. He looks leftrightleft before removing the float bag from his heavy cardigan. Emptying the bag, he glances indulgently at the shrewd locations of his shiny new Hidden Security Cameras. And looming from separate corners, four big shiny new convex mirrors preside. Bruno can see them, they can see Bruno.

He waves importantly to himself. And four smug Brunos wave back. An army.

Bruno surveys his dusty stock, then flicks on his shiny new security monitor beside the till.

He is Prepared. Really, *really* Prepared.

And it is all concurrent with the recent amendments to his updated *Retale Gide*. In Chapter One, the *Three (3) Points Vital To Retale Success* are now as follows:

1. Profit Obtained is Profit Justefied.

2. The People Will Respond Only To What They Want To Hear.

3. Anyone, Anywear, Anytime is capable of Anything.

> *Therfore (subclause):*
>
> *a) You canot put a price on Safety.*
>
> *b) No one can be Trusted. Ever.*
>
> *c) Affermative Precautions must be executed.*

And they have been.

Bruno (to quote Althea) has gone *absolutely crazy*.

Alongside the Spanish Armada of retail security, Bruno has also fitted an exorbitant alarm system in his Babyshit Ochre Mercedes. And a bigger, shiny new motor to accommodate his shiny new four-inch exhaust. A gaping chrome cylinder, Big enough to swallow any potato, Big enough to house a small dog. It even *sounds* Big, because it has to.

The Potato Incident was a humiliating ruffle in Bruno's Bigness. It reduced him; deflated his inflatable whaleness.

Shortly after The Big Bang, Bruno had been infuriated to find that his tankish Mercedes had been brought down by something so sly and small and piffling as a wedged potato. A plangent tantrum had ensued; a fat man foolminating while his car ticked and hissed and smoked beside him. *Behaving*, his wife scolded as she ducked disgusted into a taxi without him, *like a spoilt child*. He stank bitterly. Kicked the flank of his felled Mercedes, paced the street, bellowed in a crude Romanian dialect. His inlaws peered from behind the loungeroom curtain, staring at his moonlit tirade. He accused his wife. Opened the car bonnet, shook his furious red head and slammed it down theatrically. He blubbered on the kerb as dogs barked and neighbours voiced their displeasure (Shut *up!* Christ! *Bloody* Wogs!).

And then, *then*, to suffer the *ignominy* of a cab. That stung. That iced the cake. Because he'd left taxis behind, Bruno. He was bigger than taxis. As he explained to Rob the taxi driver (a tired, retired sales rep supporting five separate children): Taxis were driven by immigrants and used by a) Tourists; b) The Elderly; c) Drunken Hooligans. And he wasn't any one of them. He didn't *need* taxis.

And Rob had nodded without listening and said: That will be eight forty-five thanks, sir.

Bruno, of course, had locked his wallet and keys in the car.

Gettout an pissorf you cheap dago bastard, said Rob, flaring with fatigue.

Bruno got out, wobbling with anger and humiliation.

He spent the night sleeping with his chickens because Althea refused to let him in. Bruno seethed, as silently as an irascible loud man can. He did not sleep, being worried through the night by small ants and probing mosquitoes.

The following day, Bruno had demanded that the police thoroughly fingerprint his vehicle. Question the neighbours, conduct Tests, launch an Investigation. He demanded Justice.

However, much to Bruno's consternation, the policewoman had smiled benignly. She patiently assured him that all appropriate measures had been taken. That there was nothing else they really could do.

Probably kids, sir, she had offered with a shrug. Just a prank, I'd say.

Bruno insisted that he speak to a man.

A *prank*. Just a *prank*. Bruno could imagine some pustule-headed little weed impressing his friends with a bag of vegetables. And he could just as clearly see himself reciprocating. With a carrot. A *big* fucking carrot. A vegetable suppository.

But a prank wasn't *enough*. A prank wouldn't ever justify his childish, unnecessary rage. And it would never ease the heat of his embarrassment. It had to be more than that, it had to be *bigger* than that.

Bruno brooded and ranted occasionally. He ate. And brooded. And ranted.

He was finally enlightened while forking the heart from a stuffed artichoke.

No! he thought aloud, No Bruno! Thiss woss no ruffian prank! No! This woss *premeditated.* Deliberate. *Spiteful*, in fact. This woss a *Personal* Attack! An affront! Thiss, he said, tapping his fork against his Roman(ian) nose: this woss *Bizzness*.

It had to be.

And the longer he entertained the notion, the clearer it seemed. And the clearer it seemed, the bigger it got. And the bigger it got, the bigger it got. Bruno knew he had to Act. Immediately, he contacted the police and explained his theory. They were, as Bruno told them, Very Unhelpful. (He secretly suspected a Conspiracy.) He then emailed a local Private Investigator, who had almost immediately replied: Fuck. Off.

But Bruno couldn't fuck off. He had convinced himself he was convinced. He had decided to Take Matters Into His Own Hands. He was consumed. It snowballed. The Big Bang became a Threat. A Warning. A Vendetta. The incident itself evolved into an act of grassroots terrorism: Potato + Exhaust Pipe = Carbomb.

Espionage. Bruno was suddenly thrust back into the streets of Napoli, to the Good Ole Days, in the throes of some esoteric mob skirmish. And he was a Player again. Against an unseen Enemy.

Either way, this was Big. It had to be.

Aye mean, hafter all, he explained to Althea, arownd thiss town aye am sin assa Big Man, yes? A *successful* man. He counted on his fingers: Aye heff a bizzness, yes? Aye haff the money, aye heffa the property, aye haff assets. And aye am well *known*. An thiss, thiss success it hass *remifications*, Alteeya. And he whispered, eyes wide: Becozz aye yam still, *still*, a foreign man to some people, yes? Ho! Oh boy! Belive me, Alteeya, there are reasons. There are mowtives to bring me down, donna you worry. Is the Tall Poppit Syndrowme, aye tella you now. They go hafter the Big Man.

Althea shook her head silently.

His suspicion escalated. Before long, Bruno was taking affirmative action. He began arming his vehicle, his house, his (middleofthestreet) Cornerstore. He began checking his chickens on the hour. He rang his in-laws to warn them, to tell them Not To Get Too Involved. To Be Careful. He would not disclose his reasons, nor enlighten them as to *what* involvement they should eschew, opting instead to sigh with drama and cryptically state that It Was Best They Weren't Informed.

Althea, meanwhile, was convinced he was insane.

Bruno, this is *ridiculous!* My sister is telling me she must now check her car before she gets into it? Bruno, she is scared to leave the house now because of you. This must stop! This *all* must stop, Bruno, you are being completely irrational. You are going crazy, over one …

Bruno interrupted.

Irrational? *Irrational?* Let me tella you thiss: There hiss nothing, *nothing irrational* about Protection. About Precaution. About Prevention of a *Personal Attack*. And, he waggled a screwdriver downwards, that hiss why, my wiyfe, for the Christmas this year my giff to you is Safety. Aye giff you Piss Of Mind.

Safety? Safety from *what,* Bruno? she shrieked, her little arms flapping. Another vegetable? A piece of fruit maybe? Bruno, *honestly,* this is just some silly children having fun. You must *stop* all this nonsense.

Aye willnot.

Why, Bruno? she exasperated.

Becozz, he sighed with effort and condescended from his ladder. Truss me, my wiyfe, you muss truss me.

Well I am sorry, my *husband,* but that is not an easy thing to do.

Exactly. *Exactly*, he said, as though it had all been clarified.

What? Exactly *what*, Bruno?

Exactly. You say it juss now. No one ken be trussted anymore. It hiss not safe! Hit iss full of Danger out there! And he swept an arm broadly across the front of the shop. Full Of Danger.

Althea shook her head in disbelief.

And you are full of the *Shit*, Bruno. And behaving like a stark raving madman. A loony! Fa! She waved him away. Little boys and their toys. A little boy who has lost his marbles. Go play your silly games. Go stalk the streets with your water pistol. Make an even *bigger* fool of yourself.

Bruno's grin was thin. He twisted his screwdriver.

Well, you hed better get used to him yes? Becozz this little boy, he hiss not gong to change. Oh no, but he *iss* gong to be Prepared.

Oh no no no, Bruno, said Althea, walking away. *You* had better get used to him. And he had better learn to cook too, my *husband*, because I will be at my sister's house until you grow up.

And she is still there.

Now, with the day's heat unravelling, Bruno stands, Prepared, entrenched behind his counter in his quiet empty little store. He fiddles with the monitor. Still life in shades of grey. He flicks through a series of covert locations; the back corner, the aisles, the Frozen Section, the porn rack, the front verandah. And then there's Rhubarb Cam. He smiles proudly. Slotted discreetly into the wall, it peers through fresh thicksticks of reclining rhubarb and overlooks the potatoes. The danger area. He gloats inwardly.

The next view is the biggest camera, poised behind and above him. He can twiddle his little joystick and scan the area with it.

Across. Back. Up. Down. He zooms in to his baggy arse. Pans up his sweaty back. Up past his neckhair (brushed upwards) and reveals his thinning coilover. He notices his scalp gleaming through the cracks. So with an eye on the monitor, Bruno deftly reswirls his hair turban. Pads it down. Presses. Manoeuvres his head and admires all angles. He adjusts the focus and beams.

Bruno zooms out, and in the foreground, puffedup and higherup, he is easily the biggest thing in the store.

***

Ewan logs on as Hermit Boy.

A girl called Heather♥ takes interest in his name. She asks him the rudimentary questions, and this time his name does not scroll into oblivion. He types back.

It turns out Heather♥ is a Canadian ice-skating champion. She enjoys horse-riding and sunbaking. Nude. She coquettishly mentions her lithe, virginal, athletic body. That is because Heather♥ is really an unemployed Yugoslavian called Serge who is drinking vodka without clothing (excepting the soursmelling sock on his tumid cock).

Heather♥ asks Hermit Boy to describe himself.

Hermit Boy says: No.

Heather♥ asks Hermit Boy what he does for a living.

The question pulls Ewan up. *For a Living.*

He pauses, sees his name drowning in the tide of text. Like television credits.

Taxidermy, he types.

Heather♥ laughs (lol) because it is silly. Ewan laughs because he is bitter.

***

Little Ewan, the Recently Emancipated Hermit Crab, had been scrabbling for days, dragging its prosthetic reminder of Home, casing the joint for new accommodation. For a new caravan. It had scoured all the floor in its search for suitable real estate, dogged by the soughing of the ocean, with no luck and scarce little sleep. Not in this shell.

And now it's found it.

The mother of all mobile homes, the hermit's Holy Grail. A veritable palace, shimmering in all its glory. And it has it all to itself. Readily accessible, vacant, and crustacean friendly.

Dazed, Little Ewan gazes with bleary upturned eyestalks. Its mandibles twitch in anticipation. It sees before it a silken rise of turgid white binbags, a stack of three. All full of leaves, dewy with condensation. From here, it looks all very alpine.

The crab pauses, looks left, looks right, and clenches a nipper on to the slippery plastic.

It embarks.

Because at the peak of this steep gradient is a cave, a snug tunnel. A crab haven. And this shell was Big. A leader in World Safety, in fact. The climb is shaky. The crab crackles upwards, grappling and swinging and grappling, pinching tiny tears into the plastic. Higher and higher. And it doesn't look down as it journeys to where no crab has ever gone before: the exhaust pipe of a Volvo.

It looms. The crab clambers on upwards, finding a good purchase in a steep crevice between the bags. And then it's there.

Little Ewan reaches its nippers inside the jutting pipe, hinges in and hoists itself, dangling perilously over the lip. Scrabbles and crawls inside. Lingers before turning in exultation. Surveying the world below from his new residence.

It rubs its claws together.

Slowly the crab shucks its old shell, and pushes it far down the dusty chamber, away from the light.

***

Warren is worried. Warren is panicking. He paces, sometimes breaks into frantic cantering. His swiping tail slaps into furniture and walls. He whines. Whimpers. He's restless, Warren, with nowhere to go but the same anxious circuit through the same rooms. Except one. He's locked in, and locked out. He can't get to her, he can't get her out. The door is etched with scratchmarks. There are flecks of paint on his snout from sniffing the gap beneath the door.

Warren trots on. Farting. His ears are flat. His blinky eyes sting. His slack tongue pants sweat. Can't help coursing this same route through the house, round and round and round. And he knows he should be displaying some kind of stoic canine grit here. Guide dogs are dogged. Guide dogs don't whimper, guide dogs don't fret. And he knows it's his job, his *Duty*, to save her. But he can't. He loves her, Warren, but he can't get to her.

Fuckssake. What would Lassie do?

Get Help. Lassie would get *Help*. Quickly. With clever heroics and high entertainment value. *Attaboy!* But Warren is not Lassie. Warren doesn't know how to tip the telephone receiver, or dial three miraculous zeros. And he can't get outside to run down a convenient postman. He's not even big enough to crash almightily through her bedroom door. He knows. He's tried.

His incessant whine is like a siren. He is frustrated and helpless and hopelessly confused. He has tried getting Estelle's attention, spent hours barking at her, pawing at her, but she is *still* sleeping.

He's stuck.

And he's smart enough to piss in the shower and drink from the toilet. From previous experience he knows not to crap on the carpet. He's smart enough to eat Estelle's Christmas dinner left on the coffee table. Smart enough to paw open the cupboard that contains his Meaty-Bites. He can chew open a plastic jar of peanut butter. He can even negotiate the door of the old fridge. He's smart enough to get by. He could rival Lassie in Survival, but that won't *save* anyone.

After almost four days of constant movement without rest, Warren collapses with exhaustion and fatigue. His sleep is deep and fitful. All four legs twitch and jab and scratch. When he wakes he is thirsty. He pants, feeling woozy and weak. The festering stink in here is unbearable. Inescapable.

Before drinking, though, Warren trudges to her door. He sits and listens. Faintly he can hear her voice. It is brief and dim, like she's humming, or moaning. Suddenly excited, he stands with his ears tensed and his tail fanning erratic, scratching the door. Whining and growling and barking. Then listening again. And waiting.

Waiting until he's back pacing this perimeter, round and round and round.

HOW TO MAKE A FRETLESS MANDOLUTE

New Year's Eve. Ewan sees the morning creep and settle with his raw eyes open. He has not slept properly for days. His body is torpid and tight and heavy. His tongue is like swollen velvet, dry and foultasting. There is a congealed smear of bile on his chest and stubbled chin.

His head still throbs, but it's easing off the spin cycle.

Last night, despairing, Ewan contrived to tackle a thick six-inch bud in its entirety. To knock himself out, to stone himself to sleep. He lit, toked, held and expelled. It was joyless and methodical. He forced coughing to open his martyred capillaries.

Two-and-a-half hours later he sat with an empty bowl and a pair of sticky scissors. Very quiet and very still. He was stiff and groggy and detached, though everything else seemed to be moving. His lungs were tender; he had to ease air into them. His raw throat burned. There was no breeze, no sound, and he sat for a long time. Wasted and awake.

Then he noticed the possum leap up and out from its hammock. It seemed to do it with a fluid felinity, as though in casual defiance to the laws of gravity. They eyed each other for a time. He felt glad for its recovery. Suddenly the possum somehow cartwheeled over to where he sat, and to piping carnival music it began staging an elaborate tap routine. It then backflipped deftly several times.

Ewan wore a lax, uncertain grin. He blinked slowly. *Plink.* The sound of a soft kiss.

Opening his eyes, he saw the possum perched on an aubergine unicycle and wheezing a small accordion. He watched it do several dizzy laps on squeaky wheels.

Ewan tried to clap his appreciation but couldn't. He frowned and coughed and spat. The unicycle had disappeared now and Ewan watched closely, squinting as the possum clambered and stood teetering on the edge of his red plastic bucket. He watched as it unscrewed his conepiece with two paws. Watched it tap out the tar and ash. And watched it stare back at him, holding it aloft. It sighed. Tossed it in the air and caught it. Up and down, up and down, and shaking its head, with a highpitched maternal voice it said:

Rhubarb, Ewan. S'all just rhubarb.

Ewan stared. Blinked harder, and it was gone. Slumbering snug in a pillowcase hammock.

He sat for a long time. Wasted and awake.

Then, smirking, he rose as suddenly as the truly stoned can. Unsteady, he stumbled sluggish through the kitchen into the garage. Padded the wall for balance and a light switch. He knelt slowly, hands on the ground, and dragged a couple of turgid white binbags slowly to his lap. He split one open, a small giggle escaping.

He removed a flaccid, paling leaf from the bag. Because, according to Ewan's catatonic reasoning, the Possum's Message (and its remarkable ability on a unicycle) were not just a hallucination. It was a Sign. Oh yes.

Another Dempsey generation seduced by augury.

The crab stared evilly, shaking a livid nipper. (That, however, was surely psychedelia.)

Ewan microwaved the leaf to dry it out. He carried it outside, shrunken, limp, steaming. It didn't smell good. He sat for a long time. Wasted and awake.

It occurred to him that in his absence, the possum had politely replaced the conepiece. Another Sign. That was nice of it, he thought.

That was nice of you, he drawled, very very slowly. Thankyou very much.

He stifled another giggle and packed the flakes loosely. He lit a dull flare and drew a small greyish cloud into the chamber. Watched it churn and billow. He paused, but not for consideration. He glanced at the sleeping possum. Then he leaned in and pulled deeply with his eyes shut.

He breathed napalm and reared back violently, coughing. The taste of acid. It *was* acid. It stung his mouth, his throat, his nostrils. He hacked uncontrollably, wheezing in air as his gut bucked and he vomited into the tepid bongwater. Heaving and spitting. And he sat there, bent and sobered and wincing, recovering breath. Then, concentrating hard on his legs, Ewan clutched his stomach and lurched inside, bursting through a sheet of flywire. Yellow dribble dangled from his chin.

He hipped a chair: it crashed. He fell numbly to bed. Bellyup. His pulse thumped.

Ewan spent the night like the lid of a blender; observing the room mixing with the motion of the fanblades. Whirrwhirrwhirrwhirr. Dizziness emptied the dregs of his belly.

His mouth was glued with an alloy of acrid residue and desperate thirst, but he was too drilled to move. Tediously suspended. His body pinned while his mind spinned, like a botched anaesthetic nightmare.

He was alert now.

Wasted and awake and with no blissful, somnolent dose of Retrospect to scatter sand over his eyes and send him on his way. Its absence kindly holding open the door for its fervent, merciless brother, Introspect, to barge through and compress these walls. Interrogate and demand answers. And Ewan fought it hard, with an urgency that made him sweat, kept him awake.

You don't have to dig deeply to see that Ewan is shitscared.

He's terrified of what he's losing; his last, solid, immutable thing. That sound was all he had left. The thing he could never lose, and so he clung to it dearly. He still is. He won't let it go. He's played for it so hard these last few days his calluses have cracked and the softskin beneath has split and bled on the fingerboard. His right thumb is a blister.

He's terrified of her, and what she's opened, what *he's* opened, what they've started. What she willed from him simply with presence. What she's asking of him with her presents. What he's told her already, what he's pared back and shown her with notes and sharps and slurs and quavers. Even words. Bold and brazen.

He's terrified of this impossible, instant inversion of his life since she fucking usurped it. She didn't arrive, she burst in and she took his arm with trust and life and voice and soft warm skin. And he went. Out. Caught and tangled and dragged; she was a rip. And you had to go with it, to trust that it wouldn't drown you. And it carried you out, out, out and you were even at ease for a time. But it was a spurious force because it left you as soon as you started swimming with it. In the open. Treading water, like you were before it came, but without the safety of shore or base. And now there's nothing solid underneath, no grounding with nothing to hold.

Ewan is terrified because losing that sound is losing Everything again. With nothing bequeathed. No consolation prize. Just Loss.

And he can't. He just can't lose this sound. He needs it to get by, to survive, to slip through days and sleep through nights. Get them behind him.

But she dislodged it all, Eleanor Rigby. She ran away with it and left you as alone as you've ever been. Right there when it mattered.

He rises incrementally. Lightheaded, like his mind is catching up. He shuffles, shits and showers. In the dim bathroom he cups his hands and drinks heavily from the tap. The water is warm. It bloats him. He holds his breath to keep it down.

Blowflies have laid siege on the kitchen. The flap of flywire lies limp on the floor. For a moment he thinks someone has broken in, but he sets the felled chair and remembers. He herds the flies out waving. They are strangely compliant, as if they were leaving anyway. He closes the door.

He drinks thick black coffee and works his way through a stale breadslice. Through the window he sees his bowl and scissors and the septic sludge in his red bucket. His belly fists and he looks away.

Shaded, the possum sleeps on serene.

Ewan rinses out his mug. Grips the sink and stands and stares. It's very quiet. And very still. And this is how it's been these past six days. This frustrating collusion of restlessness and listlessness. Of energy without inclination, without direction. His routine is shot to shit with lack of sleep and sound. His days are frayed. Less assured. And dripping with Time. Aimless, he drifts.

And like always, his feet lead him down the hall, first room on the left. Like always, she's there. Recumbent, on her side, on a Turkish rug with her back turned. Ewan leans on the architrave and looks at her, as you would a sleeping lover. And he *knows* that back, just as he *knows* that front. The grain; the curves; the kicks and dents in the purfling. The small imperfections, every facet of her dimensions. But he's almost scared to touch her now. Unsure of her.

But his feet urge forward. They have to.

He takes her up and hovers over her. Her new D string gleams.

Again, she won't settle back. He doesn't even try Tu Ning for fear of not hearing.

He winds a stubborn bownut. Breathes and closes his eyes.

And it's Tchaikovsky this morning, Uncle Pete. He launches

into it hard but with a nauseous stab of dread because he hears nothing. Nothing in this room. Limbless Lilian, who has limned loud for you, for years, cannot be heard. But he persists, face taut. He plays and plays and plays, until there's no rhythm, no melody, no patience. Until it's not music any more, just notes notesnotesnotes. Just getting them out. Blood spreads through his bandaids, slippery. They work their way off. His blister bursts and stings. He leans forward, plays harderharderharder until he is off his chair holding her perpendicular, crowding over her in his erratic pace. He bends sweating. Hears only his breathing and the surreal slap of strings.

He finally stops when the thinnest string cuts into the meat of his finger and nears bone, and he bellows and heaves and sweats. His fingers are capped red and sticky. Choking her neck, he recovers the chair. He swallows.

It is very quiet. And very still.

This is all he has left:

Shaking, Ewan lightly lays the thumb of his left hand on to her highest string. He waits for calm. Breathes: and slowly pulls the bow, running his thumb softlysoftly up and down the string. Begging for harmonics. For an ethereal tinklytingly sound.

But no sparks come. He hears nothing.

He drops the bow. It clatters. The room is a whorl, condensing. There is no distance. It is just him here, just him. He staggers nowhere. Vomits glutinous diluted coffee into the bathroom sink, porcelain slap. Eyes clenched shut, spastic retch, silent scream. He spits with rancour. Sniffs. He hates her. *Hates* her. With all the strength his Loss provides. Hates her for what is happening. Can't explain it. Hates her because he is afraid. Hates her, because even in the humid fug of this bathroom, his house still bears the scent of her. And the scent of her is still her absence. And he hates her because it hurts more when there is someone real to miss. Hates her most because he doesn't hate her at all.

And so it's her insistent scent that has him spilling into this stifling New Year's Eve, out the back door. He almost trips on her esky.

He tries to keep himself busy, to drive thought from his mind. He tips the putrescent bongwater over a lavender bush and hoses out the bucket. Cleans the blood from his fingers. He kneels over the possum; on and on it sleeps. He watches the slow mechanics of its tiny lungs. He hopes it is all right. He tickles its snout. Dribbles some water over its fur to cool it.

The heat is unbearable. He is slippery with sweat. He peels off his shirt and drapes it over the rosemary bush to give the possum more shade.

Then he is standing, moving (because moving helps) and ducking under the Hills hoist and into his shed. The heat is worse, but the scent is his own. The air in here is fat and thick and difficult to breathe. An open tub of beeswax has melted by the closed louvres and the redolence of honey mingles with turps fumes and epoxy and wood dust and sweating weed.

Ewan wades. It's a sauna in here. His long navy shorts are drenched.

He touches things. His things. Sifts through his clutter of crap. A broken Bunsenburner. A history of flawed ebony tuning pegs. An oil lamp. A saucepan full of failed homemade rosin.

Rags, woodcrumbs, drill bits. He tackles the shelf space beneath the bench. Discovers an array of lost tools and fasteners. A tunnel of stacked bridges. Dovetails, emery paper, adhesives. A bag of rock-hard grass, scattered rhubarb leaves, an old weeping tin of Moonshine.

He finds bandaids. Puts them on.

Dust clings to him.

He sorts through his piles of scraps and offcuts. Finds a forgotten plank of sycamore, rare and expensive and crudely sawn. Plywood sheets. Pine. Sheets of zincalume.

He moves around. Suddenly, blessedly absorbed. He clears out his rack of thingrained poplar planks and lines them side by side. Some have split and warped with the constant heat. He pulls them all out. Some have been here years and are grey with age. He tears away the web of a redback with the last plank.

The dust is so thick he almost doesn't see it. On the ground, behind it all, a mound. A small hill, like a tortoise has sneaked in to slumber. He kneels and wipes at it. Then remembers.

With two hands he hefts it, shaking away the dust. It is the bulbous burl of an old poplar. Like a guillotined teardrop, the size of a pregnant belly. Delivered here years ago without reason. He turns it over in his hands, heavy. Dampens a rag with his sweat and smears away the remaining dust. Lays it face down. The back is a dark gnarled dome with boils of dried sap and thin tufts of stringy bark. The shape of it suddenly amuses him. He raps the timber with a knuckle.

He sits on the bench, the burl in his lap. Taking a chisel, he absently pushes at the grey flesh of the face. Just a light, idle push.

A coil of timber flares immediately. Smooth. Ewan frowns and tries again; gets that same creamy roll. He prods it with his fingernail: the timber is hard. He examines the chisel blade and it's a little blunt.

He's awake now. He tries again and again and again to the same buttercurl effect. He has the impulse to turn and see if anybody is watching. Even the angry knot in the centre peels away easily. He shakes his head. Stabs straight down into it, hard, and it gets him nowhere, barely makes a mark. Which is how it should be, like chipping concrete, or granite.

But the surface still gives effortlessly with the grain. Layer by layer. His heart thumps.

Ewan digs.

Without thought, without purpose, he just digs into the belly of this wood. Before long he's lost in it. He sits bent over on the bench, a smooth furrow gouged from the face. Flakes of timber surround him. He carves and carves and carves, easy smooth curls, gutting it.

The knot is like a frozen vortex; it thins as he deepens. Slivers of sap bleed in rivulets, and he is compelled to collect the shards in a steel mug to one side. He doesn't know why.

A vague, inchoate notion is forming in his head, though it won't reveal itself. His hair stands on end, and he knows he is going somewhere with this, he just doesn't know where. He is confused yet assured. He carves briskly, though carefully, deliberately, in wide sweeping strokes. Somehow he knows what to do as he does it. And how. It feels instinctive, almost meditative. Right. It's all he sees through this afternoon. He's on autopilot. Guided, but in control. Taking something he knows to somewhere he isn't sure.

The burl is light now in his hands, taking the form of a thick shell. The tip of the tear has remained solid. His arm aches. Sweat drips freely from his hair and his nose and his chin into the bowl in his lap.

It is late afternoon when he begins thinning it out, starting from the base. He peels away long strips of milky wood. Lightblond curls cover the bench and the floor. He sneezes. The mug is full with shavings of sap.

On the inside lip he carves a recess and leaves the walls of the bowl slightly thicker. He uses calipers to gauge consistency. The belly is almost weightless now.

In the light of a stunning ruby dusk he reaches for a ream of garnet paper. He rips strips and works cautiously, lightly. The bowl is very thin.

When he is finished he tugs the lightcord and blows out the malty dust, fine as cornflour. He rubs the bowl softly with steelwool until it is smooth to the touch.

He runs it over and over and over in his hands. Aware of its brittleness. A huge, halved, hollowed timber tear. Its hooped growth rings are like tight isobars. He smiles, feeling a cool breeze seep through a gap in the louvres. Ewan looks, touches, for a long time. Its capacity to break is beautiful to him. He feels strangely arrested. Tingly.

And it is with this weird conviction that he slides off the bench, lays the shell bellyup and takes a hacksaw. Carefully he cuts away the very tip of the tear. Then into the remaining solid wood he cuts a thick V. The bowl he leaves untouched. He doesn't know why.

He doesn't know why he has suddenly ducked outside either. It's cool. The breeze chills his sweat. He doesn't notice. He finds himself wrestling with a banksia and shuffling along the back fence. Finds himself in the back corner, trampling an abandoned herb garden and climbing the flimsy asbestos. And he's reaching into the struggling sheoak that overhangs from Beryl's backyard. He doesn't notice a curious possum, the male, surveying him from higher up. And he doesn't know why, but he's pulling hard at a dead limb about the size of his arm, the thickness of his wrist.

It comes away with a crackle and his balance. He falls into an accommodating patch of fennel and coriander.

From over the fence, Beryl's floodlights blare and then are swamped by shadow.

Ooze thair? Eh? Ello?

Ewan ducks and firewalks back to the shed.

Nah, nah. S'all right, Reg. Jussa possum love. Piss off ye liddle barsted!

The possum walks the length of a branch, craps on her lawn and scarpers.

Ewan lays the straight sheoak branch on his bench. The skin is smooth and grey. He does not think, just does. He winds his vice back, and the scroll in progress drops to the floor and remains. He sets the sheoak in place, tightens, and saws ten inches from the thicker end. Then from beneath the bench he takes a plane and begins shaving away strips the length of his forearm. He leaves room at the thinner end, where the branch tapers into long twigs.

The timber is dry and pares away easily. He planes, layer by layer, until he exposes the middle of the branch. He leaves a concave kick at the thinner end.

He stops to run a finger along the exposed surface. The grain is incredible. Medullary rays, huge and unique to sheoak; beautiful pods of light rust, laced in a web of creamy beige like loose, elongated honeycomb.

Turning the limb over and vicing it back up, he carves away three inches from the rounded base with the chisel, however, he is careful to retain the planed surface. An overhang, like a stubby diving board. Now, from the squared end of the gutted burl, he takes a measurement of the V. He then transfers this to the underside of the sheoak and using a bevel and chisel, he shapes a short splice.

Excited, Ewan takes the branch from the vice and joins the two together. The splice slots in and fits flush and perfect. He grins. It looks like a giant medieval spoon.

He turns now to inspect his lineup of poplar. There is only one plank broad enough to span the width of the bowl. It is old and thick, with dark grubby waterstains across the surface.

Ewan wastes no time. He saws off a section and cuts a rough circular border. The grain is straight and consistent, like calm wavefolds. But the watermark is like a nebulous explosion. A dark swirling ball with shifting patterns and tone. He wants to keep it. No Moonshine tonight.

On the lip of the bowl he measures the depth of the recess and scores it on to the poplar board. He begins planing, working fast and mechanical. He is consumed. And this is all he knows, this rhythm, this action. Just pushing, pushing, pushing. This is all that matters, this moment now.

It takes him an hour to strip the thickness down.

With slow care he traces the shape of the bowl on to a thin sheet of paper. Then he copies it on to the planed poplar. He saws outside the outline, then sands the timber back.

Removing the branch, Ewan drops the board into the seated bowl. He is surprised by his flukish precision. Barely a hairline is visible. Almost like it's full again.

And he knows, he *knows* that this tightfitting lid is a soundboard, just as he *knows* that the sheoak limb is a fingerboard. He knows, but the concept doesn't convene, won't unveil itself. Where it is going; what it is; what it will be. Its conclusion is still elusive. But all he knows now is the task. The doing, doing, doing.

He marks out the centre of the poplar board and marks out the dimensions for a soundhole. He attempts a freehand guide.

With coercive care he tips the thin board from the bowl. Vices it. With an old auger, he corkscrews a hole in the centre marking. Using a fine blade from a coping saw, he follows his guide and cuts a soundhole in the shape of a tear.

A hollow tear, immersed in a dark waterstain. Like the tear of a giant has fallen and burst.

He unscrews the blade.

Now he takes the first offcut from the sheoak branch. With the coping saw, he cuts a thickish medallion from the open end. He then cuts off a small piece, about a quarter of the way down, and into it, four evenspaced grooves. This will be the bridge.

Ewan pastes and screws it beyond the soundhole, towards the fat end of the belly. Perfect.

Vicing the sheoak fingerboard now, he sketches a quick guide for a pegbox at the thinner, uncut end. With the auger he drills four holes whose constellation forms a rectangle. Again, he threads through the blade of his coping saw. He cuts out four separate boxes. The twigs rattle as he saws.

He drills four larger holes through the side of the pegbox, one into each section.

Beneath the cobwebbed louvres, Ewan sifts through his bucket of buggered ebony. The tuning pegs that never made it. He chooses four, in varying states of evolution. One by one, he shortens their tapered shafts, sanding them down to fit the smaller peghole. The heads he carves into smaller shapes. Just following the grain of the wood, going with it, so that no peg is the same. And it feels strange not to be carving out a model, a copy. Even stranger to finish with four different pegs, each delicate and unique. He rolls them in his palm, admiring their detail, their newness, their smallness.

He doesn't pause for long.

He twists them into the side holes. They are a good, tight fit. The two in the back are longer than the front two. Now he cuts four grooves running from each peg to the concave kick preceding the fingerboard. Blows away the woodcrumbs.

Ewan wads a rag and doses it with linseed oil. Rubs it into the belly and into the back of the soundboard. He doses the rag again and applies it to the beautiful grain of the sheoak.

Stripping a new rag, he wipes the dust from an old tin dish, into which he mixes a quickdrying two-part epoxy. The fumes corrode his nosehairs and threaten to set his head spinning, again. With a thin stick of scrap ply, he dabs and scrapes the adhesive along the recessed lip of the bowl and then the splice and furrow. Then carefully, carefully he lowers and lays the poplar soundboard into place. Presses. Then carefully, carefully he eases the neck into the belly and holds.

The overhang of the fingerboard sits flush against the soundboard. From the base of the V he collects weeping adhesive with a rag. He resists the urge to hold it, to turn it over and over and over in his hands.

Instead he kneels and reaches below the bench to unearth a rusted camping stove. A small gas canister rolls with it, leashed by a flexible tube. On the bench it yawns open, evicting four spiders and an earwig. Ewan takes the saucepan with the failed chunks of homemade rosin and upturns it. They clack and clatter onto the floor, pinging chips. He wipes it clean.

He cranks both plates of the little stovetop with a pink Bic lighter. On one plate he places the mugful of resin, like sharp shards of dark toffee. Over a lowburning flame he slides the saucepan. Into this he gives a generous splash of turpentine. Then dollops in some beeswax, which has partially congealed. He cuts a small slab of carnauba wax and throws it in with a dash of linseed oil. He adds a mouthful of spit and stirs it briskly with a screwdriver. He then leaves it to heat through.

He finds himself back outside, striding quickly, purposefully into the house. Through the kitchen, and into the garage where, from beneath a pile of assorted crap, he removes a small electric heater.

His fridge door gasps open. He takes two eggs. Almost jogs back.

The air in the shed is fat with scent and the day's heat. His sweat tastes brackish.

Ewan stirs, cuts the gas. The resin is now the colour and consistency of treacle. Its steam is sharp. Smells a little like cardamom. Such a heady aroma in here.

He tightens an old F clamp on to the molten mug and pours the resin into the saucepan cocktail. Scrapes it out with the screwdriver and stirs.

He leaves it to cool. With a scribe now, Ewan etches a decorative border around the soundhole. Inside it he engraves some small ornate touches. Adds a thicker line round the outside. Does what he wants. The patterns are pretty, almost Incan in their shape.

Soon he can palm the base of the saucepan. It's cool enough; he can wait no longer. He cracks the two eggs and separates the yolks, the albumen spilling into the mix. It is still warm, but the eggwhite doesn't cook. Already it gives the mix a natural sheen.

Ewan tears a clean rag. He wads and dips it. And in light, easy strokes he applies the varnish. It doesn't take long to spread the thick coat.

He stares and he does not breathe.

The waterstain is a sudden satin whorl of dark crimson and burgundy and chestnut, with an espresso fringe that shifts tone with the angle of the light. His scribing remains a lighter hue, the colour of straw. It glistens wet. The surrounding timber is a wash of rich creamy honey and amber and copper. The finish almost shimmers. Again, he looks to see if anyone is watching. Contrasted with the sheoak grain, it is hard to believe this is just timber, just wood.

He stares, but still he does not linger.

He switches on the heater, sets it to high, and leans the face of the soundboard into the hot breeze, propping it up with stuffed rags and scrap wood. He wipes the sticky varnish from his fingertips.

Now: strings.

He rifles through the cavities and boxes and drawers of the shed. The best he can uncover is a length of twine, a roll of fine nylon fishing line and a handful of elastic bands. At a loss, he drifts across the lawn (ducking) and back into the house. A halfarsed glance in the kitchen and the garage and the laundry reveals nothing.

He moves down the hall, first room on his left. Slaps on the light.

He doesn't notice the bellyup cello or the scattered bow (still taut). Doesn't notice the silence in here or the smell.

All he sees is a small forgotten cellocase which rests atop the bookshelf. A halfsized case. With a midget inside. Called Kamahl.

And he doesn't know why he suddenly needs it, but he brings it down with a shower of dust and opens it. The catches are tight. He doesn't notice the trapped scent of Backthere rising up like smoke. Doesn't notice exercise books or manuscript paper or a large certificate with his name on it. Doesn't even notice the instant, precious stream of memory the little instrument evokes.

He just sees the four strings he will take with him. Now.

Without lifting the cello, he unwinds the pegs and unhooks them from the tailpiece.

He leaves.

The varnish has set, like a thin sheet of glass. He unplugs the heater and lays the strings on the bench. They are a finer gauge than a fullsize cello. He rummages impatiently through a scummy toolbox for a pair of pliers and snips the ends from all the strings. His fingers are greasy with sweat. He takes the thinnest two strings, ties a knot into one end of each. The thicker of these two he slots into the top groove of the bridge. Pulling hard, he brings the string down the length of the neck. Lays it in the corresponding groove and threads it through the first peg. He winds. Taps lightly at the string and with a surge of something hot he hears it sing. He tunes it to a rough E, two tones higher than middle C.

Almost frantic now in his excitement, he does the same with the finer string and tunes it to an A.

Ewan is left with the remaining gutstrings. Shaking he selects the fatter of the two.

He strips away the finecoiled silver casing to exposes the sheepgut beneath a sheath of cotton. The gut is light and tough and wound together in three thin strips. It is the colour of snot. And still too thick.

Ewan gnaws at it to fray an end. He peels away a single strip of the gut. Perfect. He knots the end of the two gut strings and sets them into the bridge. His hand is unsteady. He struggles to slot them through the eye of the pegs.

Tightening, he softly tunes them. D and G.

And he swallows and shuffles back.

And he has to stop now. There is nothing more to do.

He can feel his pulse beneath his skin. He reaches out but does not touch it.

It.

Looking now, he isn't too clear on what It is. It is not a lute. Too short, too thin. There are no frets, no angling on the pegbox, no tailpiece. It isn't quite a mandolin either. Too big, too long. It's single stringed with a deep one-piece belly. And it has twigs.

A mongrel then. A new mutant cousin, only just brought into the world. And it makes him smile; this crazy ambiguous thing in a roomful of replicas. So pretty and so strange. So balanced and unique and dignified and just look at that stunning, *incredible* grain. So incongruous amongst these stern looking clones.

Still smiling he lifts it off the bench. Weightless. He twirls it like a showcase, pores over it. Its detail, its newness, its smallness. He lightly taps the soundboard.

Ewan turns and hoists himself to sit on the bench. Doesn't notice the crunch of woodshavings. It sits in his lap. His thumbnail rests on the top string.

And then he strums his Fretless Mandolute and almost drops it with the shock of its sound. Very quiet and very still, he listens to it ring out.

And then he laughs. All by himself. Laughslaughslaughs. Can't help it. High and delirious until it wrings his belly. He strums again, eyes wet, slow then fast. Upstrokes and downstrokes. Swelling with volume. Still laughing. Striking into a simple one two three four rhythm. And the moment is beautiful. Myooozic. Volts and volts and volts of it. He can't stop, feels himself filling. He presses a cautious finger on sheoak and he's stumbling into notes and sharps and flats and the dissonance in between. Exploring. His trembling thumb gives it a Spanish tremolo, and it almost sounds like he knows what he's doing. He hunches over it, grinning. Absorbed, absorbing. Acquainting himself with the strings, with how it all works. He's learning all over again. And he's never heard anything like this sound. He loses himself further, fumbling and fiddling. Gathering confidence. He discovers little runs. Finds that if he twangs the gut strings hard he can get a sound much like a sitar. He finds an assortment of easy chords which riff into a folkish sound. He peppers them with shameless hammer-ons and vibrato to give it a sweet Celtic air. He tries rockstar bends and crappy lead breaks. He fucks up, doesn't care. He tries messy bar chords and suddenly he's in Tahiti, belting out some seriously bad ukulele.

Ewan lays a flat finger softly lightly over the strings and strums. He feels and hears the tinklytingly ping of harmonics and he could burst right here.

Sparks.

He fingerpicks uncannily fast, tapping Time with a dangling foot. He plays around with different scales, moving in and out of them at will. Just makes it up. From thin air. Eyes closed. No sheet music, no theory, no plan.

Grinning, he takes the pink Bic lighter from the bench and uses it to play a bluesy slide mandolute. The first of its kind. It makes him laugh. Feels like singing.

He is immersed in D major when he hears a dull crackling behind him.

He swivels and stares through the louvres, wiping away a sheet of dust.

Fireworks.

Ewan frowns. Then, for the first time since this morning, he notices things like time (midnight) and temperature (fucking hot) and thirst (desperate).

Shit Zoltan, he says. Where did the Time go?

He surfaces.

On the lawn he realises it is the New Year. The New Century. The New Millennium. He can hear broken bursts of amplified music carried on the seabreeze. It doesn't feel like the end of the world.

He watches.

Then it occurs to him that he is holding something. He looks at the mandolute as though seeing it for the first time. He stares, then remembers and smiles.

And it is in this moment that he Understands, and Everything converges. Just like that. Ewan rests the mandolute on the lawn and runs inside (ducking). Throughthekitchenfirstdoorontheleft and he's here again. And he knows why. He's reaching for another cellocase. A fullsize cellocase. Without a fullsize cello inside. But it is not empty.

It yawns open smells smells smells and he's flicking open the long felt console inside. A little yawn. And it's there, still there. And he is shaking as he takes it.

He runs.

Back on the lawn he kneels like a prayer and sets it up.

He still has that Bic lighter in his hand. It is now poised beneath the tail of a canary yellow firecracker.

As he kneels, he suddenly recalls the certificate inside Kamahl's case. He remembers the day he received it: Tuesday Afternoon. Back There. The day of his Official Artistic Licence Ceremony. And Everyone who was Everyone was there. They both had nametags, The Dignitary: Voolfgung and The Proud Recipient: Zoltan. Everyone. It was three weeks before he left.

After he received his certificate to a Warm Hearty Round Of Applause; after they shook hands and played the Rocky theme with Lilian and Kamahl; Jim had made them both a cup of tea and his eyes were twinkling because they were wet and that was when he told him that if you lose something (and he knew all about losing) the best way to help fill up that empty space was to get something, to make something to fill it with. Something new and beautiful and precious. Something even better. And to keep making things. It didn't matter if they lasted forever or a second or if they were made of air or wood or tin or gold, it didn't matter. That wasn't the *point*. It didn't matter. Just as long as you kept making things and feeling things strongly.

And Backthere, clutching his certificate, Ewan had only *sort of* got it, but he had nodded because Jim was almost crying. He didn't really Understand. Until now.

He understands that remembering the things that are gone doesn't fill up the space that they leave. Holding Memory, pinning it, stuffing it, preserving it, can't ever fill that absence. Just helps you pretend that space does not exist, he thinks. You can't fill the hole with the hole. With beautiful reprisals, with replicas, with Everything that used to be good. You get nowhere, he says aloud.

And it hurts to know that of all the things he spent his days re-remembering, until now it was the *point* he had forgotten. Creating, carving air and the making up of shit. Out of thin air. Something real and alive. Alexander and invention and parturition. He forgot it, and he has *had it all this time*, the one thing he's never lost. And he knows, Ewan, that the harmonics, the sparks, they've been at his fingertips, *in* his fingertips, just waiting. Not in the cello, not in the strings. *He* gave it life.

Ewan shicks the lighter and says Goodbye and the cracker fizzes. He dives.

It shoots straight up (boof!) and hisses into the night.

Ewan stands. Looks up.

Waits.

And waits.

And waits.

Nothing. The fireworks on the Esplanade crackle on. He shrugs. Picks up the mandolute.

And the cracker, now on a downward trajectory, smacks (bang!) into his roof and explodes (kaboom!) in a flurry of showering red and gold and green sparks that arc and list slowly. Some fizzle into the night. Some cascade on to the lawn. It is all over in seconds.

Ewan just stares.

Silence. A dog barks down the street. Behind him, floodlights blare again.

Blood-ee *hell!* Reg! *Reg!* Get the torch willyer love!

It's alright Beryl, Ewan calls.

Wot? Hello? Ooze that?

It was me Beryl. I just let a cracker off.

Oh. *Christ.* Tryan a start a bushfire are ye then, son?

Happy New Year, Beryl.

Yeah. Righto. Ewan hears her mutter something about a Bloody Queer. He grins and picks out Auld Lang Syne on his instrument.

Hosing down his hissing roof and watching the grand finale of the fireworks, Ewan laughs to himself. Because he can; and because he knows it took the blind to teach him to see. Because he understands: he sits on her rock and she inhabits his Tuesday afternoons. They fill the gaps in each other's lives, fill the hole with a whole. He thinks of her. Eleanor. And his first impulse is to share this, this, this, all of this. Whatever. Everything. Because she somehow belongs to it. He has a restless lust for vicissitude and company. He muses, thinks of going to see her now. With a turkey in an esky. Lord no! With two tickets to Turkey and a Fretless Mandolute! He has a sudden reckless vision of taking her around the world, hand in hand, and describing Everything Everything Everything he sees with this voice he's got. He could busk, ringed by People, and not be afraid.

He feels strange. Ineffable. Bloody queer.

The Russian is at the Concert Hall tonight. He intends to be there with her. To show her, prove to her he isn't useless to escape with.

But he doesn't go far tonight, because in the midst of his reverie his knees buckle and he is suddenly sprawled on this cool dewy lawn, in a deep blissful sleep.

COPIUM

Climb up Bruno's ladder in the cool of this night (but take care, the fourth step is still missing). Stand on the rusted corrugation of his verandah rooftop and turn your back on his name. Look East.

It's higher up here, so you get a good view. You can easily survey the suburban flatlands that spread tightpacked from the distant escarpment. The cubed regiments of allotments, which cast stippled lights like stars that fell. Watch them blink and snuff.

In the foreground you can hear parties, big raves and small gatherings. Some with belated countdowns. Some with muffled Hits Of The Eighties. But you aren't interested in the foreground.

On the fringes you see the sprawl of corporate communities, pushing sand North and South. Each with a Theme and a token Ethos and an artificial Landmark and two bullshit nouns plastered to a deviously wide entrance. All ticks on the Urban Residential Development Checklist.

Squinting, you can trace the roads, named and numbered, and the paths and threads of wires and fibres that connect them all. And with your back to the crackle of fireworks and music and briny breeze; you have to worry for them, worry if there are just too many out here, especially in Dark Ness, just too many that might be the same the same the same

***

Beyond all expectation, Jim died because of arthritis.

He couldn't play her any more. His joints were too weak and set and crippled and excruciating. He could no longer pick up his bow, could barely move his fingers. He shattered. And the ticking of his big Tinman heart was just a triggered bomb, counting down Time.

All he had left now were limitations that would steadily worsen. And no amount of weed or rhubarb or anti-inflammatories or lapslapslaps could help him live inside it now. All that mattered was gone. So why wait? What for? To finish up a palliative patient in a green walled room with swabs and yellow bags; an isolated contaminant, wasting away while his body betrayed him further?

He was tired of enduring pain. And he had just lost his vehicle to survive it, beat it, forget it for a precious while. And he hadn't the strength nor the means to fill its absence. Hadn't the strength left to keep pushing his ball of shit uphill.

He was just tired.

Jim approached a pyrotechnician, with a broad smile and a credit card. Jim hired a hang-glider. Jim tackled a thick six-inch bud in its entirety. Jim basted his joints in rhubarbroot balm, so he could move without wincing. Jim drove East, truly stoned, with bright wings strapped to the hood of his red Renault. And Jim staged his last exit. Flew his grand finale high above the sea.

He was twenty-three. It was three forty-five and a little cold on a dark, dark Sunday morning. There were no sippers of sweet port. No oohs nor ahhs. The clear sky erupted with colour.

***

Theo lived because extensive surgery and rigorous bouts of chemotherapy cleared his brain of malignant cells. Theo recovered because a nurse called Kate made sure of it.

Registrars came and went, but Kate was there for everything. Every stage, every process. They had become close almost immediately, easily, without thinking. Without time to balk at his prognosis. They clicked. Found each other infectious. Talked for hours sometimes after her shifts (to which she had doubled her hours). And there was also comfort in the silence they shared when he was too weary to speak or listen.

Theo refused to be administered by any other nurse. Kate obliged.

Silently, she worried over his absence of family visitation. Friends dropped by, but briefly. Kate brought him small things, and sneaked him food she had cooked from home. Theo made her eyes roll with his assortment of bad puns. He made her laugh and she shared his stubborn optimism. She caught his vomit in a bucket and stayed awhile.

She watched him sleep sometimes. Some nights she slept at the hospital, by his side.

It was Kate who had cleared away his struck matches. She kept them all.

Theo refused to call for assistance. She knew what he was doing. She had seen it before, but never ever like this. She was clutched by a mix of admiration and pity, and over the fourteen tedious months of care, Kate played his game and made him stronger.

She discreetly instructed each patient on the ward to tap out a special Code Theo on their emergency buttons (two short, two long) whenever they heard him say *rhubarb*, or even mouth it.

The patients, mostly bored pensioners, loved it. Relished it. It gave them something to do. Suddenly they had Responsibility. Theo could feel them eyeing him expectantly.

And they were on to it. It was like a tacit gameshow, buzzers in hand, to see who could implement a Code Theo the fastest. The nurses' switchboard would explode in a flurry of emergencies. But everyone, grudgingly, had come to recognise Wing C's unwritten policy.

And Kate, always Kate, would respond. The ward would subside with relief as she rushed in and pulled his curtain across. And without his ever knowing, she would reset his IV line and dim his nerves. Leach it away. Give a sedative if his pain was severe (*rhubarbrhubarbrhubarb*). She held his hand. He held hers back.

She hated his eyes. When they weren't clenched shut, the pupils were flickering madly inandoutandinandout. It was surreal and frightening to see. They would not respond to light. They weren't Theo's eyes.

She stayed with him until she brought him back. She chattered, soothing and cheerful, kissed his Temple. Often he would fall into an exhausted sleep.

Leaving the ward, she would wink at the onlooking patients. They nodded importantly among themselves, having done their Duty.

One night he screamed it. *Screamed* it. Hoarse and highpitched and scarily loud. The entire ward was frantic, bashing out Code Theos. Kate burst in, just on the end of her shift. She examined him, set his IV line to a heavy dose. Tears streaked his cold gaunt cheeks. He clung to her hand, scared, rocking violently, blurting the word over and over and over. He was farfaraway. Too faraway. She wept, too, and held him tight. Tried to still him, to calm him. Found herself trying to pray. Trying not to think about morphine.

The ward was asleep when he had quietened to a vacant whisper. He was drenched. Kate made sure the curtain was across. Then slowly, slowly, she lifted a knee on to the bed. She straddled him. Careful. Watching. She offered no weight. And then she guided him inside her. And there was satisfaction in having his eyes settle, the sweetness of recognition in them, instantly. And in having that word *stop*. And in knowing he was without pain.

Two more months of therapy, without incident, Theo was a grinning outpatient, officially in Remission. Wing C went back to normal. Kate resumed part time.

Theo didn't know magic.

Theo had an insular illusion that sapped his energy and made nothing Disappear. Deepdeepdeep he would go, uttering that placebo like a mantra, retreating to a small dark space where he could deny pain. Palliate it. Where he wouldn't let it exist. And it was Kate, always Kate, who silently treated it, silently took it away, silently pulled him out. Silently gave him the confidence to believe he was healing himself, right then when it mattered.

But he knows now, Theo, that rhubarb was just rhubarb. Just a word. That cloaked his sight and made his pupils flicker like fireworks. It was just barely surviving within it, inside it. Just a version of aversion.

And never, ever was it coping.

PROLOGUE

It's just before dawn when the phone rings.

It cuts the air. Warren stops pacing and freezes.

And Eleanor opens useless crusty eyes to a sound she doesn't recognise. For the briefest of moments she forgets where she is; why it is still dark.

Her head spins. The need for water is vital. She does not know how long she has slept. The ringing is dimly insistent behind her closed door. She frowns at the noise, then realises it's the phone.

She pushes off the bed too quickly and her weak legs collapse from under her. She bruises her elbow on a pine trunk beside her desk.

Confused, Eleanor crawls to the door and levers herself standing. The phone rings on.

She opens the door and is shirtfronted by an overzealous Guide Dog and the thickest, most horrific stench. They both shove her back down.

Warren is all over her, whimpering sniffing licking. The phone is louder now, more urgent. The dog's tail whips as she shoves him aside and rises gingerly. Stumbles into the hall and gasps. The fetid stink gives her a sudden disgusted squint. It is unbearable. Unbreathable. The phone rings out. She wades slowly now. Warily. A glutinous sickfeeling slides into her belly.

Stella? Stelle?

She can hear the television.

Stella you awake? Where are you? Voice a dry wavering croak.

She chokes on the festering odour. Makes her lip curl and her eyes wet. She shakes her head.

Estelle? she tries louder, more insistent.

She can feel Warren beside her. Hopelessly, helplessly confused, she gropes and takes his harness. *God*, she whispers and covers her nose and mouth with her hand. Her pulse is livid. She moves slowly slowly forward.

In the lounge, the television trumpets commercials. She kneels and lets the dog go. Warren sniffs a marbled leg and flinches. Paws his snout.

There is only blackness. Eleanor's hand brushes the couch. Her belly churns with a dread she doesn't fully understand. Hand traces the cushion.

Stelle? she whispers, and it's as feeble as it feels.

Hand settles on an inert lower belly. Keeps it there in the dark and does not move. She is sleeping, only sleeping. Blind Girl shakes her gently, to wake her up. Slow trembling hand reaches in the dark, touches a limp wrist.

The knowing stabs her sickly coldly cleanly with a hoarse moan as she bends and backsbacksbacks away. The room is a nauseous whorl, gushing in spires. She feels it in Dark Ness, condensing. There is no distance, Everything in. Dizzy. Her moan gives way for a sheet of hot vomit that spreads in a dead lap like a gift. She topples, head roaring, and falls again. And Warren is there, ready to save her. Her tightlipped moan resurges and follows her down the hall where panic takes her. Back to her room where Time is still. She paces the space in her room. She must move, because Moving helps. She fights with imbalance. Feels her body closing in on itself. Like it is being sucked from the inside. Nightmare, it has to be. She'll be waking soon, pissing soon, heaving soon. She bites her knuckles. The horrible wail of the autistic child. Her panic mounts until she scrabbles and snatches something that feels like paper and betrayal, and she movesmovesmoves with her dog beside her. She knows the way. She does not breathe. Shaking she hurries down the hall and rushes outside. Leaves, like her mother never did. And she is *not* her mother.

It feels like morning. She knows she can never ever come back.

Look at her.

Eleanor Rigby. Blind Midget. Bearer of bags and sad sacks and Too Many Things that she can't put down.

Watch her walking, fastfastfast, almost jogging, with a trotting dog trying hard to slow her down. Faster and faster she surges through these streets; these streets she *knows*. Concentrating hard. On roads. And paths. Pavement. Kerbs. Traffic. Trees. The things in front of her. Small and Big. And the faster they approach, the harder she concentrates. On surviving. So she doesn't have to think. Or ask questions. As though it could displace the knowing. The things behind her. Disengage it with Distance. Apartness.

Faster and faster, she heaves. She has the sudden urge to shower. Wash it off and scratch at her skin. She sweats. Gathers pace. Holding a dog that, right now, is too scared to take this shit. He lags on the lead. Falls behind. Nips at her heels (something Lassie would *never* do). But she moves on without his leading. Without his showing her where to go; where things are. And he can see the danger in her conviction, and so he totters forward, matching her speed, pissed off and afraid. Yelping his distress. She needs to be saved. He has to bump her out of the way of things, has to drag her, lean on her. Outside Bruno's (middleofthestreet) Cornerstore she only narrowly misses a ladder that has been left leaning on his verandah gutter. Warren flinches and Eleanor spills on regardless. Her face haggard and blotchy. A kink in her throat. Her footfalls jolt and it's a beat, a rhythm that her cheap sandals clap into the quiet streets.

And she doesn't know why she has this letter. Why she's taking it. But she grips it tight as she movesmovesmoves. Keeps going with kinetic need.

Roads.

Paths.

Pavement.

Kerbs.

Traffic.

Trees. Smells. Slopes. Space. The topography of things. Vicinity and proximity.

Distance.

She is close now, she knows. Her breath quickens, her chest is sore. She knows this street, this pavement, this road that she is crossing now urgently. And she trusts it and she knows now why she has this letter unread. She recognises this gate. Bursts through it recognising this path. She drops the harness. Smells mint and bougainvillea. She is watched by a bashful gnome and a leaning sunflower as she surges on to the verandah and stops. Stops *there*, because it is like hitting a wall. An edifice of air. And everything stops for Eleanor Rigby as she recognises too well the sound inside this place. Too, too well. And it is not the sound that brought her here, but she's heard it before, she's *been* there and *seen* it and is stuck here because of it and it killed her mother and she can't be here. She can't be here.

It is too much. Too much right now. All this, all too fast. Too big. And it feels like betrayal, holding this letter. The world threatens to swallow her whole. Blind panic. Dead eyes flutter she sways. Her bladder issues a threat. Everything flares and flexes. Unravels.

She loses it.

***

After her phone had rung out, Ewan had slowly returned the handpiece. A beige bob cut.

He held the neck of a fretless mandolute. He had only just woken. His bare back was itchy. There was a thin beam of light pouring from a hole in the roof.

No one had answered his call.

He laid the instrument on the table, next to a congealed plate of pasta. He went very slowly through his empty empty house. Room by room. Smelling her smell.

He felt disarmed. Open, not raw. Just sloughed of bullshit. He let himself think. Reflect even. On this day, and on the ones that preceded them to get him here. He couldn't tell them apart. He was aware of the routine now, by virtue of being outside it. He knew how each day preserved the next. Sucking stones. Nothing lost nothing gained. He felt bereaved thinking of them.

He thought about today. Tomorrow. Felt heat in his belly.

He wandered outside. Knelt at a vacant pillowhammock.

In his shed he took a sudden claw hammer and smashed his suspended replicas. Punched holes into their empty bellies. They were brittle. Easy. Too easy to break. They crackled. Chips flew and scattered. Then he smashed his moulds over the workbench. One by one. These were more difficult to break. The nailed joins groaned with disappointment. Last night's woodflakes fluttered like birdflocks. The saucepan fell and seeped. He stove in backs and bellies with his foot. Flimsy ribs he snapped in his hands. He ripped the spines of notebooks. Destroyed everything, quickly.

Almost Everything.

He charged back inside. Bent with momentum. His feet were bold and brazen.

And in the hallway there was just the swelling urge to up, up, up and leave here. And he would. He knew he would. But not yet. He wouldn't do it alone. And he knew *why* he was alone.

And he was in this room now and burning, with some kind of bitter, determined rage. He was taking her neck like an axehandle. No. Not *her*. Never *her*. Because this was never Lilian with limbs was never Jim with a heartbeat nor Eleanor with arms. It was just wood; and not the Elvish *Brabuhr* of past myth. Just wood, just maple that he wielded right there in this room. Just wood that he swung back and flung while he bellowed and watched it fly and watched it crack against the far wall. He saw the spine split. Saw the thin bridge ricochet. And he picked it up. A dislocated soundpost rattled as he lifted high above his head. He drove it slammed it into a Turkish rug wailing again and again and again. He thrashed at the broken timber with the celloneck, with strings flailing whipping and wood shattering; like a Blind Girl was shattering outside. ˙

And when there is nothing left, when Everything is gone, he is suddenly stung by shrill screams and a frenzy of barking.

***

Warren is barking because Eleanor is running.

Bolting.

He can see her: she is sprinting down this street. And he can hear her feet, so he knows it's real.

And poor Warren can't chase her, still can't save her, because his harness is snagged stuck on the catch of the gate. He almost tore it off its hinges setting after her. He pulls hard against it, standing on his hindlegs. The leather straps groan.

His hackles mohawk and his teeth are bared as he barks and barks in violent hacking bursts.

His ears are pinned.

***

When her bleary eyes had looked up to see Eleanor charging out of there, bent with momentum, *running*; she froze. Squinted to Make Sure, just as Warren was hooking himself and swinging legless. Her bum clenched up (though she'd never worry a walnut) and watched Eleanor run and run and run and round a corner. Her hands went to her mouth. She panicked.

The screaming belongs to Althea. She is across the road in her sister's frontyard. A running hose and a spill of rose fertiliser are at her feet. She is horrified. She hugs her chest and screams.

Greta blusters out, hastily wrapping a dressing gown, the sound of one slipper flapping. Her husband follows her (topless, wobbling, hungover) and they both scan the street, fearing an attempted abduction or a detonated wheelie bin or some other manifestation of Bruno's Prophecy of Terror.

So standing beside her now on the lawn, eyes darting, they are confused (and relieved) to find Althea screaming at Nothing In Particular.

At the same moment, Ewan bursts through his front door, also topless, and still wielding a broken celloneck like an ornate club. He stops and steps back, frowns at the shrieking midget and follows the dog's fierce gaze down the empty street.

The squat woman turns to direct her screams at him, glaring and pointing:

You! *You! Go!* Gogogogogo! Go now Go you Stupid, *Stupid* Man! My *God!* What have you done what what what have you done to her she is going to get fucking *killed!*

(Before now, Althea's primly pursed lips had never passed that All Purpose Expletive. Her panic latches to it.)

She's fucking *blind* you stupid useless stupid *stupid* fucking man! She can't fucking *see!* Go! Go! *Go!* Do something! Do you understand? Do you fucking *understand?* For God's sake, *Go!*

Warren barks on. So does Althea. A vein appears down her forehead (for she has been withholding this eruption for years. It merges into spousal invective. A torrent of imprecations, in broad Italian now, from a lifetime of sponging bullshit. Althea loses it).

Curious People emerge from their homes to slowly, sleepily absorb the tableau.

Greta and Alan stand stunned. Alan marches inside shaking his head.

Ewan just stares. Blankly, then

click

sickly coldly cleanly

And his pupils dilate. He drops the club like it burns. He backs away. Trips, fumbles, falls. And the entire street gathers to watch in silence as he rushes back inside.

***

Running in the dark.

Gulps in air and does not stop. Running. Distance Running. Sweat.

She should feel truly, truly scared right now. Mortal. And above all, small.

But the truth is she doesn't. Truth is, she doesn't feel anything. She is overfull. Her nerves have stalled. It's too, too much.

This blank expression is not composure. This is how it feels to lose it completely.

Like something has taken over. Guided but in control. Autopilot. She concentrates *hard* on a map and an arrow and keeps to the road. She knows Distance. With impossible accuracy. She carves through Dark Ness on these streets she *knows*. The mechanics of going, going, going. Fast. Scarily fast. And she is not slowed by the things she tows.

There is that sweeping easterly at her back, like an angry mob with pitchforks, hungry for a lynching; like a flock of hotbreathed ghosts on her tail as she flies past her old haunts. It pushes at her, urges her, and she tries to outrun it. But no one is going to catch her now. No one.

She is tripped by a devious drainage grate. She stumbles collapses slides. The road taxes the skin of her chin, her elbows, her left leg badly. Her bruise leaks. But she is up and on, on, on before it hurts. Her arms are pumping. She wills leaden legs through intersections, round bends and corners. To the only place she was ever going to go.

***

Hallway. Kitchen. He doesn't think.

Garage, cardoor, slam.

He knows the theory. Sort of. His left foot presses the clutch flat. Right foot pins the accelerator. He rushes flustered. Shaking, he finds a gear. The windscreen is thick with dust. Heavybreathed, he turns the key. The car has emphysema.

Finally it catches and roars.

Left foot pulls off the clutch. The wheels spin. And then

***

there is a collective flinch from the milling neighbourhood when they hear the crash. They all hush, even Althea. There is a sharp uniform headturn in the direction of a sudden dent in the garage door across the road.

Seconds later they hear scrabbling, then a recalcitrant groan as the galvanised door is forced open.

Mute pause. Cardoorslam.

Then a splutter and a restart. High revs. And a fan of People watches a dustcovered Volvo suddenly pitch and lurch towards them. They scatter clumsily as it mounts the kerb and swipes the letterbox (which doesn't explode) then turns unsteadily and eventually straightens, trailing dense blue smoke. It fangs down the street on flat wobbling tyres. Stuck in first gear. Whining like an empty blender.

But it's moving. And it's rounding that corner now, unconvincingly, but without stopping. Or looking. And trapped in the gap of the driver's side door is a flappingseatbelt. It spanks the road and the carbody like a frantic jockeywhip to make sparks.

***

The smoke settles, and on the lawn, beside an uprooted letterbox, Althea bends to shakily retrieve a small conical seashell that has just rolled to rest on her foot. She puts it to her ear and calms.

***

There is a victorious leathersnap, the sound of a starter's gun. Warren's harness breaks and he is off, bolting into the morning, a celloneck clasped in his mouth.

***

Ewan can't see the road either. The windscreen is a curtain of grimy dust. So he has to jut his head from the open window and squint into the carwind. His knuckles are red white red on the steering wheel. He rides kerbs and median strips and collects more letterboxes. A liberated hubcap rolls sedately into a driveway.

The Volvo rattles and shudders and shrieks and Ewan just drives. Doesn't think, just follows roads, streets he doesn't know. And it occurs to him that he has never chased before, always just lost.

Ewan is unaware of his passengers.

He hasn't noticed the two wide-eyed possums in the backseat. They had slept there last night due to a kaboom in the roof. It had sounded like the End of the World. They were lucky though, they had been in here at midnight, pilfering more plush interior for their expanding lovepit (for the recently recovered possum bears the fruit of their labour, and will give birth in days).

Shrinking back into the seat they watch the clear sky and whizzing foliage through the windows. The voyage is not smooth, and they hold each other tight and safe and still.

Inertia claims a signed, softleather bible. It slides and falls to the floor.

Outside, the crab is shitting itself.

It hangs grimly to the lip of the exhaust pipe after being bowled out of its cave by the rolling exit of its own discarded shell. It suddenly understands that size is not safety. Its hopes are pinned on the waning grip of a reflexive left nipper.

The crab is buffeted by slipstream. It clings parallel. Choked by smoke and swinging madly through bends and corners and letterbox collections. The crab is on the edge, naked, and slipping. The hot airblasts from its cave make it impossible to attempt a crawlback.

Foiled again, but the crab is holding on. And if it can keep that nipper fixed; if the crab can survive just a little longer; then in a feat of serendipity, the crab will be all right in the end. Because Ewan has just shuddered and rattled up over a crest to reveal a shimmering glimpse of ocean. He suddenly has a destination.

But he won't catch her before she gets there. No one will. She is a blur of skinny limbs down these sleepy streets. Sticky thick dark blood seeps into Peasant Birkenstocks.

Her teeth grit. But it's not panic, and she's not tiring. She just knows how close she is now. She tilts forward, forward, forward. Closer. Past warm yeasty breadsmells, past early morning coffeesmells, past rancid binsmells. Ononon she sprints, in Dark Ness. Past the cool shadow of the monolithic hospital. Blankness. Blackness. Through a roundabout. Pastpastpast. Down this street so empty, so eerie, but she *knows* where she is, she *knows* where she's going. Glass shards crackle underfoot, they cover the road like sleet. The Party Of The Century is over, but she doesn't know. Another thing she's missed. She runs through the aftermath. Past the slurred wellwishes of hardcore streetdrinkers (ayayay! Appy Noo Yee to yer!) Past random stares. She is inexorable. And fastfastfast. She veers now, this blind girl, down a desolate Essex Street. Her footclaps rebound off walls like rubber bullets to thump back pounding in her head. Couples sharing champagne from hotel balconies turn to watch stunned from above.

But past them, past them all, and now she hears the suddensqueal of locking tyres and feels the ghostblow of a near miss. But she doesn't flinch, she will not flinch, because the world will move for her today, this day of days. She will not stop and she will not be stopped. She will leave a voice trailing behind her (Fucken *ell!* Whyn't yer bloody *watch* where you're going eh? You wanna get killed or somming?) as she hurdles on to the cushioned lawn of the Esplanade Reserve.

So close. Wilted bodies sprawl beneath Norfolk Island pines and surly men detach scaffolding from a stage. She belts past them all. Grounded gulls stir and alight.

She stumbles among litter. Her left foot punts the inflated bladder of a winecask. It rises upupup and is taken in the breeze like a small silver zeppelin. Her fingertips xylophone the bars of the fenceline and she breathes salt and there is a letter glowing in her other hand. So close. She bursts through the railway crossing labyrinth. Pulls out on a taxi. It honks, she doesn't hear. So, so fast now. And she can taste it, hear it amid a fat headthump and raspy heaving and she's here. Here. She got here. Impossibly. All by herself. How far she's come and she does not stop now through all of this this this too much too many

***

Neither does Ewan as he pulls out blind and jerks on to Marine Terrace.

There's the suddensqueal of locking tyres and a near near miss. But Ewan drives on undeterred, with a crab and two possums and a tally of fourteen letterboxes, three side mirrors and almost a cat. Still in first gear. Still hanging out the window. Black smoke and sparks and a trailing voice behind him:

Fucking *hell!* Am I fucking *invisible* today? Am I? *Am* I?

At which point a slobbering Guide Dog leaps over his bonnet and scrabbles off in hot pursuit.

***

This is the unknown. And look: she's running straight at it. She leaves footprints in the sand. She should be scared.

Her ankle fizzes into the coldwet shock of her boundary. She doesn't know where or why she just knows forward, forward, forward fuck it *fuck* it she'll swim and swim and swim on to Africa Why not She'll swim on round past the Cape Of Good Hope and churn on up to the icy isles of Scotland and toss somefuckingcabersinHappyNess anywhere but here And she won't ever stop And she won't ever sink Ononon

Watch her thin legs kick watersparks as she stumbleruns in in in to take on the Biggest thing there is. In the dark. And look: there's a rare saltwater dribble that spills from a teflon reservoir and glints and drips into a flat full sea. Plip. And there's the sound much like Warren's leathersnap, the sound of a dropped bundle, and it's forward she falls and she is swallowed like a baptism. She clenches shut her eyes and the ocean is calmer than it should be and she is not galvanised by this; not like she thought she might. It coats her, washes her, scours her raw skin and it *hurts*. She drinks it in, but it does nothing for her thirst. And it holds her up as she lets a letter go; and then she is movingmovingmoving, kicks and carves. In a thicker Dark Ness. She cocks her head, breathes in hard, and bawls into the ocean. Eyes shut tight. And she thrashes and she weeps, even mourns. There is no distance. Her hands are cupped but they hold nothing. Movingmovingmoving. And it exhausts her. Muscles tight, starting to sear. Her grazes sting. Fatigue thieves her rhythm. Already. Her stroke is messy and she is lost and winding down. Lactic acid burns. Her thigh cramps but she wills herself on on on so tired so

***

The suddensqueal of locking tyres and a near, near miss. A dustcovered Volvo belts over a kerb and into a pine bollard.

A naked crab is flung. Like a flipped coin; a high, wide arc. On the listing shore it lands and rolls and settles. Eyestalks scan, mandibles twitch. The crab is home safe.

Ewan sees her. He runs, towards a Blind Girl. The seawall to his left. The beach is four steps long.

Watersparks. Cold, he dives and kicks and carves.

He is standing chesthigh when he seizes an ankle. Her eyes they open. Blue murk. She kicks, struggles, then doesn't. He pulls like a rip. Locks an arm across her breast. Dragging.

Her head above water, gasps.

And there it is. *There it is.* Cuts through Everything. Just a sliver, a bright white slice. Just a start, a small slit pared open. But enough, enough to have her clutching her face in her hands, like it stings somehow. And she's shouting, shrieking into her palms. And he's here and there's heat near her ear. Staccato. She hears and calms.

And there's Warren, lumbering in late (he got confused inside the railway labyrinth) and driven by Duty. But he's stopping short now, there on the crest of the beach. Beside a nude crab wending its ecstatic way to a waiting wall of rock nooks.

It is six thirty, the first of the first. The wind gusts but silence hangs like a gravid pause.

Warren drops a broken celloneck to grin, and he sits slumpish and solid, because no one needs saving any more.

And off the shore, soaked, standing kneedeep, you can see how they *fit* together; Tall and Short; held and holding; filled so there is no space between them, both shaking softly in the early morning light.

ACKNOWLEDGEMENTS

I am deeply indebted, fiscally and otherwise, to my parents, Chris and Rod, who have been and continue to be truly supportive and benevolent and loving. *Salut!* I also wish to kiss the feet of my guru, Glyn, for his generous assistance from the get-go. Much gratitude is expressed to all and sundry at Fremantle Press. Also to Jennifer Tingley, gifted teacher and cellist. Word out to the gorgeous and discerning sisters Khan, and some unabashed manlove for Adam Caporn. A tip of my sombrero to the Gringo and his eleven strings. Apologies are offered to Al Popov, a man of unquestionable character and aquatic celerity, and I trust he remains vigilant against the sharp knives of watermelon vendors. Thank you to Meredith Rose and Nikki Christer for valued time freely given. A special thank you to Emily O'Connell for her kind patience and patient kindness. And thanks lastly, with love, to Brooke May, the Nancy to my Ronald, who has a dodgy ticker but the very best of hearts and who inspires goodness and ambition. May we be wed in Vegas and in Reno by dawn.

ABOUT THE AUTHOR

Craig Silvey grew up on an orchard in Dwellingup, Western Australia. *Rhubarb*, his first novel, was published in 2004. It won Silvey the Best Young Australian Novelist Award from the *Sydney Morning Herald* in 2005, was chosen as the 'One Book' for the Perth International Writers Festival, and was included in the national Books Alive campaign. His second novel, *Jasper Jones* (2008), has received many awards including in 2009 the Indie Book of the Year Award and joint winner of the Western Australia Premier's Literary Award (Fiction). In 2010 awards for *Jasper Jones* included the ABIA (Australian Book Industry Awards) Book of the Year, ABIA Literary Fiction Book of the Year, the NSW Premier's Literary Award (Christina Stead Prize for Fiction), finalist in the *Sydney Morning Herald* Best Young Novelist Award, and shortlistings in the Miles Franklin Literary Award and Victorian Premier's Literary Awards (Vance Palmer Prize for Fiction). In 2011 it was shortlisted for the International IMPAC Dublin Literary Award. Silvey is also the author of a picture book, *The World According to Warren*, with Sonia Martinez (2007). He lives in Fremantle, Western Australia.

MORE GREAT READS

Julia Lambett heads across the country to her hometown where she's to help her father move out of his home and into care. But when Julia arrives, she finds her father has adopted a mysterious dog and refuses to leave. Frustrated and alone, when a childhood friend crosses her path, Julia turns to Davina for comfort and support. But soon Julia begins to doubt Davina's motivations. Why is Davina taking a determined interest in all the things that Julia hoped she had left behind? With four decades of possessions to be managed and dispersed, Julia uncovers long-forgotten, deeply unsettling memories.

FROM FREMANTLE PRESS

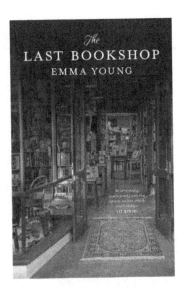

Cait Copper's best friends have always been books – along with the rare souls who love them as much as she does, like the grandmotherly June. When Cait set up her shop, Book Fiend, right in the heart of the city, she thought she'd skipped straight to 'happily ever after'. But things are changing, and fast. The city is transforming, with luxury chain stores circling Book Fiend's prime location. Soon Cait is questioning not only the viability of the shop, but the life she's shaped around it. An unlikely band of allies is determined she won't face these questions alone; but is a love of books enough to halt the march of progress and time?

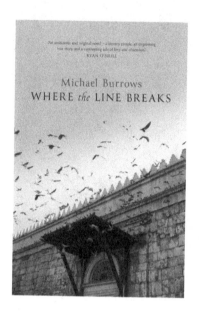

The Unknown Digger is Australia's most famous WWI poet. But for decades, his identity has remained a mystery. Enter Matthew Denton – a PhD student at University College, London – who believes the unknown digger to be in fact one of Australia's greatest war heroes: Lieutenant Alan Lewis VC of the 10th Light Horse. As the story of Lieutenant Lewis unfolds, the question of what makes him a poet, a lover and a hero becomes a troubled one. Meanwhile, in the footnotes, scholar Matt Denton is fighting his own battles with romance and with academia as he attempts to rewrite literary history.